Dear Patti,

Thank you for your
my first novel.
It means a lot to me that you want
to take time in your life, to read
my words.

Once Upon A Solar Time

May the journey the characters
take you on, excite your inner child,
your inner teenager who knows
"when I am in wonder" life is
magical, goodness abounds
and love not fear always wins.

Thanks for your friendship
Patti !!
love & light
Jeather aka
denise

What an imagination! I love the compelling adventure you took me on, and I am an adult! Your inspiring portrayal of youth gives me hope for their future.

—Mary Martin, Grade 9 English Teacher

Once Upon A Solar Time speaks to one's higher self and also to one's inner child. This magical fantasy book cavorted me down the path of curiosity because it is about possibilities—a story of creation that helps me explore and expand my own transformative, creative opportunities.

All the protagonists have unique gifts where they are creative on an energetic level. They can go beyond the physical realm of limitations and have fun in that mystical process. Also, the ant characters are enchanting, giving me a sense of the smaller and grander aspects of who I am—supporting me in recognizing the power within the magic of my world.

Once Upon A Solar Time is for those who still dare to dream. For those who believe in the circle of life—community, responsibility, imagination, and rebirth. A book that will inspire you to discover your inner fantasy place and learn how to draw on the magic within you to live in the magic around you.

—Esther Austin, Transformational Leader, Talk Show Host &
Broadcaster "On the Sofa with Esther," Chief Editor,
TurningPoint: Your Lifestyle, Your Well-Being Magazine

Awesome read! I wish the Point-by-Point Invention existed. I would sign on to do it. The details of your incredible story slowed me down to take it all in.

—Peter, 17-year-old high school student

Bless you, dear feather, for this remarkable creative endeavor. *Once Upon A Solar Time* captures your brilliance on so many levels. This book is a must-read, and I recommend we all buy two so we can give one as a gift.

—Joanie McMahon, Psychologist PsyD (ABD)
Getting Happy Together Inc

Once Upon A Solar Time

feather
aka
denise bertrand

 FriesenPress

One Printers Way
Altona, MB R0G 0B0
Canada

www.friesenpress.com

Note: The author is Canadian, so Canadian spelling is used in this book.

Editor: Lynn Thompson, Living on Purpose Communications
Book Cover: FriesenPress Design
Book Cover Photographer: Dany Lajoie
Author Portrait Design: Macrae Creative
Interior Photographs: referenced in book

For information, contact: onceuponasolartime@gmail.com

ISBN
978-1-03-914774-4 (Hardcover)
978-1-03-914773-7 (Paperback)
978-1-03-914775-1 (eBook)

1. *Fiction, Science Fiction, Adventure*
2. *Fiction, Visionary & Metaphysical*

Distributed to the trade by The Ingram Book Company

DEDICATION

Children hold the keys to the future of humanity.
I hope, in some small way, the seeds of creativity
I have planted in their consciousness will support
their brave hearts throughout their lives.

FOREWORD

This delightfully precious book, *Once Upon a Solar Time,* written by my friend, feather aka denise, is brilliant. I know feather's work with children, whereby, each year, she gathers children interested in theatre expression. Then, from scratch, they create a play for an audience that embodies the children's ideas, opinions, dreams, and intuitions. Gifted teacher feather directs, writes, and produces the plays. It's challenging to accomplish so much with a group of children in a short time. However, attending many of her original plays, each filled with fun, wisdom, and grace, entertained me.

And now, feather has taken her love of teaching, music, nature, humanity, and the spiritual world and woven everything into this captivating, highly-creative book that teenagers, young adults, and grown-ups will love. Colourful, mystical, and magical—clearly the work of a brilliant thinker and writer. Her writing is so visual that I imagine her book becoming a significant movie for humanity.

Once Upon A Solar Time is packed full of creativity; one character is Relaxella, a name that embodies the need for more trust, knowing, inner calmness, and genuine loving. As a psychologist, I recognize the necessity for human expression that leads to enlightenment and the restoration of the body and soul; it is powerful. Relaxella's sensitive nature purposefully demonstrates what is possible to help others grow.

Through the video-like game, Point-by-Point, feather teaches essential elements of the body and the importance of keeping ourselves clear so our true nature can shine through; she expresses the concepts with elegance and engaging dialogue during this intriguing story.

The author's love of nature is clear and prominent throughout this masterpiece. One of the fourteen-year-old girls says to her friend, "I still talk to the sun rays when they touch my face each morning. I haven't missed a sunrise for over one year."

The writing is delightful, educational, and charming. Such beauty of expression in a single paragraph; feather expresses so much in just a name or a word. The richness of each sentence takes your breath away. For example, "Oh Light, may the gentleness of your magnificence bless our hands as we prepare the abundance of food before us into a nutritious meal. Keep our thoughts joyful while working together, so we can infuse this nutrition with wholesome elements for all who partake."

I can go on and on in my excitement about this precious work of art where feather expands our use of language through original songs and endearing expressions that melt our hearts and minds.

Bless you, dear feather, for this remarkable creative endeavor.

—Joanie McMahon
Psychologist PsyD (ABD)
Getting Happy Together Inc.

INTRODUCTION

*I*t all started with the—conundrum of ants. Not the most sought-after insect. Most people prefer butterflies or bees, apparently. Although a Google search will reveal over 10,000 quotes about these famously industrious, self-organizing little creatures who have been sharing nests in harmonious co-operation since eons before the first humans worked out how to rub sticks together to make fire.

Ants certainly bring me into the moment when I find myself entranced by their perfectly regimented collective movement in the garden, along pathways visible only to themselves.

The ant is, the scientists tell us, one of those species whose lives constrain them to almost endless suffering. The scientists like to say negative feedback, although we might more simply call this feedback—pain. Ants experience pain when they find an item of food and a slightly different form of pain when they don't. Pain forces them to leave the nest—pain forces them to return, and pain forces them to fight each other at times for the best morsels! Yet, for all of this, the ant survives—prospers, even, in its small way—one presumes, without complaint. What perseverance! What a conundrum!

I dare to say those six-legged insects, talk to me! I have also said a few not so gentle words back to them. Honestly, I am *confident they have spoken to me in various moments in my complex life.*

Explaining this "ant business" is not easy. Perhaps a true story about a real ant encounter might help you understand why they are part of my novel project.

Once in 1989, while investigating my inner landscape at an Ashram in Sicily, a queen ant visited me. I was invited to the head table, sitting beside the Guru of this human colony, waiting for the lunch to be served. Plenty of eager seekers like me gathered. Beautiful young giggling women waited in the wings, anxious to serve us an abundance of sumptuous delights. After a brief group meditation, I opened my eyes, and there directly in front of me on the table, a huge black queen ant was balancing gracefully on her two back legs. Her trembling front legs appeared to be waving to me and asking for a cuddle!

Now I can hear you, dear Reader, thinking, Odd! Weird! As if! Honestly, this is what I saw! I felt almost strangled by her intelligence, begging me to do something. It looked like a long way to the floor, and I did not have the heart to knock her off the table. I glanced around to see if anyone else had noticed her. No one seemed to be bothered. I was alone with this queen ant and had to decide her fate. I struggled not to attract too much attention to myself. I slowly lifted my spoon and gently presented it next to the queen's body. Unlike most ants, which naturally squirm when some giant object is threatening their very existence, this queen approached the spoon without any resistance. I thought she knew I wanted to rescue her, not destroy her, as I have done to many ants. This situation was exceptional!

She slid into the spoon, legs up. Amazing! I had her. Again, I contemplated putting her on the floor, but I calculated someone would easily trample her while she wandered around the table legs, looking for an exit.

Since I was in an Ashram, learning to give reverence to worlds seen and unseen, I felt called to set an example. A bit tough, though. Remember, I was sitting beside the Guru, and indeed it was considered an honour to be by his side. What reason could I give for leaving the table before lunch was served? "Ah, sorry, may I be excused to release this queen ant outside?"

I did not ask for permission. I made it my mission to rescue the queen! I covered the spoon with my left hand, held it close to my body, and walked to the balcony to release her. Inquisitive eyes and frowning brows watched my every move. I didn't care what they thought; I knew what I needed to do.

Some asked me afterward if I had become sick or had felt faint. When I announced I rescued a queen ant, some laughed with me and seemed rather proud of my deed. Others, well, I read their judgment in their eyes. "How dare she! What nerve! You were at the head table with the Guru!"

This certainly wasn't the first time in my life where I have stepped out of my comfort zone and did what I felt compelled to do—raise some brows!

Will I elevate your brows as you wander through the trails of my written words? Will these seedlings of words carve garden paths in your imagination that an ant the size of a seed could follow? Will you be curious and journey with me in this imaginative world I have written that does have ants as characters? Fret not; Once Upon A Solar Time is not peppered with them, and anyhow they do not appear in full force until Part II.

Now I must tell you a grand honesty—I started writing this book when I was 18 years young! Dare I admit the book is already 45 years old! Sometimes I think of my novel as a wonderfully-aged treasure chest, finally being discovered. Indeed, one may critique why it took me this long to finish writing. Trust me, I have been the most demanding critic on the timeline. Part of my hesitation for years had been because I was not sure if I included ants as characters, anybody would want to read my novel. Somehow though, I couldn't get rid of them.

In my teens, I nourished my own idealism, wherein friendship ranked very high on my list of needs; what teen doesn't? Herein I wrote a story about two friends called Girlfriend and Neighbour. These characters stayed with me and are the two main characters in Once Upon A Solar Time. *I know, strange names, but because these characters are not based on particular friends in my life, I gave them these "code names." I wish a computer program existed in E-books that allowed you, the Reader, to substitute the names of these two characters yourself, perhaps based on a great girlfriend or a kind neighbour you have or had.*

In some ways, maybe I have waited so long to get this book published because it is my private jewel feeding me and tempting me back into its secret world over time. Maybe, I am shy? Once again, my inner critic finds a way to surface.

I have travelled a lot, lived and worked in Asia for 14 years, created numerous Drama Clubs for children in Canada, Singapore, and Thailand. For 41 years, I have worked (and played) as a Theatre Director, Playwright, and Producer of original shows wherein the children are the actors. The plays are written based on the children's ideas, dreams, and intuitions. The delightful imaginations of hundreds of children I have taught have certainly influenced the fantasy world of Once Upon A Solar Time. *Characters in my book often speak aloud as if they were on stage reciting a monologue. I loved exploring their inner landscapes and giving them a voice.*

I never set out in my life to be a professional writer. Ironically though, I have written an abundance of journals, original plays, and newsletters, and I have loved to pen poetry for years.

Once Upon A Solar Time *is an imaginary journey taking many turns. The main character is "The She" with another name for those in her inner circle—Relaxella. It might take a little getting used to reading her with two names. I wrote her this way because I believe we have the constant shuffle of duality in ourselves. You get the idea: good and bad, light and dark, positive and negative, higher self and lower self. Two principles, however, that intrigue me constantly are—masculine and feminine. Every day these principles are weaved into balance and harmony within us, creating our unique tapestries. Many have written books on masculine and feminine principles, a study I have undertaken for years now. The fractures duality creates often disrupt our sense of psychological unity, and from these fissures, creative inspiration is born.*

There are two twenty-one-year-olds, Tesshu and Kaleb, whose character development supports the plot of this story. Will they finish going through The Point-by-Point Meridian Figure "game" the inventor The She has created to help anyone interested in clearing themselves?

By Chapter 10, Girlfriend and Neighbour (also names to get used to) will be adventuring through the Woods of Facuzi. The Woods of Facuzi was an actual place I explored with my Ashram friends in Sicily. The correct spelling is Ficuzza. Anyone can visit these woods between August and October to pick wild edible mushrooms. Picking wild edible mushrooms left a lasting impression on me in my life then (not psychedelic mushrooms); thus, I made mushrooms come alive to the point they became at least two feet tall with personalities! They are called the Cuzies. Girlfriend and Neighbour will eventually meet Sir Rush in the woods. He is one of my favourite characters.

The antagonists are the Vog—the government of the times. They are edgy. There will be tension when they show up; nevertheless, I will admit this is not a bloody novel. There are no murders, kidnappings, rapes, tortures, or deep, evil gritty chapters. There is some angst when the Vog gangs appear; however, they are only cowardly bullies with powerful mouths.

If you, dear Reader, are more inclined to read stories about painful betrayals of love, gore, or war, then perhaps this novel is not for you. However, if you prefer a fiction novel written to inspire: soul-searching, inner psychology, humour, duality, community relationships and consciousness, an underground world, a quest for a golden age, and good old-fashioned friendships, then I hope my book, Once Upon A Solar Time *will be your newest page-turner.*

PART I

As a thinker and planner, the **ant** is the equal of any savage race of men; a self-educated specialist in several arts, she is the superior of any savage race of men; and in one or two high mental qualities she is above the reach of any man.

—Mark Twain

CHAPTER 1

RELAXELLA aka THE SHE

Relaxella is busy making last-minute notes to herself in the back of her journal. She flips to the front to look at her to-do list created daily by her primary assistant Jenerrie. Herein she notices unfamiliar handwriting in gold ink:

This is a gentle reminder,
you have a council with Girlfriend and Neighbour,
and their respective parents today at 11:00 a.m.

Who wrote this? Relaxella wonders. Jenerrie is her only assistant permitted to make additions or appointments in her journal, and this is not her writing.

Relaxella is slightly annoyed at this meeting reminder, as she had scheduled to get the next phase of the Invention rolling at 11:00 a.m. with the two twenty-one-year-old newest challengers, Tesshu and Kaleb.

Relaxella flips a few more pages and discovers a sealed envelope. She examines it closely and intuits the Invisible Mentors have dropped in. She immediately puts the envelope back into her daily journal. *Later, I will open the letter and read what they say. For now, though, I must go to the mini-theatre to make sure everything is in place for Tesshu and Kaleb. I can't back down from today's scheduled objective.*

Many months have passed since The She lingered in this particular setting—the mini-theatre, a little room within a larger space. She had certainly seen many clear out their inner drama in here. Everyone in her inner circle has been through a Meridian Figure; it is a prerequisite to work or associate with her. Today will be different, though, as two Meridian Figures were designed and are now ready to be played simultaneously. She turns on a handheld recording device to draw comfort from her voice speaking aloud.

"I am here now, in the mini-theatre, to be with my Invention alone. I have refined my design over the past fourteen years, and today the plan is for two males to begin their process to be clear. Tesshu and Kaleb have signed on to explore a game I call Point-by-Point that was once only a vision. This is the first time two challengers will simultaneously work with two Meridian Figures. If they complete the game, they will then be initiated

feather aka denise bertrand

into The Echoes of the Sun Community as Echo Youths, if they choose.

"When I use the word 'game' in context to my Invention, I am not suggesting this activity is for amusement or diversion. Its strict definition is more like a physical and mental competition conducted according to rules. The participants assume they are in direct competition with each other; only the truth is, the competition is with themselves."

The She walks around the mini-theatre, imagining she has an audience. Although she used to give speeches in the past, these days she has too many responsibilities, thus she rarely leaves her Estate. She understands speaking out loud improves memory skills and increases one's confidence; hence, she continues vocalizing details she knows by heart.

"Tesshu and Kaleb will travel through the Meridian Figure via a computer console, which utilizes interactive programming from games in the past, such as Nintendo Search and X Box. My game conveys an energy network is inherent in every human being (Meridians[1]) that is not exclusively male or female. Thus, the Meridian Figures appear androgynous. The interactive system that gathers information about the contestant's current emotional and mental states is part of the Figures' artificial intelligence.

"Hmm, I rather like articulating in the theatre; the excellent resonance makes it feel like a rehearsal. I will have to share many details about my Invention with Tesshu and Kaleb soon. I will enjoy imparting more particulars. I am excited, though, at the same time, distracted, wondering why I am to meet with the parents of Girlfriend and Neighbour. Did I double book meetings? Jenerrie would have noticed sooner. Am I being

---

1   An energy system in and around a human being. Any of the pathways along which the body's vital energy flows according to the practice behind acupuncture.

4

tested? I shouldn't be upset; after all, Girlfriend and Neighbour are wonderfully gifted Echo Youths, and it is always a joy to see their parents. However, the timing is not great. I must be short-circuiting one of my Meridians! I will clear the block before 11 a.m. if I don't forget! It's time now to deep breathe to calm myself. Then I will return to my quarters and read the contents inside the sealed envelope."

Relaxella turns off the recording device. She sits in front of the two Point-by-Point Meridian Figures glowing in their theatrical lighting and imagines every breath she is taking is giving life to them. When her meditation is finished, the overhead illumination is bright enough so she can see her way out.

A calendar falls to the floor when Relaxella closes her private sitting room door. The words "Spring Equinox," written in large gold lettering, catch her attention. Everyone knows today is the opportune time to start something new in The Echoes of the Sun Community. Many community members ask for blessings from the Invisible Mentors to consider their project, dream, or insight. The Invisible Mentors study all requests and then decide which one seems worthy of the graces to be delivered on this day. With certainty, in the deep regions of Relaxella's mind, she is in this moment conjuring up a way of securing two blessings instead of one. Relaxella picks up the sealed envelope and opens it carefully.

Dear Relaxella aka The She,   March 21

We call your attention to the following matter:
You know, fourteen years to the date of this document, we began The Golden Bow Project underground in the Realm of

Thagara. This inside-the-earth project has many Echoes of the Sun Community members working favourably on our collective vision. One of our most steadfast leaders, whose nickname is Dig, is investigating why Level 4 in the Realm has moved ever so slightly. The seismometer located in the Woods of Facuzi has recently recorded an unknown current moving through the Level. It is not considered severe; however, please make a memo of this observation and store it under Level 4—The Heart of Communication.

We know that the Realm of Thagara is now ready to receive the two fourteen-year-olds who have cleared their Meridians and have the gift of shape-shifting well-developed for their early age. You are well aware of the two Echo Youths we are speaking of, called by their code names, Girlfriend and Neighbour. We are most interested for you to arrange permission from their parents for them to go into Thagara. Please hold council with all of them on this Spring Equinox at the 11th hour. We, known to you as the Invisible Mentors, who have chosen this form to do our work for The Echoes of the Sun Community, request all other projects be put on hold. We are aware your Invention has been scheduled to start up this day, too; still, we ask you to favour our request and postpone the initiation date until the Summer Solstice. We trust in your co-operation.

We remain, The Invisible Mentors

Relaxella slams the document on her desk. She speaks out loud.

"Summer solstice? Impossible! It's too far away. Tesshu and Kaleb have signed all the commitment papers. How could you ask this of me? Thanks for giving me plenty of time to consider your request!"

Relaxella leaves the letter under the desk lamp and starts to pace around the room, occasionally stretching to unwind her tense muscles. Nevertheless, anxiety rapidly slips in and overrides her calming technique—deep breathing.

Relaxella begins to emote for the second time this morning.

"When I received the intuition to start this Spring Equinox, I worked hard to arrange everything with Tesshu and Kaleb, and now when they arrive, I will have to tell them they must wait another three months! No! I hear what they request of me, but, even so— Oh, I am frustrated and wish sometimes the Invisible Mentors would trust me! I know I have enough experience to be able to oversee two major projects at the same time! Yes. So be it! I will contact the Mentors to discuss this issue before the 11th hour. If they agree, then Tesshu and Kaleb will start after lunch. Yes! I feel this is what I need to do! I feel strong now, and I will do as I feel!"

Relaxella stops talking out loud; Jenerrie knocks at her door. Relaxella knows Tesshu and Kaleb have arrived. The door slowly opens. Before Jenerrie has a chance to speak a word—

"Good morning, Jenerrie. Give me ten minutes, and I'll meet all of you in the Greenroom."

Jenerrie quickly shifts the intense feelings she picks up from Relaxella to her mental body and sends her a thought-wave of peace.

When I was five years old, I saw an insect that had been eaten by **ants** and of which nothing remained except the shell. Through the holes in its anatomy one could see the sky. Every time I wish to attain purity I look at the sky through flesh.

—Salvador Dali

CHAPTER 2

GOOD MORNING

Girlfriend stirs inside the yellowish-orange, early spring morning light, which frames her face and light brown hair. Before opening her eyes, she hums to herself and places her hands on her solar plexus.

Neighbour, Girlfriend's best friend, is dancing in the sunbeams on the window ledge, watching her latest shape-shifting form absorb the rays into her multi-coloured wings. This morning Neighbour is a butterfly.

"Girlfriend, Girlfriend, wake up, wake up, it's me, Neighbour. Open the window, Girlfriend. I want to give you a morning hug."

Girlfriend gently wiggles under the covers and continues her somewhat of a morning ritual of visualizing any of her Meridians, which have a path of movement through her head. Today she chose the Governing Meridian. She imagines the rest of her Meridians waking up with the sunlight too. Her feelings are acute. When she senses her energy circuits are activated, she bolts out from under the indigo duvet and dashes for the window. She opens the window wide, sticks her head out, closes her eyes, and breathes in the scent of fresh morning dew.

Neighbour takes the opportunity to flutter around her friend's beautiful face. "Good morning, Girlfriend."

Girlfriend hears a tiny voice saying good morning to her. She smiles enchantingly. She extends her hand and watches the butterfly flutter to a stop. Girlfriend proceeds to stroke the energy around this tiny insect. She welcomes the gorgeous butterfly into her room, balancing it on her baby finger. She carefully tucks her head and upper body back through the window. She joyfully consumes one of her shape-shifting symbols and visualizes a butterfly body for herself too. Instantly, Girlfriend giggles herself into her new temporary form. At the age of seven, she learned that laughter would ease any shape-shifting procedure. She follows the butterfly and tries to imitate its flight patterns. Flying across the room, together, they move in and out of the sunlight rays. She suspends herself above her favourite purple amethyst stone that sits on her table of unique crystals. Neighbour flutters beside her.

"Neighbour, it's you! All along, I thought you were a real butterfly saying good morning to me. What an awesome wake-up call you have given me! Thank you! I mean, wow, this is great! I have never seen you like this before."

The two friends laugh and watch the aura of their butterfly bodies mingle with the ambiance of the amethyst crystal.

"I must admit I have never seen a butterfly wearing purple pyjamas. I wanted to come through your window, land on your nose, and wake you up when I arrived. Unfortunately, your window was shut when I got here. I am glad you decided to transform too. I rather like being in a butterfly's body, but we have a meeting with Relaxella, and somehow, I don't think she would appreciate seeing us this way. You know how she always warns us about over-indulging in this 'thing we like to do.' I can even hear her voice in my tiny butterfly brain saying, 'If you use the Science of Transformation[2] too much, you will weaken your Meridian system, and your abilities will decrease.'"

"Well, my friend, should we change over and get real?"

They both nod yes with their butterfly heads.

To return to their bodies, they touch each other on what they imagine are their butterfly foreheads, using their right wingtips for balance. When the touch is secure, they beam to each other the thought of their regular forms, and as they arrive back in their bodies, a sunbeam caresses them. Their pointer fingers are rubbing the spot in between their eyebrows. This spot secures their change. Sometimes they touch forehead to forehead to facilitate the same result. They breathe deeply together until their heart rates stabilize. Slowly they open their eyes.

To come back into one's body is a skill that took both girls only seven years to master. They had many lessons with Relaxella. Shape-shifting at such a young age was considered rare by the Elders of the Community. For many members of The Echoes of the Sun Community, not until a person turned twenty-one were they able to start learning the skill of shape-shifting. Members born outside of the Community and later willingly became part of the Community were gifted one chance to shape-shift.

---

2   A conversion from one form to another. Any change in an organism that alters its general character and mode of life; biological transformation or metamorphosis.

Instantly, Neighbour reached for her friend and gave her a warm hug. "You know this is what I really wanted to do when I saw you lying there so beautifully under your indigo duvet."

"Geez, Neighbour, today has been one of the better morning awakenings I have experienced in a long time. Oh my, I slept through sunrise meditation! I don't know what happened."

"Neither do I, Girlfriend. I came here because I didn't see you at the meditation rock, and it is the first day of spring. Were you up late reading, or—?"

"Hmm, nothing in particular. I guess my body needed some extra sleep. Neighbour, will you stay and meditate with me?"

"Sure, how can I refuse? I love to go into a solar state of mind!" Neighbour's morning enthusiasm is notable.

Girlfriend arranges her special purple velvet pillow she sits on for this journey to the world of silence. She offers Neighbour a blue velvet pillow, knowing it is her favourite colour.

When they first met each other at the age of four, Girlfriend saw the colour blue all around Neighbour. Neighbour saw the colour purple all around Girlfriend. They would call each other by birth names: Girlfriend is Lilac, and Neighbour, Azure. The Invisible Mentors gave them their code names of Girlfriend and Neighbour at age ten.

Young Lilac had asked her mother, Estel, why she saw blue all the time around her friend. Estel told her daughter the colour blue has a link with music, poetry, and visual art; everything artistic and positively creative comes from the colour blue. One can receive the bounty of blue daily simply from looking up at the sky. Estel told Lilac that Azure would grow up to be an artist one day. Of course, at the age of four, Lilac didn't understand all the variety of artists one can become. Lilac wondered if she had blue around herself. Estel told her daughter she has every colour *inside* herself. "You have an inner spectrum of colours, and so does Azure. Your predominant colour, though, is purple."

Lilac loved this image. Her mother continued to explain to Lilac that when children have a predominant colour seen at an early age, their destiny is to help and inspire others.

"You will grow up to help many people because you will always want them to be happy inside. You will understand how magic is essential in our lives. You are a passionate soul, and whatever you do in your life, people will feel your enthusiasm for truth, love, and even mystical love. Your devotion to a spiritual path will be with you all your life."

Surely, Estel knew that her daughter did not grasp everything she told her about the colours blue and purple at such a tender age. Nevertheless, she felt it her duty as a solar-conscious parent to introduce concepts early, such as the cycles of seven years[3] philosophy that is fundamental in The Echoes of the Sun Community.

"Neighbour, let's tune into the colour blue today as we immerse ourselves slowly into the magical solar view."

"Girlfriend, I love this idea. I want to feel expanded like the sky!"

When they finish their meditation, they will be ready for the day ahead of them, which they would soon find out, is the start of the next six months of their lives.

---

3   Cycles of Seven: Rudolf Steiner's philosophy of the 7-year cycles of life
    Ages 0 to 7: From Oneness with Mother to Growing Autonomy
    Ages 7 to 14: A Fight for and Commitment to Life
    Ages 14 to 21: Wild Emotions, Raging Hormones, Sexuality
    Ages 21 to 28: Play That Turns Toward Responsibility
    Ages 28 to 35: The Body in Full Bloom
    Ages 35 to 42: Crisis and Questioning
    Ages 42 to 49: Soul Searching and Wonder
    Ages 49 to 56: An Ever-Growing Vision and Understanding of Life
    Ages 56 to 63: The Crossroads: Mastery or Re-evaluation
    Ages 63 to 70: A Time of Harvesting and Spreading the Wealth

It is certain that there may be extraordinary mental activity with an extremely small absolute mass of nervous matter: thus the wonderfully diversified instincts, mental powers, and affections of **ants** are notorious, yet their cerebral ganglia are not so large as the quarter of a small pin's head. Under this point of view, the brain of an **ant** is one of the most marvellous atoms of matter in the world, perhaps more so than the brain of a man.

—Charles Darwin *(On the Origin of Species, 1859)*

CHAPTER 3

ARRANGEMENTS

The She is sitting in her favourite chair in the Greenroom sipping a cup of peppermint tea when Jenerrie opens the doors, inviting Tesshu and Kaleb inside.

"Good to see you again, Tesshu, Kaleb. Please have a seat. I trust it was easy for you to find us, even though our location is tucked away from the mainstream."

"I didn't have a problem," replies Tesshu.

"How about you, Kaleb?"

"Well, I did run into a few dead ends that weren't on the map Jenerrie gave us the other day in the city. I live on the east side, and I hadn't anticipated this place being many kilometres away from me. Lucky I started out early. When I turned up the driveway, I saw Tesshu, so we walked up the path together. Wonderful entrance gardens."

"Thanks, Kaleb. There are plenty more gardens out back, which you will visit in a short while. I am glad you both made it here safely. Do either one of you have any questions regarding the instructions?"

"Yes," Kaleb says, nodding. "I have read your guidelines three times, and I still need to know why Tesshu has to be in the same room with me. Don't take offence, Tesshu. I don't even know you. I guess I am feeling a little apprehensive about being thoroughly observed by your assistants and with Tesshu beside me—" His eyes meet The She's. "I'm sorry, I'm rambling."

"Kaleb, I sympathize with your apprehensiveness. Any new therapy can be frightening to open to or even embarrassing. However, I know you will be deeply involved with your own process; you will often forget Tesshu is in the same room. From a technical point of view, it does not work for us to have you in separate rooms. Sometimes we anticipate you will assist each other. We will always leave time for discussion before and after your sessions, if need be, okay?"

Kaleb nods his head in agreement.

"Since there are no more questions, I apologize, but we will have to delay your start time today until after lunch. I have an unexpected rendezvous at the 11th hour, and I must prepare myself for the meeting. In the meantime, Jenerrie and Parli— another assistant whom you will meet shortly—will show you around the Estate, particularly our gardens. After the garden tour, lunch will be served. Again, I apologize for the delay. I do hope this is not a disappointment to either of you."

Kaleb replies, "Is there some last-minute adjustment you have to make to your Invention? Is this really why we can't start as indicated on the signed Acceptance Documents?"

"Kaleb, there is absolutely nothing wrong with the Invention. Many have gone through the Point-by-Point Meridian Figures. A lot of time, resources, and people have helped me make this project a success and what it is today. I told you the truth regarding our delay in starting. I am grateful you are excited to begin; still, I warn you, it is of utmost importance to have an attitude of flexibility regarding procedures around here. We do our best to keep to schedules; however, sometimes, urgent matters take priority, like today."

The She stands up. "Tesshu, Kaleb, I must take my leave now. I look forward to seeing you at lunch. Jenerrie, please connect with Parli for the tour. Enjoy the gardens."

The She leaves the Greenroom with authority and arrives back in her meditation room with an hour to spare before her other guests arrive. She will need fifteen minutes to prepare herself for the Invisible Mentor's communication wavelength. Even though she feels a little hurried inside now, the vibration of her birth name—Relaxella—always brings her back to calmness.

Five candles are strategically placed in her meditation room. Relaxella walks from candle to candle, lighting them. Her pattern across the room traces the form of a five-pointed star, a pentagram.[4] As she lights each candle, she thanks the Princes of the Elements: Fire, Air, Water, and Earth. She thanks the force within herself as she lights the last candle, uniting her with this ancient ritual. She lays down in the middle of this unseen star shape she has walked out to begin the preparation for becoming a clear channel to communicate with the invisible world. She visualizes each of her fourteen Meridians, starting with the Lung Meridian, which follows a clock pattern discovered by the Chinese culture. She honours this ancient wisdom. At the 10th hour of the day, the Spleen Meridian rules transformation and transportation. Playfully, she says out loud, "Okay, Invisible Mentors, I am ready to communicate; I am ready to go for a ride."

She sees the currents flowing through her physical body with her eyes closed. Within seconds, the energy moves into her astral body. A body of light appears, and a "shield" forms around her physical body, so, while communicating, no negative entity can enter her energy field and affect her. With the shield in place, she mentally calls the Invisible Mentors by their sacred names and asks for their council. In this state of consciousness, all communication is non-verbal. After she clearly mentally states each sentence or question, she knows how to pause to allow and receive the communication from the Mentors.

Gently yet assuredly, she states her qualifications for handling two significant projects at one time. Relaxella tells the Mentors she is certain Tesshu and Kaleb are thoroughly prepared to begin working with the Invention, and it will be a great disappointment for the young men to delay their start date. They have signed contracts. She articulates her concern for Kaleb, as he already displays anxious energy; he may not

---

4   The Pentagram is a symbolic representation of the path of the human soul to perfection. The rays of the pentagram represent love, wisdom, truth, justice, and kindness.

want to return if the Mentors insist on a Summer Solstice start time. She knows that if Kaleb backs out, she will have to start all over again to find another youth the same age as Tesshu with the right complementary personality, and this alone could take six months. Six months she cannot afford to waste. Relaxella knows they have to begin today on the Spring Equinox.

The Invisible Mentors are pleased with her courage, conviction, and tenacity. They acknowledge the letter was a test of her dedication to her intuition. They open the ninth point on her Heart Meridian as a gift to her. A pulsating light enters her mental body and scatters any lingering particles of sorrow that had previously scarred her Heart Meridian. This gift now gives her a direct and quick open line to the Invisible Mentors' plane; thus, she no longer needs to go through the ritual of the five-pointed star to communicate with them. The pulse of light slows. She feels blood rushing through her heart on the physical plane. In this one brilliant moment, she also sees the clock of the Heart Meridian kick in at the 11th hour. She quickly brings the shield back into herself. Tears of gratitude naturally release. She breathes deeply, and when she feels fully in her physical body, she places herself in a devotional pose, gives thanks once again, and rises from the floor with a new sense of profound grace. Before walking out of her meditation room, she whispers, "I am so glad I can break my own rules because I will be a few minutes late for Girlfriend, Neighbour, and their parents."

Anti-acid: What **ants** use to get high.

—Unknown

CHAPTER 4

DISCUSSION

Estel and Eos Ernel are sitting on the couch looking over the latest heritage seed catalogue when Girlfriend bursts into the living room.

"Mom, Dad, are you ready? We've got a meeting in thirty minutes at Heart Quarters." Girlfriend is excited.

"Slow down, love. Of course, we are ready. We can continue later deciding what seeds to order with the ones we already have for this year's garden. We heard a few extra footsteps earlier this morning. Has Neighbour gone home? What were you two doing?"

"Yes, Neighbour went home. This morning, she visited me in a butterfly's body, and I couldn't help it; I changed into a butterfly, too! At first, I didn't even know the winged being was Neighbour and—"

"Darling daughter, you are talking too quickly," her father says, attempting to calm her. "Have you forgotten what Relaxella asked you both regarding shape-shifting? You are only fourteen years old, and you know the creation laws around doing this too much can be harmful to you."

Girlfriend walks over to her father, sits beside him, and gently rubs out the frown marks of concern on his forehead. Girlfriend takes one hand of each parent and speaks gently, yet with conviction.

"Please don't worry about me burning out, with my ability, my gift. You have to trust me. I am at a stage in my young life where I need to understand the power of shape-shifting. I promise I will not abuse the gift. I am a different generation than you. As you know, I have read the laws many times formed years ago by the Invisible Mentors. Relaxella knows we are clearer than you were at my age, and naturally, the clearer one is, the more access they have to this particular state of consciousness. Mom, Dad, I have to ask you a question—are these feelings of concern coming out for me because you both will not be seeing me for some time after today?"

"Dear, how do you know? Relaxella asked us not to tell you. Did you overhear us speaking about your upcoming journey? Did Neighbour tell you?"

"Neighbour and I figured it out on our own. We were reading about our history in *Once Upon A Solar Time*—you know the part in the book where future visions are described in poetry?"

"Relaxella allowed you both to handle the only copy left of *Once Upon A Solar Time?*"

"Yes, Mom, she did. Lately, in our weekly lessons, we have had to learn about the history of The Echoes of the Sun Community. Then, three weeks ago, she asked us to memorize and perform the poem for her."

"Perform the poem? Interesting."

"Last week, we finished the book."

"You read the whole book?" Eos asks, surprised.

"For sure. Would you like me to recite the poem called 'Two Echo Youths'?"

"Definitely!" Eos and Estel exclaim simultaneously.

There is a consciousness we all know.
It is not bound to the physical plane.
It may shift into a flower before us.
Those who fear it will go insane.

Two Echo Youths will know it,
more than many who have come before.
Their keenness will kindle kindness.
Their joy will be forever adored.

They are destined to go on a journey,
to meet Echoers in the Realm.
They must pass through the Valley of Boji
and then reach The Hillock helm.

No villains will greet them while walking
or other dark and negative beings,
an abundance of light and gladness
will follow them on wings.

We who honour the cycles of seven,
know from a deep, heartfelt space,
the two Echo Youths who have been chosen
are souls, which cannot be traced.

Girlfriend's recital of the poem moves her parents to tears of joy. Their only child, now a teenager, constantly gifts them with her "wisdom." Estel and Eos respect her fearlessness and understand her expression addresses their own anxiousness.

"We love you!" Estel unashamedly tells her daughter. "You don't know how much we will miss your presence."

"I hope you both know how much I will miss you too. I have an idea. Let's make a conscious effort on every full moon to tune into each other's frequency throughout the day. This way, I will receive news of you, and you will receive news of me."

"Oh, darling, such a brilliant idea! Will it work?" asks Eos.

"For sure! I practice telepathy[5] with Neighbour all the time. Mind you, we have been training for a few years. Still, I know you both will get the hang of it. My thought transference is quite strong. I guess you'll have to wait and see, oops, I mean hear," says Girlfriend with a grin.

"Hello, is anyone home?"

The Ernels jump up from the couch and run to the kitchen to greet their visitors. Phoenix, Neighbour, and Davey are standing at the open door with their right hands held up near their Heart Chakra,[6] palm side facing their friends. This standard greeting used by The Echoes of the Sun Community symbolizes the giving of light from one's heart to another's. The Ernels stop and mirror their friends. Everyone is smiling and looking into each other's eyes.

Phoenix, Neighbour's father, then breaks the silence. "Are we having fun or what?"

Everyone laughs. They all exchange hugs and kisses on the cheek. Girlfriend grabs her packsack. Estel carries a strawberry pie in her knapsack, and Eos has a jar of last year's honey from their first beehives. He also takes a gift-wrapped box of goodies

---

5 Communication from one mind to another by extrasensory means.
6 The Heart Chakra is the fourth of the seven primary chakras. It is represented by the colour green. The Heart Chakra acts as an individual's centre of compassion, empathy, love, and forgiveness.

for their other daughter, Jenerrie, in his bag. Phoenix has a basket of cut flowers to accompany the other gifts to give to Relaxella and her assistants.

"Looks like we are ready," announces Eos.

"Yes, our timing is perfect," says Phoenix.

The Ernels turn off the lights and close the door but don't lock it. It is not necessary. Girlfriend and Neighbour stay behind a few meters to allow their parents to talk. Davey runs slightly ahead of the adults. Although he is only six years old, he is intensely independent.

The pleasant stroll to Heart Quarters takes the group twenty minutes at a steady pace. They take the path through a large field of wild spring flowers, which will soon bring them to the back entrance of Relaxella's Estate.

"Neighbour, my best friend, could you do me a favour?" asks Girlfriend.

"Sure, anything for you."

"Could you ask my dad innocently to tell you the story of how he met my mom?"

"Okay, but I have already heard this story."

"Yes, I know. However, I feel if my dad is re-stimulated with the memory of the moments when they first fell in love, it will ease the heartache they are experiencing now because they know we will not be coming back home for a while."

"Girlfriend, did you tell them?" Neighbour asks in a loud whisper.

"I had to. After our last class, Relaxella took me aside and told me to tell them today."

"I wonder why she never told me to do the same with my dad?" muses Neighbour.

"I don't know why, Neighbour. Relaxella always has her reasons, unless, of course, she simply forgot. We know how her memory does not always serve her, don't we?"

"Yes, we sure do. Who am I to judge? I will ask your dad."

"Great, you're a real friend, Neighbour."

"Takes one to know one," Neighbour replies.

They run to catch up to their parents.

"Eos, would you mind telling us the story of how you met Estel?"

"Right now?"

"Sure. You are a great storyteller, and we have time while walking. I feel like hearing this story. Come on, Eos, please." Neighbour walks backwards in front of Eos, facing him, hands held together tightly as if pleading.

"If there are no objections." Eos looks at Phoenix, assuming he may want to question his daughter's request. Phoenix has nothing to say. He smiles in agreement.

"Estel?"

"Eos, I never get tired of you telling; just the same, don't exaggerate."

Eos has a glitter in his eyes that will last throughout the story.

"Many years ago on a Saturday night, magic happened. Every weekend, the adults planned activities for the youth of our times. There were dances with recorded or live music, theatre and comedy nights, choral singing events, sports fun days, cooking parties—so many activities; however, the event many participated in was Synchronicity. That is where I met Estel—in the Synchronicity game."

"Yeah, I know *where* you met—*how* you met her interests me most," demands Neighbour.

"Hold on, Neighbour. I'm getting there. I have to set the stage."
Everyone laughs, knowing Neighbour is being over-anxious
on purpose.

Eos continues. "In those days, the consciousness of what
it takes to make communities work started to form. Many
systems had their trials and huge learning curves. We didn't
have the same ability as you both have to perform shape-shifting. However, the beginnings of the Science of Transformation
happened in our generation. Our experiential nature has
proved to be the groundwork needed for the geniuses of the
next generation to expand this Science, which can still only be
explored by those who are open, receptive, and willing to work
for the collective consciousness.[7] Our generation learned a lot
of theatre exercises, games, and techniques. So, through the art
of theatre, we practiced an organic form of shape-shifting, and
thus, for most of us, it was easy to act out a character, improvise, and have fun!

"Everyone loved the Synchronicity game. Upon arrival, The
Sync-Caller gave a card to those who wanted to participate.
On one side of the card was written an emotion and a character; for example, an angry salesperson, a happy teenager, or
a frustrated secretary. On the other side of the card was an
image from the ancient playing card deck; for example, three
of hearts, ten of clubs, or eight of diamonds. The Sync-Caller
established an environment for the players to improvise the
scene and would call out six cards per round. Those who held
the called-out cards would go into the creative space and have
a two-minute huddle wherein they told each other the details
written on their cards. Then, someone would volunteer to start
a scene. The others chosen for the round would enter the stage

---

7   Collective Consciousness (simply defined) is a state of mind and heart
     wherein everyone values truth, honesty, peaceful actions, and respect
     for all living beings.

when they felt they could contribute content to the dialogue. The Sync-Caller always gave a one-minute warning bell that informed the players to end whatever they were improvising.

"Often, politics of the day would be acted out or other current events. Sometimes the character and emotion were similar to the person acting, and a real story would transpire therein.

"Many rounds of play would take place throughout the game. However, only three times in an evening two people improvised together. No one else could join them. The night I met Estel, Nova was The Sync-Caller. She had the exceptional quality of bringing single people together. I hoped Nova's magic would find me. First, she picked my card. Then, I saw Nova give Estel a wink when she called her card too."

Eos changes his voice to mimic Nova. "It is now time for a scene with these two players. The environment is a full moon night, early evening, and the characters are meeting at a soda shop, time frame, 1958."

Eos winks at the girls and continues in his regular voice. "My character was a biker with a hardened heart; her character was an enthusiastic roller skater who recently won a championship. I was the three of hearts card, and she the ten of diamonds.

"Estel walked gracefully onto the stage. She had on a mauve silk dress. Her long, brown silky hair caught the light just right. She didn't have much makeup on, unlike many women present who did. In fact, she was rather plain-looking, which attracted me.

"While we were in character, she made me laugh, even though I acted like a bitter, tough guy. We ended the scene with me promising to give her a motorcycle ride with her roller skates on. We casually walked off the playing area, holding hands. Everyone clapped loudly. Her eyes were sparkling when she thanked me. Nova's magic worked! The rest, my dear friends, is—her-story, but there is no more time to tell it, so it will remain—"

Estel finishes his sentence, "—His-story."

The children cheer. "Thank you, Eos! Awesome storytelling!" Girlfriend and Neighbour shout simultaneously.

"Thanks, Eos. It's too bad Synchronicity events aren't happening anymore," Phoenix laments.

Neighbour replies. "What do you mean, Dad? They happen all the time with our generation because we are in sync! You had to create it artificially to understand its value in your generation. With us, it is a part of our nature. Girlfriend, I'll race you to the estate."

"Sure. No shape-shifting!" yells Girlfriend.

Davey runs after them. "Wait for me!"

Watching the children run away from them, Phoenix addresses the Ernels. "I want to thank you both for letting me know earlier that our two precious daughters will be gone for a while. There will be an empty space in my house without Neighbour," says Phoenix sadly. "I know Davey will miss her terribly; he loves his sister immensely. I will have to break this news to him gently later today."

"Yes, I understand," Eos says, nodding. "Even though Jenerrie doesn't live with us anymore, she loves her sister and will miss her. Lucky for Girlfriend, Jenerrie is Relaxella's right-hand assistant, so she will ensure all of their arrangements are in order."

"Truthfully, this journey is a chance of a lifetime for them," said Estel. "I am confident Relaxella will assure us."

Ants are so much like human beings as to be an embarrassment. They farm fungi, raise aphids as livestock, launch armies into wars, use chemical sprays to alarm and confuse enemies, capture slaves. The families of weaver **ants** engage in child labour, holding their larvae like shuttles to spin out the thread that sews the leaves together for their fungus gardens. They exchange information ceaselessly. They do everything but watch television.

—*Lewis Thomas*

CHAPTER 5

A WALK IN THE GARDEN

Late morning sunlight gently bounces off the brilliant red, hardy azalea flowering shrub border standing seven feet tall, providing a visual barrier to The She's Estate. A hexagon-shaped wood and glass cedar home is about a hundred feet beyond this border—where Relaxella lives. Circular solar panels, artistically mounted on the east side of the roof, shimmer above Shasta daisies, double hollyhocks, blue flax, sweet lavender, and purple coneflowers surrounding her place. Clematis vines with buds of yellow and blue flowers drape her home's arched entranceway.

Tesshu and Kaleb walk on each side of Jenerrie, with Parli keeping in step, slightly behind. Parli walks many a guest through the gardens with Jenerrie; she has yet to be designated spokesperson. Jenerrie has been with Relaxella for five years, compared to Parli, who recognizes the virtue for her to master patience in her second year of assistant training.

As the group looks around in awe, Jenerrie speaks softly. "And on the east side of The She's home is her vegetable garden. We will pass by all its beauty by the end of our tour."

Jenerrie and Parli sense the usual excitement approaching the first view of Relaxella's home. For some reason, every time this moment arrives, these feelings they initially experienced occur repeatedly. However, for Kaleb, the first view is an altogether different and unsettling experience. He stops abruptly. While intensely gazing as if seeing an apparition, Kaleb hears Jenerrie coaxing him to explain his feeling.

"Feeling? You mean seeing, don't you?"

"Feeling, Kaleb. What are you feeling?" encourages Jenerrie.

"Well, I'm feeling my heart beating faster than normal. My legs are a little rubbery. My palms are sweaty, and my mind is trying to piece together fragments of thoughts, rapidly firing information at me. Man—ah, excuse me, woman—this is too much!"

Jenerrie instructs Kaleb to close his eyes. She places her right hand on his Solar Plexus Chakra[8] and then indicates with eye contact and a nod for Parli to quickly come to her other side. She puts her left hand on Parli's Heart Chakra and asks them

---

8   The Solar Plexus Chakra (third chakra) is associated with the element of fire and directly links us to ourselves through our willpower. Its associated color is yellow, hence its link to fire and, more broadly, the sun.

to breathe deeply. Even though Kaleb doesn't quite understand what she means by breathing deeply, he doesn't voice it. Instead, he breathes the way he knows how. Jenerrie sees he is still shallow breathing because part of her hand is not undulating at his plexus. She chooses not to repeat her question and to watch what transpires.

"Kaleb, when did this feeling first hit you?"

"Hit me is the right word! Exactly when I saw the symbol on what I imagine is the entrance door to The She's home."

"You mean the blue circle with a blue dot in the middle?"

"Yes."

"Where did the feeling come into your body?"

"Exactly where your hand is."

"Is the energy gentle or harsh?"

"It is not so gentle. It is not intense like a punch in the stomach; even so, it is like a door opened really quick, something went in, and then the door slammed shut."

"Can you trace what went in?"

Kaleb searches for the answer with his eyes closed. His body occasionally gives off spastic energy. Finally, he breathes deeply for the first time. Jenerrie senses the heat returning to his Solar Plexus Chakra and says, "You found it. Tell me what you think happened."

"This may sound weird, but the symbol went inside me. It is like, right now, your hand is sealing it in. I guess my anxiety is that I don't know what the symbol means."

"Kaleb, the circle with the dot in the middle represents the sun, or Solar Consciousness.[9] Imagine," Jenerrie says, her voice

---

9   A simple meaning of Solar Consciousness is a state of mind, heart, and body wherein fear does not have any roots. It is also called clear consciousness, linked to joy and gratitude through service to humanity. Honouring the sunrise every morning always activates and sustains Solar Consciousness.

steady. "Matter is inert and formless until spirit descends into it to vivify it. A point symbolizes a spirit, and the matter that surrounds it is the circle. Cosmic Intelligence places this figure of a point surrounding a circle throughout the Universe. We see it in fruit (the flesh around a central core or seed), our eyes, and certain parts of our bodies. We even see it in the structure of a cell and the solar system. Kaleb, you have just received a gift."

"A gift?"

"Yes. The area where my hand is on your body is called the Solar Plexus Chakra. This chakra is leaking vital energy, which could mean you require excessive control, or you often have feelings of helplessness arise. Focusing positively on the Solar Plexus Chakra can help us connect to Solar Consciousness; it can help us feel calm inside and increase our willpower. Truly, you are lucky to have had this experience before you start working with the Meridian Figure Invention."

Kaleb opens his eyes and roughly pushes her hand off his body. Jenerrie accepts his response and makes a mental note to tell Relaxella. Jenerrie knows she cannot tell him anything else unless he asks. Parli, on the other hand, excited by what just happened, charmingly takes Kaleb by the elbow and leads him to the east side of the house, delicately distracting him from going deeper into the experience. Parli senses this young man will undergo profound transformations once he gets "playing" the Point-by-Point game. Relaxella assigned Parli to Kaleb, and Parli already likes him. She is always attracted to those who have an internal fight going on inside them.

Meanwhile, Tesshu, throughout the whole exchange, remains calm and non-judgmental. He admires the Estate's gardens and how Jenerrie handled Kaleb. Soon, once again, he wordlessly falls into step beside Jenerrie as she leads the group to the next activity.

Ants live safely till they have gotten wings.

—Unknown

CHAPTER 6

PREPARING LUNCH

"Tell me, Coral, did you get a good look at the new contestants?" Omni asks with a slightly jealous edge.

"As a matter of fact, I did. Jenerrie introduced me to them."

"Where? I thought only Jenerrie and Parli were to take them on the garden tour. How come you got to go?"

"Omni, you are jumping to conclusions. I didn't *join* them on the tour, and besides, they are in the gardens at this very moment. We all crossed paths as I came to the kitchen to start the lunch preparations. We exchanged eye contact, handshakes, smiles, and a few questions and answers. I detected they both have sharp jawlines, a sure sign of being able to use their willpower. Tesshu has mixed blood, Japanese and Anglo-Saxon. Kaleb has light-coloured hair and hazel eyes, and he mentioned briefly he comes from Scottish ancestry; however, he isn't purely

Scottish. Kaleb is also edgier than Tesshu. Tesshu appeared shy and had a softer feeling than Kaleb. I particularly enjoyed Tesshu's corner of the mouth lines when he smiled. Both have smooth skin, and Kaleb asked more questions than Tesshu. Is there anything else you want to know, Omni?"

"No, not really. You might have said too much already. I'll form my own opinion when I see them. So, since you are the head cook for today's special lunch, how can I assist you?"

"Before you assist me with anything, I will appreciate it if you get rid of some of the attitude forming on the edge of your phrases. Relaxella insists when we are cooking for others, we participate with care and clarity. The twins, Vera and Vital, should be here any moment. If you prefer, I could ask one of them to be my main assistant for today."

"No, please don't, Coral. I've always wanted to work with you. It is true what you say about my attitude. I'll change right now."

"Omni, I must admit, I admire that aspect about you—your ability to adjust quickly to what is best."

"Thank you, Coral. I need to hear this. Shall we synchronize, sister?"

"Yes, Omni."

The custom for those working in the kitchen is to recite a prayer or poem before making a meal. By enhancing collective harmony, the cooks believe the food tastes better.

Vera and Vital arrive just in time to add their voices to today's prayer.

Oh Light, may the gentleness of your magnificence
bless our hands as we prepare the abundance of food before us
into a nutritious meal.
Keep our thoughts joyful while working together,

so we can infuse this nutrition with
wholesome elements for all who partake.

"Vera and Vital, you both look beautiful," says Omni.

"Thank you, sista." The twins speak together.

Coral adds a comment to the twins. "I must say your timing is perfect. It is hard to believe you have been with us for only six months. You always seem to know when to arrive! It will be a pleasure to co-create with you today in the kitchen. Vital, I know you are talented at designing salads; you always remember not to soak the leaves for long, so they keep their vitality. There should be enough alfalfa and arugula sprouts in the sprout room for today's meal. Relaxella informed me you could go to the greenhouse and pick some fresh lemon balm, basil, and oregano to add to the salad dressing. Vera, you can decide what dessert you want to make, and Omni will assist you after she has helped me prepare the main dish."

"How many are showing up for lunch, Coral?"

"Good question, Vera. There will be fourteen guests altogether. By the way, you and your sister will also be responsible for setting the table. Are there any more questions before we begin our work in silence?"

"Silence? Coral, could we sing while we are making preparations?"

"Of course, Omni. Singing is a form of silence, the silencing of useless chatter. Does anyone have a song suggestion?"

By the time Jenerrie and Parli finish giving Tesshu and Kaleb a tour of the gardens, they are all ready for a hearty lunch. While Parli checks with the kitchen staff to see how everything is going, Jenerrie decides to create an ambience with music in

Seashell Lounge, since today is a special day to serve lunch here. While the young men are chilling out, she puts on one of the first recordings Sungram Records produced. The music dips and curves excitingly. Tesshu and Kaleb saunter around the Lounge, absorbing as much visual stimulus as possible. Their senses are deliciously over-stimulated. When they reach their comfort zones, they simultaneously snap their fingers to the music. A look and a wink to each other assures Jenerrie's good taste. Upon recognizing this synchronicity, Jenerrie smiles at them.

"Great choice of music, Jenerrie," Kaleb acknowledges.

"Yes, real fine, Jenerrie, real fine. Sungram's first micro tape release, Details on a Wing. It sure became cool when micro tapes finally came to par in quality with high-definition CDs."

"Do you also happen to have the vinyl recording?" asks Kaleb. "I've never seen the sleeve before."

Tesshu answers first. "Kaleb, if you ever want to come to my house, I can show you my collection. I have everything Sungram has ever recorded." Tesshu speaks loud enough for Jenerrie to hear while she is looking for the album jacket on a shelf nearby.

Kaleb replies, "Tesshu, this is the moment, and Jenerrie is getting it for me." Kaleb emphasizes the word *me*.

Jenerrie enters their conversation again and gives Kaleb the vinyl album, Details on a Wing. "Please be careful; it's a collector's item."

"Sure, I'll sit on the leather chair and ease into the information."

Vera, Vital, and Omni enter the lounge to make sure the table settings for the lunch are in place; Parli follows them in, carrying a tray of glasses of sparkling water.

Walking over to where Tesshu is standing near Kaleb—who sits examining the album sleeve—Parli asks, "Would you both like some sparkling water?"

"Yes, please," says Tesshu, who quickly drinks all the water and places the empty glass down.

"I would love a glass too, Parli, thank you."

Parli then serves Vera, Vital, and Omni glasses of water and exits.

Kaleb gestures with his hand for Jenerrie to come to his side. "I have a few questions to ask you."

Jenerrie kneels on the floor beside the chair.

"Is the other woman on the album jacket with The She her twin sister?"

"We are not sure ourselves. There is a rumour: The She has a twin, yet no one has seen her."

"The She had a different name back then; why doesn't she use it now?"

"Various reasons."

"It seems odd. Doesn't The She ever desire to stay in contact with the friends she must have had when she was younger?"

"They are never far away, Kaleb. We all know thoughts do travel." Jenerrie giggles. "I guess, The She meets up with whom she needs or wants to, and her long-time friends connect with her when they have a need or desire to be with her. I know for a fact, though; her name did make her comfortable in many circles awhile back."

"She was the back-up vocalist and band dancer, cool. I love the name of the band too—Inner Faces. How old was she?"

"Early twenties. The She attended university to become a physiologist at the same time." Jenerrie stands and closes her eyes briefly. "One moment, Kaleb."

Kaleb is watching her.

"Kaleb, sorry, I feel The She approaching with our other guests. I must greet them. Please excuse me."

Kaleb's thought forms are now jumpy. He watches the three beautiful women, wearing light cotton summery dresses—almost see-through yet not provocative—flagging Tesshu on all sides. Suddenly, Tesshu's laughter fills the room. Kaleb isn't inspired to join them. The women hold water glasses while they smile and chat together with Tesshu.

Kaleb thinks to himself—*I wonder what he is talking about to keep them all alert around him. Wait a minute. What's he doing now? He's scrunching his face. He's making quick movements of his head, and they're all giggling. Now he mimics the shape of a rectangular box and imitates someone writing something. What a lucky guy, making all those women laugh—what a charmer. And here I am, sitting in this chair, no one noticing me. Is it because I have an insistent independent streak in me? I did pull myself away earlier. Maybe, I'll walk around the room slowly and eventually make my way to their circle of conversation. I will take my time and scan The She's art collection. The artwork has an identical symbol inscribed in the right-hand corner with no name. Interesting. If I feel brave enough, I will ask The She about her art collection later.*

Parli comes back to the lounge and indicates with her eyes for the kitchen staff to make last-minute detailed arrangements for the lunch they are about to serve. While Parli talks with Tesshu to keep him company, the three women move like one mind, never bumping into each other or making useless chatter. The harmony of their movement is transparent and angelic.

Coral is the last to join the group in the lounge. Noticing Kaleb, now wandering around the room alone, she moves towards him slowly. Since his back is to her, she waits for a natural pause in his movement before she will say hello. Coral liked the initial feeling with him when they met earlier in the hallway. Coral knows lunch will be served in a few moments; however, she wants to at least talk to Kaleb a little bit to show him her smile and beautiful hazel eyes. Something they have in common.

Being more of a nervous type, it doesn't take Kaleb very long to feel someone's presence near him. He is unsure if he should turn around in case it is The She, since he would have to make conversation with her—surely an awkward one-on-one. Even though Kaleb fantasizes about how he would like to talk with The She about anything, he knows he isn't confident emotionally to feel secure talking with her alone. He pauses to study one of the paintings.

"Hi, Kaleb. How are you doing?"

"I'm fine, thanks. Ah, I met you already, didn't I?"

"Yes, I'm Coral. We met in the hallway just before you and Tesshu went to the backyard gardens. By the way, did you like the tour?"

Kaleb fidgets before answering. "It—it was fine," and adds quickly, "beautiful, too."

"Listen, I want to let you know; if you have any questions or need anything whenever you are here and can't find Parli to help you out, let me know, okay?"

"Sure, Coral. What do you mean if I can't find Parli?"

"Oh, I thought you would have been told by now. Parli is assigned to be your primary assistant each time you work with the Invention. I will probably be assisting her in a day or two, so you will see more of me." Coral giggles shyly at her comment.

Kaleb laughs nervously, too, and says, "Thanks for letting me know. Is Jenerrie going to be Tesshu's assistant?"

"Yes, and Omni will be assisting Jenerrie when the time is right. Do you have any other questions before I bring you to your seat for lunch?"

"Yes. I hope you don't think I am nosey—do all of you beautiful young women live here on the estate?"

"Thank you for the compliment. Yes, Kaleb, we do live here. We have chosen to come and participate in the work of The She, and it is our pleasure to serve her and the Invisible Mentors.

The She is so in tune with them, it's awesome. Maybe I can fill you in on more details about this place some other day. By the way—" Coral whispers in Kaleb's ear, "—The She's other name is Relaxella." She steps back and smiles at him. "Best, though, you call her The She. Maybe one day in the future, she will invite you to call her Relaxella. I had to wait one year before she invited me into her inner circle. Now I can sense her arriving, and as we prefer to have our guests seated before her, I must bring you to your chair. Please follow me."

Coral pulls slightly on Kaleb's hand and leads him into the dining area of Seashell Lounge. Tesshu is already seated between Jenerrie and Omni. Coral indicates to Kaleb to sit beside Parli. She will sit across from him. The She enters the room, as anticipated, with Girlfriend, Neighbour, Davey, and their parents. Vera and Vital show the guests to their seats. The She, graciously smiling at everyone, finds her place at the heart of the table.

This is the **ant**. Treat it with respect.
For it may very well be the next dominant
life form of our planet.

*—Empire of the **Ants** (the movie)*

CHAPTER 7

THE BUSINESS OF INVENTING

The She is sipping peppermint tea while watching all her beautiful assistants gathering for the after-lunch meeting. Tesshu and Kaleb returned to Seashell Lounge after the heavenly meal. When everyone settles, The She begins.

"I want to thank you, Coral, for being responsible for today's lunch. Everyone moved with grace while serving our guests. I hardly noticed any of you were even there. The savoury tart and salad were amazingly on point."

Her assistants giggle when she says *point*.

"Speaking of points," says The She, amidst more laughter, "you are aware that it is now time to bring Tesshu and Kaleb into the mini-theatre so they can begin their initiation. I need to emphasize how important it is for those who will not be with us to take responsibility for their emotions and thought forms. The more you can sing together in harmony or by yourself, the more you will stabilize a clear and gentle state of mind in yourself. I anticipate the first session will end by the 17th hour of the day. Tesshu and Kaleb will then go to their respective homes, and I will need private time until after tomorrow morning's meditation, wherein we can all meet for breakfast. I trust you will rise early for our sunrise practice. Are there any questions?"

"Yes, Relaxella," began Coral, "do you envision needing Omni and me to assist Jenerrie and Parli tomorrow as we discussed a week ago?"

"Yes, thank you for remembering for me. In fact, it would do you both good to re-read The Second Assistant's Manual tonight."

"I have been studying it ever since you told me I would be helping this time." Omni is proud of her announcement.

"Excellent, Omni. Nevertheless, I trust your passion for being correct will lead you back to the books tonight for the buzz of certainty."

"You know me too well, Relaxella," Omni replies.

"A few more details. Coral, please go now to Seashell Lounge and bring Tesshu and Kaleb to the second floor. Also, I almost forgot to inform whoever is not at this meeting that singing lessons with Sophia will be at the 16th hour of the day."

Coral leaves.

"Vera and Vital, you are the guardians of Girlfriend and Neighbour for the remainder of the day. So, for now, until I come back to talk with their parents, let them be together. At that time, you can take Girlfriend and Neighbour out and get them settled in the guest rooms. And Indigo, thanks for being at this meeting, too, and volunteering to do the dishes. As coordinator for child activities around the Estate, I trust you can entertain Davey when I talk to the parents later."

"It will be my pleasure, Relaxella," Indigo says with a warm smile.

Relaxella leaves the room with Jenerrie and Parli. "Are you both excited to see Tesshu and Kaleb go through the game?"

"Oh yes. I had a great connection with Tesshu. He is eager to clear his pathways."

"And you, Parli, any thoughts?"

"Despite the experience in the garden that we shared with you earlier, Kaleb seems to have settled somewhat after lunch. I trust he, too, is eager to clear his Meridians."

The three women walk side by side through the large hallway.

Tesshu and Kaleb are waiting with Coral on the second floor.

The She stops near them but not too close. "Tesshu, Kaleb, I am glad you spent some time with Girlfriend and Neighbour and their parents before you begin your journey with us. Soon, you will understand how the Echo Youths are an integral part of our work here. For now, we must focus on your purpose. It is the 14th hour of the day and time to be introduced to the Point-by-Point Meridian Figures. Are you excited?"

"For sure!" exclaims Kaleb.

"I haven't been so stimulated in a long time," adds Tesshu.

They follow behind The She, Jenerrie, and Parli. As they turn from the red-walled corridor into the orange-walled hall, Kaleb suddenly grabs Tesshu's arm and pulls him to a stop as the women walk ahead of them.

"Hey, what's happening, Kaleb?" Tesshu asks in a whisper, a little shocked at Kaleb's aggressiveness.

"Well," Kaleb replies urgently in a quiet voice, "I want to talk a little with you before we get going on the game. Tell me what you think of The She—so far."

"Sure, let's talk, but we better walk simultaneously. I'll keep my voice low. I like The She, Kaleb. She seems to be very organized. She is intelligent. She has many social graces, and I can feel she cares deeply for everyone working with her. What are your first impressions?"

"I am a little edgy around her. I know she knows too. It was weird during lunch. Man, I never ate in silence with mostly women before. It felt like my thoughts were a megaphone inside my head! At one point, I looked at Coral, and she was looking right at me with a sparkle in her eyes. I then looked at The She, and she looked at me and quickly glanced at Coral. Meanwhile, Coral had lowered her head, so she did not see The She looking at her. Sometimes it feels to me, The She is inside my thoughts or knows them before I think them!"

"Well, Kaleb, I wouldn't ponder about it too much if I were you. Synchronicity happened a couple of times to me too, but with Jenerrie. Go with the flow, man. Chill."

The She stops in front of a green door. She turns and smiles at Tesshu and Kaleb as they approach.

"Before we go in, I need to ask you an observation question. Close your eyes momentarily and tell me, what are the three colours of the floor tiles in the blue corridor we are presently in?"

The She waits for their answer; however, the young men do not remember.

"Open your eyes. Being aware of details in the moment—including your thoughts—is a huge part of the training you are about to undertake."

Tesshu and Kaleb gulp. Kaleb controls himself not to laugh out of nervousness.

Jenerrie opens the door to the mini-theatre. Parli activates the lighting panel. Slowly, the lighting illuminates the Figures. Tesshu and Kaleb follow The She down a ramp towards the Figures.

They are stunned at what they see.[10]

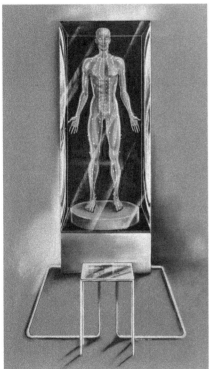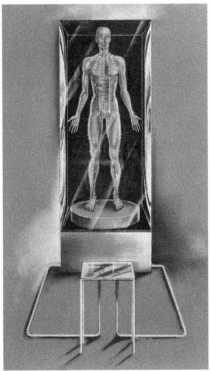

Tesshu's eyes grow wide with amazement.

Kaleb feels his heart beating faster, and he doesn't understand why he is perspiring. He can smell the toxic residue of the coffee he had early in the morning coming through his armpits.

The She says to the young men, "Please make yourself comfy in the theatre chairs."

---

10   The Image of the Meridian Figure Game is from the author's archives.

Kaleb and Tesshu glance nervously at each other as they walk over and settle into the seats.

The She nods to Jenerrie, who walks to a console, presses a button, and the enclosure around the Meridian Figures slides down. The She stands beside one of the Figures. Her assistants remain by the computer consoles.

"I hope your memory skills are sharp as I have many details to impart. Please listen closely. First of all, my Invention is finally at a place where two challengers can operate the Figures independently while seemingly competing with each other. My assistants and I are very excited to have you both 'playing this game' simultaneously—most of the time. All my team and many Community members have been through other versions of The Point-by-Point Invention. These two Figures are adaptations of the original prototype. It is the fourteenth year of my study; thus, programming the Figures has become more transparent and easier each year. You are the first two *outsiders* from our Community invited here to enhance our research.

"From time to time, your assistants might ask you if you are winning your game. In other words, to win your game is to clear your Meridians, your points, your pain, confusion, lies, predictable patterns, institutionalized patterns, and useless dogma. Any mindset that blocks your intuitive flow will be opened for clearing. Our mission with anyone who works with a Meridian Figure is to calibrate your vibration to inner joy, gratitude, self-renewal, and clarity.

"All the data recorded on your process is private. If you want to retrieve your info, you will have free access later. However, not many who clear their Meridians need or want to look back at what they 'went through.' When you know you have accomplished a change that enhances your vibration, elevates your consciousness, and inspires you to serve a higher ideal, it is not necessary to dabble over what you have safely realized.

"A favourite saying amongst The Echoes of the Sun Community is: 'I don't look back. My heart is talking to me right now. I give my full attention to its voice. I am responsible for making it feel even more alive every waking moment. And with this joy, I give back. I am in service to my higher purpose.'

"Any questions, comments, so far?"

"I'm good," states Kaleb.

"I like your favourite saying," Tesshu comments.

The She nods and continues. "It is now time to show you the Proto-Type Perfect Program. We created this program to illustrate the movement of the fourteen main Meridians, and their corresponding points, when in complete harmony. It is an elegant visual developed to inspire in you a commitment to clear your Meridians, in other words, to finish the game.

"Even though the Meridian Figures are androgynous, meaning not masculine or feminine, each one has already been programmed to reflect your dimensions: height, skin density, water content, skin elasticity, and colour pigments. Tesshu, you will work with the Figure on the left, and Kaleb, yours is on the right.

"If you recall, we gathered this preliminary information on you when we met in our downtown office a month ago. The indentations for facial features on the Figures can resemble any challenger. Still, our research shows that it is harder for contestants to look at *their* facial features while playing the game, so each Figure's face is neutral with eyelids always closed.

"Without a doubt, your participation will substantially advance my work. Again, I want to emphasize how grateful I am to you both."

Kaleb raises his hand to ask a question.

"Yes, Kaleb."

"I remember you were talking about some bodysuit we would be wearing. Is this still going to happen?"

"It sure is. Presently we have the suits hung up in the fitting room. I thought it best first for you to view a replication of your Meridians' potential through the Proto-Type Perfect Program before you put on the suits. Tesshu?"

"I would like to say that I feel honoured you have selected me to participate. I hope I can provide more insights for your research. I am also pretty keen to watch my Meridian potential flow. Perfection is hard to achieve in life but worth aiming for."

"Lovely, Tesshu. Okay. I think we are ready. Parli, dim the lights. Jenerrie, please activate the 'Meridian show.'" The She takes a seat in a theatre chair behind the young men. The assistants sit on either side of Tesshu and Kaleb.

The timing of the theatre lights going out synchronizes with both Meridian Figures' ambient lighting turning on. Then, the Figures start to move ever so slowly. A deep masculine voice-over narrates.

"Welcome to the show of how Meridians flow in your body. Even though you cannot see your Meridians, they are part of you. There are fourteen major Meridians to clear. Twelve of the fourteen Meridians are related to a specific organ in your body. These organs are the lung, large intestine, stomach, spleen, small intestine, heart, bladder, kidney, circulation sex (associated with sexual organs), triple warmer (associated with the thyroid), gall bladder, and liver. The two Meridians unrelated to body organs are the central and governing Meridians. We discovered through our research that these two Meridians are the first ones to develop in a growing fetus. As you can see now, every major Meridian energy pathway is on both sides of the body. The exception to this rule is the central and governing Meridians. There is only one pathway of each."

As the voice-over articulates information, one by one, each Meridian and their corresponding points—known as acupuncture—light up. Each Meridian has a different colour. There is also a musical soundtrack playing gently in the background to enhance the feeling of what they are seeing. The voice-over continues.

"The computer console in front of the Figures is your control panel. You must use it to key in any Meridian you want to explore. You do not have to worry about how many points are on each Meridian because the number will stay lit on your console throughout the time you travel through it. Please observe the demo carefully now."

At this point, a 3D image of a contestant is super-imposed and standing in front of a console. They watch this AI (Artificial Intelligence) "person" key in "view Kidney Meridian." First, they see the perfect image of the Kidney Meridian, and afterwards, all the blocked points on that Meridian slowly light up.

"As you observe in this demonstration, points 7, 11, and 19 are blocked. As a rule, start by clearing the point with the lowest number. You may often find that clearing the lowest number first will trigger the release of the remaining blocked points. You will be wearing your bodysuit every time you are playing this game, and since the Figures are like a mirror of yourself, it will not be difficult for you to locate the points on the bodysuit because each one has a sensor connected to your Figure. For help with any blocked Meridian pathway on your back, you can ask your challenger or your assigned assistant to press this point on your behalf until you pass through it.

"Unquestionably, you will know when you have cleared an issue by various accompanying reactions or symptoms: crying, a substantial vocal sigh, a yawn, or a momentary pressure in the brain. These reactions are pain-free. When the reaction goes away, it brings freedom in your mind within a few seconds.

"Other times, you will inevitably find yourself in a recall of an incident that made an imprint in your life and which, in turn, blocked you. You may be surprised at how vividly you recall memories. Occasionally, you may experience stronger reactions, like trembling. Rest assured, your assistants will be at your side immediately. They will support you with their healing skills until you pass through the transition. At any time, if you cannot hold the triggered block, know it is safe to let it go. You can return to the particular blocked point another time. Please do not allow negative thoughts like 'if I do not get through this point, I am a failure.' This thought is a false belief. All your actions are part of the process.

"Another possible scenario is you will receive a glimpse of an event that has not yet taken place on the physical plane. These premonitions are rare; however, if you receive one, it will be accompanied by a feeling of joy. Our research has shown all clairvoyant images of the future contain positivity only.

"For the remainder of the Meridian show, you will see the beauty of light we can each emit when all of our Meridians are clear and flowing."

The soundtrack comes up in volume, and Tesshu and Kaleb watch in awe the Proto-type Perfect dance of light of the Meridian Figures.

The completion of the presentation finds both Tesshu and Kaleb in an introspective state of mind.

The She stands up and walks to the Figures. "Please, join me here. I want you to touch the Figures."

Tesshu and Kaleb move to their assigned Meridian Figure. As they approach, the presence of the Figures is powerful.

"Jenerrie, can you kindly lead the second part of the demonstration?"

"Gladly. Tesshu and Kaleb, please place a hand on your Figure's arm. Feel the smoothness of the texture, how it resembles human skin, though not rough skin. Now, gently pull the surface layer out one inch and release it. Look closely. It never makes a mark, a bruise, or a wrinkle after you let it go.

Also, you will see the Figures are void of hair, moles, freckles, and scars. Our designers perfected the quality of 'skin' of the Figures to such exactness there are rumours the skin breathes. Some also rumour that only The She can detect this breathing. You can choose to believe this or not." Jenerrie smiles at them.

Standing nearby, Parli giggles; she doesn't remember the detail about pulling the skin and makes a mental note to try it when no one is looking.

The She glances at Parli briefly. Jenerrie continues.

"Like in the show we just watched, the pedestal your Figure is mounted on moves slowly to help you see where the Meridians are on your body. You can activate the Proto-Type Perfect program on the console and view the light show again whenever you feel you need inspiration or encouragement."

Jenerrie turns to The She, who speaks again.

"Thank you, Jenerrie. Kaleb and Tesshu, there are just a few more details to share, and then you can put on your Meridian bodysuits and begin your first session today. I will be in and out of the mini-theatre throughout the various times you are here. I thoroughly train my assistants, so they will find me if there is an emergency. If you want to speak with me privately, your assistants can arrange an appointment. Once again, I want to express how pleased I am, Tesshu, and Kaleb, that you are here and helping us in our research; this is indeed a monumental time for us all.

"May the seeds of wisdom that reside in your cells open you gently to your individuality, your records, and your soul's beautiful symphony. May you come to understand the meaning of 'we are beings of light' one day."

With her focused telepathic communication, The She tells Jenerrie and Parli to bring the young men to the fitting room. The She exits gracefully.

Jenerrie and Parli hand Tesshu and Kaleb the bodysuits, wherein the details of their fourteen Meridian roadways and points thread the fabric. The suits have built-in openings for fingertips, eyes, mouth, and nostrils with an invisible, delicately fashioned zipper so contestants can get in and out quickly while not interrupting the detailed Meridians. In addition, the suits have a very smooth feeling against their skin.

Since the material of the suits is highly flexible, it does not take Tesshu and Kaleb very long to put them on. They are soon outside the fitting rooms looking at themselves in full-length mirrors. Tesshu is stroking his arms. He likes the feeling of this "new skin."

Kaleb is excited. "Gees, Tesshu, you look amazing in the bodysuit! You're small-boned; however, your muscles look strong."

"You are really fit, Kaleb! Do you work out every day or what?"

"I go to the gym every other day. I wonder what kind of work-out we will get with the Invention?"

"You guys look great, are you ready to begin?" asks Jenerrie.

Both Tesshu and Kaleb forgot their assistants were watching them. Jenerrie could detect a slight flush of colour on Tesshu's face when she spoke. On the other hand, Parli observes that Kaleb tucked his buttocks in at the sound of Jenerrie's voice.

"We'll zip up the face hoods momentarily," says Jenerrie.

The assistants lead the young men back into the mini-theatre and place them in front of their consoles. When their face hoods are on, they look at each other and laugh. Their assistants join in the joy momentarily, and they all leave for the observation room. Parli takes a Kirlian photograph[11] of their energy fields,

---

11 A technique for recording photographic images of the auras of living people.

Meridian points, and respective blocks. Within minutes, the Kirlian photo information translates into computer code, and Tesshu and Kaleb watch the Figures melt into the exact dimensions of their physicality. Finally, the blueprint appears, revealing all of their blocks.

"Tesshu, this may be the longest video-like game I have ever played. I can't believe what I am seeing! And that Figure is me! Wow!"

"I hear you. I do. Good luck, my new friend."

"What Meridian are you going to go through first?" Kaleb asks with a measured amount of anxiety in his voice.

"I am not into communicating about what I will do first. My brain is giving me tons of messages! If I continue to talk, I may not hear where I should start! Trust yourself, Kaleb."

Tesshu's decisiveness is encouraging, notes Jenerrie. The observation room is wired so that the assistants can hear every conversation. Jenerrie sends a thought-form message to The She, telling her the contestants have begun "their" game.

The **ant** is knowing and wise, but he doesn't
know enough to take a vacation.

—*Clarence Day, Author*

CHAPTER 8

SAYING GOODBYE

Relaxella is holding court with the parents of Girlfriend and
Neighbour in the Greenroom.

"It is never easy to say goodbye to someone you love, whatever age you are. However, with goodbyes come new beginnings. Girlfriend and Neighbour will be going through a rite of
passage as they journey through the Woods of Facuzi and then
into the Realm of Thagara. The trust you have given them and
me is admirable, for I know all three of you have such great
relationships with your children. Phoenix, your lovely wife
Arul would be proud of how you have raised your daughter
and Davey by yourself for the last five years. I am sure it will be
tough on you, Phoenix. So, please know that you are welcome
to come and hang out here at any time of day, even if I can't

visit with you. Of course, Estel, Eos, my offer is extended to you, too."

All three parents simultaneously say, "Thank you."

Everyone chuckles at the synchronicity.

Relaxella sees six-year-old Davey looking sad, so she reaches out to him.

"Davey, come here." He sits on her lap. "I wonder if you would like to join me on Sundays and be my personal garden assistant."

Davey, who already loves to save seeds from fruits and vegetables, quickly agrees. "Can we try and grow some of the seeds I have been collecting?"

"For sure."

"Dad, when is it Sunday?"

"Two days from now, son."

"Will you bring me here to help?"

"No problem. In fact, if any of the seeds that you care for grow, I will buy you the bicycle you have wanted for quite some time now."

"Really, Dad? Cool!" Davey jumps off Relaxella's lap and falls into his dad's arms.

"Indigo, please take Davey outside for a short while," requests Relaxella.

"Yes, Relaxella."

Estel speaks a question for all three parents.

"How long do you think it will take before Girlfriend and Neighbour complete the task you have set them out to do?"

"Estel, we hope they will complete the first stage of their work in the Realm in six months. Then, if all goes well, they will be back with us on Autumn Equinox, the day we celebrate our annual Pit Festival. Not very long, really. This task is much bigger than I even know. When the Invisible Mentors orchestrate change, we can be certain that many events will unfold when we least expect them. Your children will be thoroughly protected. I give you my word. Once they are in the Realm of Thagara, communication will not be easy since they will be underground. The networks of communications in the Realm of Thagara are extraordinary, to say the least, although from time to time, we do have problems. Once they are there, do you know they will have to shape-shift for a good portion of their journey?"

Estel is nodding. "We thought they would have to shape-shift. That is why we have been keeping an eye on Girlfriend for some time now. We have seen her shape-shift quite a lot, recently. She insists she is only practicing. We did remind her this gift should not be overused. She knows. I think she is also somewhat anxious about this journey abroad. This morning, Girlfriend said, 'I have mixed feelings because I love you both so much it is tough to leave home; however, I know I am destined to go. I will be wise with my abilities. Don't worry, okay?'"

"Girlfriend and Neighbour are exceptional Echo Youths. I know they will bring The Echoes of the Sun Community vision through a new chapter," Relaxella assures the parents. Then she stands, and the others do too. "I must take my leave now. It has been wonderful to share some quality time with all of you. Tesshu and Kaleb are also beginning an exceptional journey today. What an amazing Spring Equinox! The Invisible Mentors have gifted me so incredibly I have to conjure ways to pay them back—if you know what I mean."

They all answer at once. "We sure do."

Phoenix, keeping quiet most of the time, asks, "How can *we* pay you back for giving our courageous children a chance of a lifetime?"

"Trust me—is all I ask."

"Done," says Phoenix with no hesitation.

"Echo," say Estel and Eos.

Cheerios: Hula-hoops for **ants**.

—Unknown

CHAPTER 9

GOING THROUGH THE GAME

Three weeks have passed since Tesshu and Kaleb came to Heart Quarters to work through their Meridians. Today, Tesshu is determined to get through the Lung Meridian; unfortunately, all eleven points show up blocked. The first five points, however, clear surprisingly quickly, which gives him hope he can accomplish his wish for today.

He is having trouble now getting through point 6. He places his index finger softly on this point on his left arm. It is tender to his touch as if bruised. His eyes are closed. His heartbeat pulses loudly in his ears. His facial features register frustration. Jenerrie notes he is trying to hold back tears. She knows he is going through an emotional release due to the imagery he is experiencing. She gently speaks to him privately through an intercom system installed into the suit's face hood.

"Tesshu, I can see you are stuck in point 6. This will be your first time going through a deep recall. Talk to me. Tell me everything you are seeing, even if it doesn't make sense. Please trust I am here for you. Kaleb is on a break right now, so you can feel more vocally free. Any emotion you want to express is okay. I am here for you."

Tesshu goes deeply into a memory. "I am six-years-old, lying in a large room in a hospital bed twice as long and wide as my skinny body. The partition curtains are a dull beige colour. I don't know why they are closed, as no other child is in the room with me. A thick-walled oxygen 'tent' of opaque plastic encases me. It is hard to see through. It gives me a faraway feeling that I do not like. I am already too great a distance from my real bed at home. I don't want to hear the sound of the shortness of my breath being echoed back to me in this tent. Sometimes, in the middle of the night, I wake myself from my noisy chest rattling. The oxygen tent is the scariest, then.

"A nurse reaches in and administers an adrenalin shot to my right arm. This drug helps break up the mucus causing my lungs to 'attack' inside. I can smell her perfume right now." Tesshu sneezes.

Jenerrie whispers, "Good, Tesshu—that's a perfect release. I am here."

Tesshu takes a deep breath and sees more pictures lining up like a film reel needing editing. He continues. "Within seconds of her releasing the needle, my heart quickens measurably. I am also on an intravenous drip. To keep the drip steady and the needle in place, my left forearm has a board underneath it secured with white gauze tape. Earlier, in the emergency room, it took a nurse three times to find a vein on this arm large enough for the needle to go in.

"For a few days after returning from this asthma attack, my Grade 1 classmates whisper together and stare at me like I am strange. Then, finally, one boy asks me, 'I heard the ambulance siren the other day, were you inside? Why do you have three bruises on your left arm? How come you were gone for so long?'

"I always came back with eyes more deeply set into my sockets. I am breathing faster now. The adrenalin shot has fully kicked in. I am breathing deeper. I watch my sternum rise and fall. The drug, though, manipulates my mental imagery and my heartbeat. I look at my right upper arm where the needle went in. I see raised bumps around the tiny needle puncture. The bumps pulse.

"Spittle runs onto my chin onto the blue hospital gown. Tears fall too, and the gown turns a darker blue here and there. These are tears of fear.

"I try to open the oxygen tent zipper. It is stuck! Maybe I can't open it from the inside. Perhaps I am trapped! I lie back on the two propped-up stiff white pillows. I close my eyes. I can feel the heartbeat in my arm. I am afraid to look at it again.

"Suddenly, an image of cowboys standing around smoking cigarettes appears behind my closed eyes, then noble faces of natives. I tell the images to go away. The oxygen tent echoes back my voice— 'go away!' I then hear a calm voice in my head, 'if you open your eyes, the images will go away.' I open my eyes and look at my right arm. The heartbeat pulse is more prominent and louder! My breathing faster! Not asthmatic, though. The adrenalin shot is working. I know the oxygen tent is causing all this fear. I have to escape!

"I pick up my heavy boarded left arm with my small right hand. I remember the nurse with the perfume smell saying, 'Don't raise or move this arm too high, Tesshu. You must not see blood going up the intravenous tube.'

"I watch the tube with every inching movement I make with my little body. I realize, though, I have to turn onto my belly to slide out of the tent first and then down the long, long bed. I turn myself over. The intravenous stand shakes. I moved too quickly, but my left arm is now on the other side where my right arm was when I lay on my back. I slip down the bed a little more. I look up. Only my head, shoulders, and outstretched arms remain inside the tent. My torso, legs, and feet are out of the tent but are still under the heavy green flannel blankets.

"Surely, I can reach the floor and make my escape before the cowboys and natives appear again, before the heartbeat on my arm pulses louder. The back of my head touches the thick, unclear tent's plastic. I feel the zipper edge on my left shoulder. I loosen the tightly tucked covers with a kick. I cough up phlegm from this action. Even though they often tell me, 'Get that stuff out of your lungs,' I dare not spit it out, so I swallow the thick mucus. I momentarily rest my head and close my eyes to breathe. BANG! BANG! The cowboy in the white outfit with a shiny belt shoots his gun in the air, creating a new surge of fear in me. I kick my feet harder to release the tucked covers. My head pops out of the oxygen tent—the intravenous pole jerks. I feel the needle. My boarded left arm is still in the tent! My heartbeat rapidly reverberates back to me as I lay on my chest and belly.

"I look into the oxygen tent from this new viewpoint. It is hard to see plastic through opaque plastic, but I see red! Blood is going up three-quarters of the tube! I kick my feet harder out of extreme anxiousness. This action brings my upper body closer to the end of the bed, yet I am still under the blankets; only my feet are free. I carefully glide my left arm from under the tent frame. My feet rest on the cold iron hospital bed bars, which soothes my tension. I breathe a deep sigh. I close my eyes. No sounds. I sense where my body parts are. My torso still needs to get out from under the green blankets. I rest my head on the bed. It is warm. I breathe in my smell. I rest. I gather inner strength. My eyes are closed. A picture of a cat appears. I automatically bring my legs under myself. The heavy green blanket slides off my back. One of the clasps on the blue hospital gown opens, exposing my back to the room air. I like the feeling of exposed skin to air. I sit up like a cat. I put my boarded left forearm on my lap. Blood in the tube goes down. I wipe away tears. I am getting braver, like a cowboy, like a noble native, like a heartbeat consistently in time with deep, cellular memory. I extend my legs over the bed bar. The coolness of the bar is invigorating on my tummy. My feet search for the floor. I wiggle them wildly. I am too short! I never thought of this! I know I will have to push off with all my remaining strength. I look at the amount of blood in the tube. It is still low. Good. Now, I notice the intravenous needle for the first time. I think, 'maybe it has always been in me like that.' Then I see the heart-beat on my arm. I know the needle is not in correctly! It is not straight in, like a landed arrow! I don't care anymore! I don't care about my arm, the water, my blood, the tent, my mucus, the board, my lungs, my smell, the zipper, the cowboys, the natives, the tent, or my heartbeat! I push myself off the bed. The intravenous pole leans and hits the double bed bars. The intravenous bottle doesn't break. It dangles. The white plastic tubing is bloody inside, stretched to its limit. Before the pole reaches the floor, the nurse with the perfumed smell catches it. She picks me up slowly, carefully. She holds up my left-boarded arm; otherwise, the needle would have ripped out my skin. My forehead is touching her nametag. I feel tiny on her big body. Somehow, I can feel some of the tubing between my little chest and her large breasts. She slowly starts trying to put me back in the tent. I am sobbing and shouting at the same time. 'I don't want the oxygen tent. I can't breathe inside it! I don't want the tent. I can't breathe inside it!' I take in a full frantic inhalation filled with her perfume."

Tesshu sneezes again in the present time. He comes out of the memory. He is breathing quickly, and his heart is beating rapidly. He shakes his body as if shaking off the ghosts of this recall. He slowly stretches his arms up. Fresh energy pours into him. He turns his head slowly, and amazingly Jenerrie is right at his side. He accepts her touch on the middle of his back. He breathes deeply and connects with her hand, gently calming him. Tesshu's body releases shivers. He slowly turns to face her. He smiles shyly and mouths the words, "thank you." Jenerrie blinks away tears of compassion for him.

"Do you want to continue, Tesshu? You don't have to if it is too much."

Tesshu says with a smile. "I will take a little break. I need to get out of the suit for a while. But I will continue after, Jenerrie. Thanks for listening to me and then showing up at the perfect moment by my side. I hope this powerful recall has cleared the remaining points on my Lung Meridian."

"Your inner strength is admirable, Tesshu."

Ant colonies are remarkably similar to cities. No one choreographs the action, not even the queen **ant,** but **ant** behaviour is controlled by swarm logic—put 10,000 dumb **ants** together, and they become smart. They will calculate the shortest routes to food supplies sniffing out pheromone signals from other **ants** and Johnson says people do the same thing in cities using low-level interactions of people on the street.

—Alex Cukan, Stories of Modern Science
United Press International, October 8, 2001

CHAPTER 10

THE WOODS OF FACUZI

Girlfriend and Neighbour each have a "fit to my back" knapsack with enough supplies for a journey through the Woods of Facuzi. They can explore the Woods provided they reach Sir Rush's home by sunset. He is expecting them and will have a nice hot meal ready when they arrive. Relaxella gave them a map showing various places of interest in the Woods and the location of The Hillock.

By day three, with the help of Sir Rush, they will hopefully reach The Hillock before the sun peaks at high noon. The Hillock is the hidden entranceway to the Realm of Thagara.

Being young and carefree, the Echo Youths play leap over the logs, match my actions, and whistle like the birds. Relaxella pre-warned them that the Woods of Facuzi are incredibly alive these days because it is spring! Girlfriend and Neighbour welcome the education of nature, watching wildflowers open before their eyes, seeing animals and insects coming out from hiding, and inhaling new earth smells. The Woods of Facuzi echo feelings of freshness and curiosity. Anyone who has these exact qualities feels safe and right at home.

Cuzies[12] are the predominant life form living in these woods. Girlfriend and Neighbour have read stories about Cuzi culture in *Once Upon A Solar Time*. According to some rumours, Cuzies are actually members of The Echoes of the Sun Community who used the Science of Transformation a long time ago to change themselves into these characters to help with the community vision in their own particular way. However, if one questions the Elders about how the Cuzies help out, they will never tell you. Instead, they often say, "Go into the Woods yourselves and figure it out."

Other stories explain that Cuzies exist to remind the Echo Youths that the magic of nature never dies. And still, other stories say the Cuzies live to teach the Echo Youths how not to become like them. There are various sizes of Cuzies, with the average one measuring two feet in height. The Cuzies are colourful and uniquely textured. Some are leathery, and some

---

12 Cuzies are Community members who have the job of working on their "emotions" that are too excessive. There are Cuzies full of fear, anger, and sadness. Some are unmotivated. Being in the Woods gives them an opportunity to get over these stuck emotions so they can contribute to The Echoes of the Sun Community in a more positive way.

have a fuzzy feeling, while others prick your hand if you touch them! There are several really hairy ones, and others are cold to the touch; old ones, young ones, soft ones, and hard ones. The hard Cuzies are also the largest, and often, guests sit upon them in the woods. The hard ones always have a story to tell because they love to hear themselves speak. Anyone resting on them soon discovers they can go on and on and on!

The Path of Olor that Girlfriend and Neighbour walk and dance on sparkles, twists, goes up, down, and around Cuzi homes and open-spaced playgrounds. The path has a colour unknown to their eyes. However, they also say one's perspective can easily alter here in the Woods of Facuzi.

While Girlfriend and Neighbour move in and around the various shapes, a continuous smell of lavender fills their nostrils.

"Girlfriend, even though I am not quite sure where we are in relation to the map, I rather like the atmosphere here in this part of the Woods. The frequency in the air is very vibrant."

Girlfriend twirls around in response; she, too, feels Neighbour's joy. Girlfriend, though, is very careful not to spin off the path. Somehow, she associates twirling off the trail with walking into someone's home when they are not home. Something curious happens, though, when Girlfriend stops spinning. She thinks she sees something move.

"Neighbour, do what I am doing and look carefully."

Together, they twirl. Now Girlfriend notices pairs of eyes are looking up at them. Even though they are in their regular body shapes, the Cuzies suddenly come up to their knees in height. Girlfriend and Neighbour find this odd.

"Neighbour, do you see what I see?"

"Yes, Girlfriend, it is strange."

"Let's really get into this moment through our breath."

They hold hands and begin their practice. They inhale for a count of eight. They consciously direct their breath through the abdominal, intercostal, and clavicle areas of the lungs. They then hold their breath for four counts. When they exhale for a count of eight, they release the breath, starting from the abdominals, then moving through their intercostal muscles, and finishing through the clavicle area. They hold their breath for another four counts. Little do they expect the whole scene to change ever so briefly! Now the shifting of the Cuzies seems to last the length of one breath! This is indeed odd!

They continue to experiment with respiration. After six deep inhalations and exhalations, they both start to see a pattern forming regarding what they are viewing in front of themselves. For some reason, every time they hold their breath, a tiny violet-coloured house appears to the right of their vision. Every time after exhaling, they can see something moving its hands or what they think are hands over a yellow piece of—something—to the left of their vision. Due to their experimentation with their breathing, they are confident the image will change the next time they hold their breath, yet they really don't want the picture to change. So, they hold their breath for a count of eight instead of four. They ask with the power of their minds for the moving image to stay still. And it does! Girlfriend and Neighbour go back to regular breathing. While they are absorbed in what they are now seeing, they don't hear a voice ordering them to identify themselves.

"For the last time, if you don't tell me who you are... I'll... I'll—!"

The two best friends suddenly fall onto the soft grass. They don't hurt themselves.

The loud, angry voice shouts again, "I said, this is your last time!"

A predominately red and white Cuzi stands directly in front of them. The violet house seems closer now and—tiny. They sniff the air and immediately know the lavender smell comes directly from the house. However, this Cuzi takes up all their attention. It has a substantial purple mouth and pale blue eyes, which are too broad and too large compared with the other features on its face. Two orange sagging stains highlight its cheeks. A brown frown mark between its eyes gives this Cuzi an angry disposition. Its unkempt hair sticks out straight for about four inches, and then a slight curl can be seen on the end of each strand. They take in this presence with awe. Its arms are tiny, yet it has huge hands busily shuffling a yellow piece of material from one hand to the other. The digits on the hands are of various sizes, and there are six on each hand! The colour silver takes over the rest of its body. However, the most amusing feature is its feet. They are bright, bright yellow with purple toenails. Girlfriend and Neighbour are quite tempted to laugh when they realize they both see this part of its body simultaneously. Luckily, they don't laugh because this Cuzi is not happy. Girlfriend quickly thinks of something to say.

"Excuse me, whoever you are. Sorry, I think it has taken us a little too much time to adjust to the frequencies in these Woods. We didn't quite hear you until we—"

Girlfriend can say no more. She and Neighbour are baffled by the look of this Cuzi, now pulsing in front of them. Its cheeks turn a deeper orange, its eyes a different shade of blue!

"Hey, what is happening to you?" shouts Girlfriend.

Not only are its cheeks turning a deeper orange and its eyes a different shade of blue—its feet are swelling!

"Hey! Please stop those contortions!" begs Neighbour.

The Cuzi doesn't hear Neighbour. It throws the yellow piece of material on the ground. It runs in a circle, then a square, then a figure eight. While it is running, this Cuzi is also punching the air. The noise coming from it is not very welcoming, and Girlfriend and Neighbour at once wish they were back in the comfort of Heart Quarters.

The Cuzi makes everything a blur as it runs around, even the tiny violet house! Finally, it stops and sits right in front of them, then begins to remove a pink and white substance appearing all over its body. It comes off like dead skin. Even each hair strand has a drop of this ooze at the end of every curl! After removing the ooze, this Cuzi plays with what seems like putty of some sort. In a brief period, it sculpts the alphabet "E" with this substance that it excreted out of its body. It carefully places the E on a small rock nearby, nods to them, and says, "Hi, I'm Myrette. Welcome to the Woods of Facuzi."

Girlfriend and Neighbour are overwhelmed by her response after what they just witnessed. They cautiously move back slightly, and Neighbour replies, "Hmmm, well...ah...I am Neighbour...and this is my best friend, Girlfriend...and...ah, we are Echo Youths from The Echoes of the Sun Community...ah... pleased to meet...ah...see you through your...whatever you just did...ah sort of...I think...well...I mean, we hope we didn't surprise you, or...disturb you...we...ah...really meant no harm...I guess we will be on our way now..."

Neighbour swallows deep and noticeably.

"It's me who needs to give you both an apology. I have not been very welcoming. It is a wonder you didn't run away! I would have been afraid of myself if I were you. Let me explain.

"You see, today it is my turn to be 'On Watch' for the next successive eight sunrises and sunsets. On Watch means two of us sit in or out of the tiny violet house and keep an ear and an eye out for any number of different things that could happen. My partner for this Watch is Winto. He went yonder to fetch us some supplies. He might be back before I finish talking. They gave me the nickname Mouthy Myrette because I tend to babble from one associative thought to another, and I expect others to understand what I am saying immediately. If you have courage, you'll shout at me to stop when you can't bear to hear me anymore. Anyhow, I don't like the job of being On Watch. The position is boring because lately, not a lot has been happening. I also didn't want to be on the lookout for the next eight sunrises and sunsets because I have started working on a new costume for the upcoming Pit Festival.[13] I don't want to get too far behind.

"You see, because I am stubborn, I wore half of the costume I had finished to last year's Pit Festival, and it was very noticeable that I didn't complete what I started. So, I got mad at myself throughout most of the Festival, and I didn't have a great time. But I am determined to have a full costume for the festivities and a good time this year.

"When I am On Watch, though, it means I have to make the costume by hand, so it takes me longer and requires much more patience, and you have witnessed I have little of that! I can sense you wonder if we have sewing machines here, and yes, we do. Solar energy powers any object that makes tasks go faster.

"Even though Sir Rush told me making my costume by hand would calm my nerves, I still don't like doing it. You might meet him later if you can catch him before he runs and does something or helps someone. If you think I move fast, wait till you see Sir Rush in action—and he isn't even a Cuzi! He advised me to use yellow for my costume because yellow also works on the nervous system, whether you are a Cuzi or an Echo Youth like yourself.

"So, when Winto left to fetch us some supplies, I knew I could put in a good amount of time on my costume before he came back. He is always distracting me! Then you both arrived just when I found my rhythm with hand sewing. Now I am obliged to talk with you. I don't want to get too far behind with

---

13 An annual Festival where The Echoes of the Sun Community participate on Autumn Equinox.

my costume-making. Whoever is On Watch has the responsibility to let newcomers understand a few basic rules about our part of the Woods. So, what do you want to know?"

Girlfriend and Neighbour feel a little breathless after Myrette finishes talking. Everything she said seems like one hefty sentence! Oddly enough, they understand. They are still slightly unsettled by her actions, and neither one is in any mood to witness the same "explosion" again.

Girlfriend cautiously speaks. "Myrette, excuse me if I am intruding on your personal affairs; I would like to know what the "E" over there means?"

"Certainly. If I don't explain at least my basic problem, you will never understand anything about this section of the Woods of Facuzi. This spill is my fourth one, and I only have one more spill to be clear of my habit of anger. When I am rid of this toxic energy in me, I can then return to the Community outside of the Woods if I choose to. The E over there is the E in the word anger."

"What do you mean by spill, Myrette?" Neighbour asks.

"A spill is simply a build-up of some emotion—anger, grief, self-pity, shame, fear—a feeling considered as a lower frequency. A spill is something to be proud of in our culture. It indicates that we are working on ourselves and trying to overcome the negative parts, which hold us back from our positive parts. I have an abundance of anger. After we 'have an episode,' we are obliged to sculpt the toxins released into something that we can throw in the Pit at the Pit Festival. I happen to like talking, and talking is made up of words, so I decided the very first time I spilled—at least 1,000 sunrises ago—I would sculpt the word 'anger.' Funny, the first time I tried to spell the whole word, I couldn't. I wasn't ready.

"I understood I would probably have four more times in which I had an opportunity to clear myself. Now, I am almost complete. The process is really where I am learning the most to tell you the truth. Each time someone spills, we understand that it aids all the others living here. It is like the feeling humans experience after a child has stopped crying. Everyone is relieved and happier; the child is calmer. We all can feel the vibration when someone is spilling. It doesn't mean we will run to their side and help them. No, no, no. It is often a private experience and actually, for some, rather embarrassing. You both are the first ever to witness one of my spills. For this year's Pit Festival, the whole Community in the Woods of Facuzi is determined to participate because—"

"Stop!" yells Girlfriend.

"Well, good for you for cutting my communication. I am a rambler." Myrette smiles for the first time. "Now, what do you want to know?"

"Myrette, I want to know how long it takes for the average Cuzi to finish spilling," asks Girlfriend.

"I am not sure. Some Cuzies have been living here for ages, and still, they are not transparent. You might also wonder why we don't go through the Invention. The simple answer is we can't. We are too blocked emotionally.

"And as you know, the Invention supports clearing one's mind first. The She really tried to help us, and then she realized it would be better for those with deep-seated emotions to live in the Woods. So, after we complete our spills, we can fine-tune ourselves with her Invention by clearing the thoughts and memories where these emotions originated.

"Anyhow, no one jumps around and yells, 'I've arrived,' or 'I'm clear,' because we really aren't entirely. It is understood. We can all see and feel the difference when our friends go through an emotional spill. However, let me tell you, there are a lot of Cuzies who are full of fear, and there are a lot of doubtful ones, like Winto, for example. The more you visit the Woods, the more you'll recognize the varieties. Others like me have a similar mark or frown between our eyes. Each time we decrease our packed emotions, our bodies will change. Of course, this is all gradual, but we can feel the difference.

"I will warn you, though, beware of the doubtful ones because they tend to shrivel when they are doubtful, and neither one of you would want to be held responsible for stepping on one because this would surely be the most unexpected way of being transparent! Cleared into another existence!"

Myrette is amused by what she said and giggles loudly. She then looks up and asks with a severe overtone, "Do you two understand? I am getting through to you both?"

"Yes, I...I mean, I think we understand. I find you fascinating," admits Neighbour. "What do you think, Girlfriend?"

"Myrette, I've never meant anyone like you before. I also learnt about the history of Cuzi Culture in our ancient texts; still, I never imagined I would ever meet one. When we were studying with Relaxella last winter, she said many of you have dispersed deeper into the Woods. She didn't think we would encounter any on this journey."

Myrette starts fiddling with the yellow piece of material again. Finally, she looks up at them. "Are you on a mission or something?"

Girlfriend answers. "Myrette, yes, we are. Relaxella instructed us to go to The Hillock, located outside of the Woods of Facuzi, in the Valley of Boji. Before we journey there, we will stay at Sir Rush's house tonight. The She asked him to guide us to The Hillock tomorrow. Once we find The Hillock, we have to go inside and do some work in the Realm of Thagara."

"You mean you know Sir Rush? I wonder why he never told me about both of you. Wait till I see him again; I will let him know how I feel!" Myrette frowns and tugs at her piece of yellow material.

"O, Myrette, please don't get upset; we don't *really* know Sir Rush. Seriously we will be meeting him for the first time today. We will gladly tell him about our encounter with you if you would like," consoles Girlfriend.

"If you want, you can. I just don't like it when I don't know what is happening. Anyhow, I have to work on my costume before Winto comes back. Sorry, but I do not want to talk to either of you anymore. I am being honest and abrupt, which a lot of us angry types are. We also enjoy time alone to finish projects."

Myrette stretches herself. When she returns to a relaxed position, Girlfriend thinks she sees a part of the frown between her eyes disappear. Neighbour does not want to ask another question. They both don't want to stare at Myrette because this would not be polite. It is time to move on. They thank her for sharing her story, and tell her they hope they will see her again. Neighbour in particular rather likes Myrette, especially her feet.

The two young friends continue to walk east on the Path of Olor. The map shows it will take them approximately two hours until they reach the final route to Sir Rush's house.

"Neighbour, it is too bad Myrette finished our conversation the way she did. I had another question; however, I didn't dare ask."

"Yes, I know what you mean. I felt sorry for Myrette at different times. It seems like one would have to embody a lot of compassion to be able to support her and her emotional problems. I am glad I can practice shape-shifting, but I don't think I would want to become a Cuzi for a day. Do you know what I mean, Neighbour?"

"I sure do. However, I would change into a Cuzi for a short while if I knew I could help one. Wow, she's the first character we met on this adventure! Do you want to make notes on her, or shall I?"

"I will," says Girlfriend. I remember Relaxella saying: 'Everyone's experience can be a part of someone's research. You never know when someone will read your words.'"

"Do you want to write now?" asks Neighbour.

"Sure. Look over there. I see two tree stumps carved into chairs; how perfect. Let's sit there while I write impressions of Myrette."

"Great idea, Girlfriend." Neighbour takes out her journal too.

"Are you going to write also?" asks Girlfriend.

"I thought I would read some past notes while you are writing. Maybe I'll find a secret I detailed and tell you about it later."

"Thanks, Girlfriend, for being my best, true friend."

Girlfriend answers, "It's not hard being a best, true friend with you. You're so much fun!"

We are closer to the **ants** than to the butterflies.
Very few people can endure much leisure.

—Gerald Brenan

CHAPTER 11

SIR RUSH

One can never underestimate the effect—the quality of enthusiasm—one person can have on others. It is mid-afternoon. Sir Rush is super excited because two Echo Youths will visit him today. He loves Echo Youths. He adores mentoring them and just hanging in the moment with them. For him, they are refreshing, even if they get into emotional messes from time to time.

After he decided to leave the big city and big business, his one true wish for himself was to serve The Echoes of the Sun Community in the best possible way. After numerous meetings with The She, he finally concluded that—having not been born into the Community—once he consumed the one symbol gifted to him, he would make himself only four feet, four inches tall.

He used to be six feet, ten inches tall, thus a massive change for him! In the presence of The She, he consumed the symbol and became smaller.

Today with pure enthusiasm, Sir Rush is dabbling from one thing to the next, preparing his home for his imminent guests. And he loves to sing!

I'm rushing, I'm rushing,
I'm rushing when I get out of bed.
I'm rushing, I'm rushing,
I'm rushing the thoughts in my head.

I'm rushing, I'm rushing,
I'm rushing all day long.
I'm rushing, I'm rushing,
I'm rushing when I sing my song.
la la la,
la la la,
la, la, la, la, la, la
la la la,
la la la,
la, la, la, la la la."

I'm rushing, I'm rushing,
I'm rushing when I'm all alone.
I'm rushing, I'm rushing,
I'm rushing to get back home.

I'm rushing, I'm rushing,
I'm rushing all day long,
I'm rushing, I'm rushing,
I'm rushing when I sing my song.

la la la,
la la la,
la, la, la, la, la, la
la la la,
la la la,
la, la, la, la la la." [14]

Savi, the Horticulturist, hearing him sing joyfully, peeks in Sir Rush's cabin window and smiles quietly, watching him dancing while singing his song as he prepares his home for the Echo Youths. Savi has been helping Sir Rush for the past few years to beautify his surroundings with plants, flowers, fruit trees, and a garden of vegetable delights in the summertime. Like Sir Rush, she wasn't born into The Echoes of Sun Community. Although she has not consumed her symbol to alter her "look," she has worked hard to change addictive habits and thoughts over the years—from almost always negative to almost always positive. All her inner changes give her more beauty than she ever imagined would come to her.

When Savi almost finishes planting gladiola seeds in one of the eight window boxes surrounding his home, she sticks her head through an open window for a second time and interrupts him.

"Sir Rush, I love it when you sing! What's on the menu for tonight?"

"Ah, Savi, I'm glad you asked because I would like to have someone else decide for a change. What would you like?"

"O, you are kind, but I don't know what you have in your fridge or pantry. I am also one of your guests tonight." She winks at him.

---

14 See musical arrangement in Appendix 1 at the back of book.

"I am sure I can create whatever a pretty young lady such as yourself would enjoy. Could you give me some ideas?"

"If you insist. I would like a salad made with any leafy vegetables on hand; hopefully, watercress, red or green leaf lettuce, arugula, and cilantro. I like tomatoes and cucumber thinly sliced if you have them. I would be pleased if you could make a salad dressing that includes tahini, tamari, garlic, lemon, and avocado oil. I'm getting hungry imagining this delight."

"I am on board with your order! What do you say we go into the Woods soon and find some wild fiddleheads? I think they would be complementary to the salad. Yes?"

"Yes, I could use a walk, and yes, to the fiddleheads. How would you prepare the almost emerald green furled wild vegetable?"

"First, I will steam them, and then I'll make a sauce with yesterday's freshly churned butter and garlic for dipping."

"Sounds fantastic. What about the main course? You know how we love to eat."

"How about pesto pasta?"

"I always add diced sun-dried tomatoes."

"When do you add them?"

"After we plate the portions."

"Yes, let's add this touch. Would you be fine with sliced carrots cooking with the noodles? Makes for a nice burst of colour with the pesto."

"Sounds good to me."

"Do you have a suggestion for dessert, Savi?"

"Me? Sir Rush, you know I don't care for sweets too much. So, I really don't have any ideas for dessert."

"O, come now, Savi, there must be one dessert you like...."

"There is one... I am not sure if you can make it in time."

"Tell me, woman; they don't call me Sir Rush for nothing."

"Okay, if you insist. It's called strawberry shortcake."

"Savi, this is not a problem at all, at all. I always have frozen strawberries in stock because they are my favourite berries. Since I won't toss the salad until ten minutes before we are ready to eat, I'll start on the shortcake right away. Once the dessert is finished baking, we'll head out and find some fiddleheads. Our two important guests should arrive by the time we return. Maybe we will even see them on the Path of Olor. Sound good?"

"Perfect. In the meantime, I'll finish planting the rest of these gladiola seeds, and I'll make sure to tidy up the yard, and I will even take your laundry off of the line and fold it if you want."

"The last little task is my pleasure and personal responsibility. If you finish before I do, I invite you to relax, be your beautiful self, and observe me rushing around. When you have your eyes on me, I feel I do my work better. I remember when I worked in the Big City, I thrived on pleasing others. Some habits take a while to die, even if you shape-shift!"

"No matter what shape you are, Sir Rush, your company is always a pleasure. Hey, I have been meaning to ask you, when was the last time you saw Una?"

"Two weeks ago, I harnessed him up, and we galloped to one of the self-pitying Cuzies; it almost drowned in its own tears! I guess I have been busy with spring cleaning and such; I hadn't noticed he hasn't come around lately. What do you think of it, Savi?"

"I saw him four days ago. I stopped to communicate with him, you know, by asking yes or no questions. I found out rather quickly that he was on his way to visit Relaxella."

"This doesn't surprise me. It never fails; each year around the Spring Equinox, Relaxella gets herself into a major project of some sort and needs the comfort of Una to get her through."

"Have you, ah, ever seen Una—in a man's body?"

"Sure, I have. Una doesn't have too many chances left to shape-shift. He is getting older; he has a limited supply of symbols to consume to transform himself back into a human, so he lives in a horse's body most of the time. Una chose the horse form long ago as he believes he is more helpful to serve The Echoes of the Sun Community in this way. He has known Relaxella for many years. I only wish he could talk when he is in a horse's body. I find it tiresome always to ask questions that must sum up in a yes or no answer. Once, he stayed with me in his human shape for a month. We had such a good time. And we joked about how he 'ate like a horse.' I honed my culinary skills during his visit. He almost convinced himself never to return to his other persona. He thanked me dearly for the 'vacation' before resuming his responsibilities—as a horse. Strange folk we are, eh, Savi?"

They both laugh.

It is the **ant**, not the lion, which the elephant fears.

—*Matshona Dhliwayo*

CHAPTER 12

TELLING SECRETS

"I'm finished writing about Myrette, Neighbour. Did you find any journal notes you might want me to know?"

"Yes, I did. In fact, I knew I wanted to tell you about this experience before we got too far into our adventure. So, I guess this is the moment."

"You seem apprehensive. You don't have to tell me anything if you are not ready." Girlfriend puts her arm around Neighbour.

"Thanks, Girlfriend. When I re-read what I had written, it stirred up some profound feelings. I often don't know how to express myself when this happens."

"Perhaps, if you tell me your experience rather than reading it, would this help?"

"Maybe."

"Would you like to walk and talk?"

"No."

"Hmm, not the moment?"

"No. I mean, yes. I mean, yes, it is the moment. I won't read my notes. I'll tell you what happened." Neighbour takes a deep breath, sighs, and begins speaking again. "O, I have so many secrets in my heart, Girlfriend. I still talk to the sunrays when they touch my face each morning. I haven't missed a sunrise for over one year. And I am glad we share this common practice. What a wonderful sensation—the first rays! I imagine I am storing the fine gold particles the rays distribute to a secret chamber in my heart. I am still inspired to draw each morning. I love stretching my body into shapes that massage my inner organs. At these times of sensitivity, I imagine I can feel my heart repeatedly dividing its cells. O, my fine friend, these are a few of the somewhat familiar feelings—"

Neighbour pauses and takes in another controlled deep breath. Upon releasing it, she continues.

"Last month, I decided to sleep outside with the full and glorious moon. I had been rather anxious all day long. By being in nature, I knew I would be able to calm myself enough to sleep. I was cushioned in the 'blue burrow,' which I call my sleeping bag; nevertheless, I think I saw it."

"Saw it? What do you mean you saw it? What is 'it'?" Girlfriend questions.

"I saw it. I saw the 'Glow.'"

"Dear best friend, is this the same Glow you dreamed about a while back? Is it really the same one? Tell me more." Girlfriend repeats, "Tell me more."

"Do you remember in the dream when a cocoon popped out of my chest and went through a metamorphosis right before my eyes? Do you remember?"

"Yes, I do. The day you had that dream, you turned thirteen. You told me that in the dream, the air smelled like oranges, and you reached forward wherein you held the cocoon with your right hand as if it were the last diamond in the world, and then it began to open. When it opened fully, you were holding, what you called, the Glow."

"Yes, Girlfriend, you do remember! Before falling asleep under the stars, I had a curious feeling. Because I had a hectic day, I decided it would be best to actively imagine something new, something not yet fully explored. Then I remembered that dream. Immediately the distinct feeling of the Glow came to me. It went all through my body. Shivers rippled through me. Shortly after, I had an overwhelming sensation of calm descend on me. The opening of the memory triggered the aroma in the dream, and I could actually smell orange in the night air. I felt I could see my mother's eyes watching me, even though she died five years ago. Then it began."

"What, what began?" encouraged Girlfriend.

"The beat began. At first, it was soft, like a baby when sleeping. I lay with my eyes shut slightly. I fell inward to what seemed like a faraway land. I wanted to hear more. The more I listened for the beat, the farther it seemed I went into this land. When I arrived at the entrance of this place, of this faraway place, the volume of the beat increased—I saw a drummer keeping the rhythm and a dancer dancing to the beat. There were flowers with such brilliant colours my eyes could not absorb such pigments! I saw several beings with names delicately written on their foreheads: dignity, imagination, joy, obedience, and love. All these beings smiled at me. The warm air touched me like a gentle grandmotherly presence. Suddenly, my right foot kicked the end of the blue burrow, and I felt pushed forward to the centre of this land. Then, I saw it. I saw the Glow!

"I walked through the centre of this Glow, stopped, and raised my head to drink the sun's rays! As the beat got louder and louder, my chest seemed to grow beyond my contriving skin. Then, again suddenly, my right foot kicked, asking for another direction, another image. Instead, I opened my eyes and instinctively went inside the blue burrow. Herein began another visual experience, yet this time my eyes were open!

"O, my friend, a multi-coloured orb with a gold dot emerged from the middle of my chest, and it glowed! My lungs breathed in rhythm to this exquisite beauty happening all around me. I knew I was awake, but I thought I *must be dreaming*. When this thought entered my conscious, the Glow disappeared into my chest where it had originated. I lay still, very, very still. My heart was beating rapidly, so I breathed with all three parts of my lungs. It took a while; eventually, my heart returned to an even pulse. I know now; I saw my secret while awake."

Girlfriend and Neighbour looked deeply at each other. Then, they moved towards each other to embrace.

Girlfriend whispered, "What you have experienced is very fortunate. You know now, the Glow is your ally. Linking yourself with the Glow image will continue to give you gifts. The more you practice inviting the Glow, the easier and easier it will be to manifest it. The more you acknowledge its presence, the more it will acknowledge you. How lucky you are. When you talked about those beings lining up in a row, I think you visited the Domain of the Invisible Mentors."

The two Echo Youths release their embrace. Neighbour feels shy. Yet Neighbour knows Girlfriend accepts everything she spoke. Girlfriend has a considerable capacity for unconditional love.

"Girlfriend, do you have a secret you want to tell me?"

"I sure do! I knew I wanted to tell you a secret, but I didn't know when it would be appropriate. It's funny how it often never works the way you imagined when you try to plan the moment. Do you recall the poem I recited to you entitled, The Presence of Space?"

"I recall a feeling of expansion when you spoke it. But, sorry, I don't recall the words."

"No problem. The words are kind of random. I am, though, grateful you remember the feeling. I want to tell you my secret now.

"One night, I was confronted by an officer from The Vog while walking with Ginger, my cat, through the silver-pointed bushes on the East Side of Lake Lookout. When too much fear is building up amongst their own kind, The Vog start making petty arrests of the positive kind, usually Echo Youths, whom they attempt to bother first.

"Ginger and I were having a friendly, playful conversation. I began to laugh. The silver-pointed bushes echoed my happiness, and they briefly lit up. When I caught my breath, the officer from The Vog appeared on our path. He held a shield. When I saw the shield, I knew I would have to do some explaining. Ginger leapt behind me and maintained a composed cat form—you know how The Vog, dislike cats. He said to me, 'Stop right there. It is late! Who were you laughing with? You know our rule about speaking to no one in sight.' 'O, I am just laughing in the space,' I told him. I hadn't thought about what I would say before speaking. Suddenly—he disappeared! Briefly, I saw veiled beings applauding me. However, I did not feel I did any harm to him because immediately, calmness came over me.

"I know now, Neighbour; when I say the word, 'Space' with intention, energy shifts around me and takes on a different dimension. That night, I had the power to move someone to another space! At least, that's what I think happened. I certainly don't want to entertain thoughts that I have eliminated this 'he' shape. The Vog can be quite trying at times; however, it is not in our best interests to determine the end of their lives. Even though he disappeared, his shield remained on the path. Ginger put her paws underneath the shield, coaching me to pick it up. Coincidentally, my experience occurred during the most recent full moon because when I picked up his shield, the moon reflected on its surface. I think it is perfect we have both acquired something new and powerful on the same day. I brought the shield to Relaxella's, and she told me she would have it liquidated in due time."

"Wow! Now I understand if I say the word Glow, it will be like a power."

"Perhaps because you received your gift through a visual experience, you will glow when you can be of assistance or in danger. How frightening it would be to one of The Vog in the dark! Of course, you must use your magic wisely. I am sure you already know this."

"I will be patient and see what happens when I bring on the Glow." Neighbour giggles. "Girlfriend, please share with me again your poem called Space."

"Sure."

"Over there,
Over there,
And over there too,
There is   Space
And over there,
And there,
And there too,
We are always in
The presence of   Space."

Neighbour shouts, "I love space!"
Both friends laugh.
Girlfriend admits, "Ah, perhaps the poem needs a little more work."

They laugh again. Neighbour tells her it sounds a "little spacey," and they laugh some more.

Girlfriend grabs Neighbours hands and suggests they dance in the space. By this time, they finish dancing the two are laughing so hard, tears of joy are falling. Finally, they stop and put their hands on their knees to catch their breath.

"Thanks for shining your Glow in my Space."

"O, Girlfriend, stop! I am bursting! I have to pee!"

"There are plenty of stumps to water over there, and over there and over there too, there is Space to pee!"

Neighbour barely makes it to the nearest stump, and the strength of urine coming out of her is enough to wake up any sleeping ants below! Girlfriend finds her own stump and squats, making sure the puddle she creates doesn't splash onto her clothes. When they are both finished urinating, they find their composure.

"I think we better start looking for Sir Rush's house. If I remember correctly, Relaxella said if we kept a steady pace, we would reach it before suppertime," says Neighbour.

"I hope Sir Rush cooks us a yummy meal," says Girlfriend, and joyfully grabs her friend's hand. Together they skip down the Path of Olor.

Ants can live together in solidarity and forget themselves in the community. In a normal capitalist society, everyone is an egoist. In the **ants'** civilization, you are part of the group; you don't live for yourself alone.

—Bernard Werber

CHAPTER 13

TESSHU'S PROJECT

Tesshu and Kaleb walk along Laird Avenue, one of the latest streets where another "Rumble" is forming. The wind is chilly in the late afternoon. They feel fortunate to live within three blocks of each other because strolling alone through any Rumble area is asking for trouble. They sidestep the many cigarette butts scattered on the ground. The young men are also careful not to step on wet spit splattered on the concrete. A Rumble is an area where The Vog create housing for people who have nowhere else to call home. They are known as Rumble X1, X2, X3, and of the current fifty-four Rumbles, gangs occupy twenty. The Vog supply the Rumble residents with basic housing needs and a steady supply of processed foods high in starch, white flour, white sugar, and chemicals with easily forgotten names. With very little fresh food content, their diet makes the residents restless, aggressive, hostile, and prone to addictive behaviours. Through "empty" food, The Vog know they can control them emotionally and make use of them as needed for their own aggressive purposes. Oddly, these gangs carry no weapons that could harm a body. They are, however, exceptionally equipped with sharp words that can penetrate and disrupt one's soul. Two years back, The Vog set up gun and knife patrols, so now, these defence tools rarely appear in the streets. Instead, members of Rumble gangs train in fist fighting and martial arts. These defensive arts were once honourable—but not anymore. Words and bodies are the weapons of these times.

In this territory, Tesshu and Kaleb walk similarly, hands deep in their blue jean pockets. Their steps are synchronized. Even though someone occasionally shouts something obscene or threatening, they walk on. They don't give the voices from a distance a chance to see them up close. Tesshu breaks the silence between himself and Kaleb.

"I want everything small momentarily. So small, I would have to crawl around to be able to relate."

"Are you all right, Tesshu?"

Tesshu stops. He can hear hammers banging on a steel surface. The sound grates on his nerves, but he doesn't let on to Kaleb.

"I'm all right, Kaleb. I am somewhat tired from today's processes with my Figure. What's going on in your head right now?"

"I have been thinking how the sessions lately are certainly stretching my consciousness. Somehow, walking through this Rumble doesn't bother me right now. I know I am in control. I cannot be abused. I have been collecting Advanced Technology magazines for the past two years, and I have definitely not seen articles about the Point-by-Point Meridian Figure Invention. The She is absolutely under the radar. I suppose this is best for her since what she is doing is experimental. If her strategy with us proves successful, we might have some recognition. What do you think, Tesshu, would you be into giving interviews? The media is a great way to get known, don't you think?"

"Get known! For what—revealing our personal life? I'm not interested in having any media mongers delve into my data. Kaleb, I know I don't know you very well. I've seen you around town before. I want you to know I do not see you as my competition concerning the game we are playing. We are having a common experience. I am excited over the possibilities for personal growth, but in the immediate moment, I feel serious. What I went through today with her Invention will never come back to me again. My recall of a particular asthma attack was so intense I thought I would need an inhaler! I can't believe I had such a vivid memory of pain without the pain."

"If you don't have any plans, you can come over to my place now, if you want."

"Thanks, Kaleb, but I need to go home. I feel like taking a warm, soothing bath with linden and lavender flowers. Then I might get into the latest book I have started to read on astronomy. Or maybe I will take an enduring look into my colony before sleep. I will give them the remaining reflections I have inside of me of today's experience. They can take from me whatever images suit their needs. Let the variety of colours find a home in their eyes. I will sleep well tonight. I will be back with The She and her assistants tomorrow. You and I will be back there tomorrow."

"Tesshu, you sound like you're talking poetry to yourself. What do you mean you will *take an enduring look at your colony*? Are you with me or on another planet? Talk to me straight."

Tesshu stops again; he looks intensely at Kaleb.

"I'm talking about ants, hundreds of them by now. I've lost count. It began as a simple science school project. The colony takes up much of my time and attention—'in a good way'—my dad says. I am sure my ma thinks I am a little weird. At first, my ma encouraged me. Now that I am in my third year of the experiment, she thinks I have carried on too long. She hasn't told me those exact words; it's what I feel from her. I show the colony to those who have honest curiosity, and lately, this is not a quality my ma has with me. Anyhow, sorry I got carried away there. I could show you, though. How about tomorrow morning? I live at 11 Runner Avenue, three blocks west of here."

"I know where Runner Avenue is. Do you mean it, Tesshu? I hardly know you." Kaleb is sincerely intrigued.

Tesshu reaches for Kaleb's left shoulder and gently squeezes his deltoid. "Yeah, I mean it, Kaleb. I would like to get to know you, too. Perhaps tomorrow, our questions and answers will be in balance. I have to go now."

"Yeah, sure, Tesshu."

"You live by yourself, Kaleb?"

"Yes. It's lonely at times. I manage, though. I will tell you more another time. Hey, you seem ready to run—go, Tesshu! See you tomorrow morning."

Tesshu walks quickly away and doesn't look back. He is not wavering in his direction. His gaze is straight ahead. His pace is confident too. The hammering on steel has stopped. He hopes the Rumble gangs have gone inside for their dinner. He imagines he is translucent, to not attract any attention to himself.

Kaleb crosses Main Street, where this particular Rumble ends. He lightly jogs through an alley. Soon he will cross a set of unused railroad tracks and follow the faded path leading to his street. He is glad this route is still intact, even in the city. He is glad he will be in his own apartment soon.

"Hungry, Tesshu?"

"Only slightly, Ma."

"There is ginger-garlic tofu and veggies in the oven. There is also a tossed salad without the dressing. I know how you like to choose your own dressing. Your father and I ate earlier. We thought you would be home sooner to have dinner with us."

"Thanks for keeping some food for me. I feel like taking a bath first, though, and then I'll satisfy my stomach later. You're all dressed up. What are you up to this evening?"

"We are going to the Sumachs. Your father and Zambi need to discuss the latest project their firm is about to undertake. There has been a fair amount of controversy over your father's role in this new development. Josie and I will probably talk about how we would like to lose a little weight by the summer. We want to hike into the mountains—without getting out of breath. We might also make new discipline charts, which outline various foods we need to eat more of, and vitamins we need to take daily; then, we'll set up a chart for an exercise program and maybe even a separate one that will help us keep track of our daily water intake. Then we will find an excuse not to keep the disciplines up."

Amber self-consciously laughs a little too loud. "Tesshu, you've heard me speak like this before. I am sure it doesn't matter to you."

She reaches for him and rubs his hair, smiling. This action he knows ooh too well, something he does not like anymore. He never considered his mother overweight. He figures she is caught in some beauty myth about what a real woman should look like. He isn't in the mood to tell her again not to be hard on herself.

"Ma, I want you to be happy. If making charts inspires you, great."

"Are you going anywhere this eve, Tesshu?"

"No, I am into hanging out with the colony. I'll note some observations, calculate some past notes, read a bit—" Tesshu turns away from Amber to go to his room.

"Why do you still have such an interest in the colony, Tesshu? I know I have asked you this before, but what does it do for you now? Do you think it still has a purpose?"

Tesshu stops and slowly turns to confront his mother. He realizes she is in one of those moods, a little more curious because she'll be socializing soon. He senses she has had a glass of wine, which also helps her speak to him. He knows she only has time for a brief explanation. However, he is not in the mood to give a short synopsis. "Come on, Amber, I don't want to go into details presently. I'm tired, and someday, I will let you in on my records. Perhaps only when I see more honest curiosity without—" he hesitates, "—judgment."

Tesshu walks into the hallway. He doesn't look back. His intention is to go and run the water for his bath. Tesshu leaves Amber at the kitchen sink. Kenji, Tesshu's father, passes Tesshu in the hall.

"Good evening, Son."

"Good evening, Dad."

Kenji senses his son is not in a mood to talk so he goes into the kitchen. Amber is putting away the dried dinner dishes; her head is bent. Kenji squeezes her shoulders gently and kisses her neck. "Are you ready to go out, love?"

"Yes, my coat is on the chair."

Kenji helps his wife into her favourite suede coat. There is no need to say goodbye to Tesshu. Mr. and Mrs. Tanaka leave through the front door.

Tesshu is speaking to himself out loud, which is a habit his parents still generally have a hard time accepting as part of his personality. When he was younger, they constantly reminded him not to speak aloud to himself when people were visiting their family. He knows that in social situations people would experience discomfort to hear him talking to himself. He is smart enough now to carve words when no one else can listen. He continues speaking to his ants and thinks they are great listeners.

"How can I surpass this hot water feeling, soothing once again my back muscles? There is nothing in here to contemplate except the flower herbs floating leisurely in only the movement of my casual breath. I like it when I am not overthinking. I like this kind of emptiness in my mind feeling. I enjoy watching the herbs cluster around me. I welcome the flower smells uniting with the last rays of the setting sun coming through the window. Smooth out, tense muscles; you have been through a lot today. You deserve this kind of gentleness. Thank you, hot water, for relaxing my muscles and releasing and devouring the stored toxins in my brain. Yes, today, my brain muscles went through a lot of shifting and stretching with the Invention, Jenerrie, The She, and Kaleb. What a day! What a challenge remembering some moments of physical pain my body went through as a child. I can't believe I re-lived one hospital stay from when I was only six years old! I trust now those memories have stunted their impact. I guess I had to see them again to help me release those fears. I'm glad there is now space for lighter thoughts to circulate feelings of joy in my mind.

"I swish you, herbs, surrounding me, caressing me. Finally, I feel I am relaxing, especially my stomach muscles."

Twenty minutes lapse and Tesshu steps out of the tub. He watches the water-soaked herbs circle towards the drain. The screen is in place to catch them to avoid plugging the pipes. The water suction sounds pierce the silence of the flickering candle. He imagines when he blows out the candle, it releases a scream into the darkness. Not a cry of fear, though. Candles shine light. After he dries his slender body, he stands in front of the open west window and feels the gentleness of fresh air, completing the drying off of his skin. He isn't hungry now. He will put the leftovers in the fridge, as he knows his ma doesn't appreciate anyone leaving food in the oven.

He puts on a baggy pair of pants, a T-shirt, and soft slippers for the evening. He knows that when he watches the scurrying legs of his underground friends, idle thought chatter will not persist. This sound is all he wants to hear—scurrying legs and antenna touching. Eventually, he'll fall asleep to their personal wanderings—maybe even right on the floor beside them. It has happened numerous times. His dreams will blink along with their antenna. He will devour their sweet edible dream substance one more time. The earth's movements will make him renewed and charmed for another tomorrow.

"Why are you quiet, Amber? It is unlike you not to get excited and chatty before we visit the Sumachs. I know how much you enjoy their company. What's happening?"

"O, I'm still a bit puzzled over a comment Tesshu made to me before leaving the house. He's changed my mood. He told me he is into hanging out with the colony this evening, and I asked him what it means to him, referring to the colony, of course. I know I've asked him this before, Kenji; I also indicated this to him. I questioned him if he still thought it has a purpose. Part of his answer, which is the most upsetting, is he said, 'When I see more honest curiosity without judgment, I will let you in on my records.' I found his remark a bit cold, undeserving, somehow. I don't think I show dishonest curiosity, do I, Kenji? I don't think I have judged him about his hobby, have I?"

"You and I for quite a while now, have not truly shown much interest in his project. When he requested to build an ant colony, we were also not that keen from the start. Now, though, it has proven quite a success for him. It generates much enthusiasm and keeps him off the streets. It really does gather his attention. It's true, though, that lately, we are not very interested. Maybe genuine curiosity would be a better choice of words. I am to blame as much as you. I'm sure if I had asked him the same question at that moment, the remark would have fallen on my shoulders."

"Perhaps, Kenji. Thanks for recognizing my mood shift and asking about it. I love your sensitivity. Now, what did you want to tell me about your firm and the partnership they are considering? And what did I overhear you saying to Zambi—something about Warea Ridge?"

The morning is exquisite. Dappling sunlight dances across maple trees, which frame 11 Runner Avenue. The manicured gardens are not overdone. No silly lawn ornaments are shouting for attention. Kaleb is on the sidewalk, readying himself before walking up to the door. Tesshu's house is more significant than he imagined. He likes that there are only seven houses on the street the same size as his, wherein his street has sixteen houses and two small apartment blocks. He wonders if one of the five windows facing the street is Tesshu's room. He rings the doorbell while brushing his feet on the straw mat. Amber hears the bell—rare before 8 a.m. on a Thursday.

"I'll get it," she says to her husband, then opens the door. "Good morning. Can I help you?"

"Good morning. I am here to see Tesshu."

"Have we met before?"

"No, we haven't. Ah, my name is Kaleb."

"Where did you meet Tesshu?"

Tesshu, hearing the exchange between his mother and Kaleb, dashes down the winding stairwell between Amber's last question and Kaleb's pause.

Tesshu thinks to himself—*this is not the moment to tell Ma where I met Kaleb.*

"Kaleb, all right, you made it here bright and early. Come on in." Tesshu waves Kaleb forward.

"Sorry, Tesshu, I didn't hear you upstairs."

"I forgot to tell you I invited Kaleb over this morning for coffee. Do you think we could have a cup of your fabulous home-brewed?" Tesshu knows how to distract his mother when necessary.

Sometimes Amber doesn't like to make coffee for Tesshu or Kenji. Sometimes she wants to see them make it for themselves.

"All right, I guess I'll have time to make a pot for you. Do you take cream and honey, Kaleb?"

"Coffee cream will be fine. Thank you."

"Good to see you, Kaleb. Follow me to my room. Amber, give me a shout when it's perked, okay?"

"Sure, Tesshu. Have a nice visit."

Kenji seems to appear out of nowhere. "The house has certainly come alive all of a sudden. Good morning, Tesshu. Who's your new friend, Son?"

"Dad, this is Kaleb. You look like you are ready for a serious meeting. Have a good day."

"What's your rush, Tesshu?"

"I would like to show Kaleb the colony, and it might take a while, and we have to be somewhere by the 10th hour. Anyway, you and Ma are off to work. I'm sure all four of us will have a better opportunity to talk soon. Come on, Kaleb, this way."

Kenji does not respond. He rather likes it when Tesshu is bubbly and extroverted. He has often encouraged him to have more friends visit, but Tesshu always insists he prefers to be alone.

"Tesshu, I didn't think you still lived with your folks. But, I mean, it is okay. You're lucky you have them." Kaleb speaks in a low voice as he follows his new friend.

"Kaleb, you can stop whispering. It's all right living here. I respect them, and usually, they respect me. I'll be leaving soon. I can feel a big change coming to me. I sense they know it, too. We don't talk about it much. They are good friends, so I often call them by their first names. Anyway, welcome. Here is my room."

Kaleb enters slowly, taking in the entire atmosphere of Tesshu's room. He is quickly satisfied that the things he sees are in accord with his tastes. Tesshu is discreetly observing Kaleb's observations; at the same time, he puts on the newest overseas release of the Sungram Recording Series. Tesshu has every micro-tape, disc, and LP Sungram has produced. The music is slightly meditative with enough edge to support creative processes.

"Recognize the music?" Tesshu inquires.

"Yes, Sungram's latest release by the Alarm Points. Great tunes! I see you have an old Underwood typewriter. Do you actually use it?"

"It's only a reminder of yesteryear. Most of my writings are hand-written, although I have a modern computer—who doesn't? I still prefer the intimacy of pen to paper. Besides,

I don't have much rhythm in my fingers. The computer will be handy when I start formulating mathematical theories on the colony."

"Cool. I like your room."

"I don't know about you, Kaleb, but I had some pretty interesting realizations last night and feel amazingly renewed today! Something is moving in me, which is rather bold, uplifting, and—" Tesshu pauses, then speaks shyly, "—sacred. However, I still feel some apprehension."

"I understand, Tesshu. It is definitely sacred. It is almost post-human or more human if there is such a way of describing a human being!"

They laugh.

Kaleb quickly asks, "Where's your colony? Or, eh, perhaps I should ask politely, may I visit your colony, Tesshu?"

Tesshu smiles. "Of course, Kaleb. Don't feel intimidated. I apologize for putting out a controlled feeling yesterday. Sometimes, when I am overwhelmed, I go inward. I talk awkwardly. I think about my colony more than anything else when I am away from it. When I am here, I spend a lot of time investigating it, recording observations and images. I could tell you a few stories."

"Tesshu, coffee is ready." Amber's voice times perfectly with the ending of the first Alarm Point recording.

"Hold on, Kaleb."

Tesshu leaves and, in a short time, returns with two hot mugs steaming his olive-coloured skin.

"Here."

"Thanks, smells good."

Tesshu leads Kaleb to the southeast corner of his room, wherein there is another door to another room he explicitly made for this project.

One floor-to-ceiling one-way window facing east lets in necessary sunlight. There are at least a dozen charts on the wall intermixed with various sizes of handheld magnifying glasses and a selection of tweezers that have padding on the ends. The room is quite tidy—like a sanctuary. The ant colony is enormous. The glass covering has no finger smudges on it. There is one brass hinge and lock on the top of the glass box. The frame is made from hand-carved applewood. There is also ample green life hanging, sitting, and giving a fresh fragrance to the room; Kaleb even feels the kiss of dew. The room's temperature feels like a summer day at about 10 in the morning. Kaleb is intrigued and enchanted. He fixes his gaze on the seemingly random motion of the ants. Kaleb allows the silence to fill his ears. While their movement is silent to Kaleb, it is not to Tesshu. Tesshu hears the 6 x 6 legs scurrying—he knows their dance. The Alarm Points have concluded their harmonies, at least in this room. Yes, it is soundproof to the outside.

"I can't believe what I am seeing, Tesshu! This colony is a masterpiece! A living, breathing spectacle of awesomeness! Fabulous! It's crazy! It's exhilarating! It is defiantly brilliant! Congratulations!"

This project has humbled Tesshu. He is not into bragging. Somehow, he knows this work he is doing connects to magic.

"Why the glitter, Tesshu?"

"O, the glitter. You see it already. Good eye. The sparkling actually came to be purely by accident. Have a seat. I will tell you the story."

Kaleb settles into a comfy chair in the corner of the room; he has a good view of the ant colony. The tunnels made by the ants are numerous. Tesshu has artistically placed pieces of wood with holes, so the ants can go in and out of them. Kaleb thinks to himself, *perhaps this is a form of entertainment for the ants.* He comes out of his imaginings when Tesshu clears his throat to get his attention.

"Two winters ago, I collaborated with an artist friend on an artwork called 'We Could Go Out Tonight.' The materials we used were sparkles, glue, and scraps of leather. Dean left me to clean up because I wanted to carry on for a little longer. When he departed, I had an urge to see the colony. I hadn't seen the ants all day because of school and such, and back then, I wasn't into letting others view it with me. I carried the sparkles in my left hand and went in for a peek. However, matters definitively switched out of my control. I tripped on the rug, and my left hand smashed right into the glass, cracking it and causing it to break open. Sparkles were everywhere, including inside the colony. Amber heard all the commotion. Back then I didn't have a soundproof room. When she came in to see what was going on, she was furious. It turns out tripping on the rug almost ruined my beginning! Nevertheless, Amber helped me clean up the glass. We put a temporary wood cover over the area I had smashed. We bandaged my hand; I had not cut it too badly, but I had to babysit the colony all night long to ensure no ants escaped into my room. Due to my frustration, I wasn't particularly interested in removing the sparkles. The next day I didn't go to school so I could purchase the right-sized piece of glass. After listening to Amber's complaints and later Kenji's, I left the sparkles and watched how the light in the room refracted and danced on them. The sparkles calmed me. Inevitably, they remained, and much to my surprise, the ants started using them—truly using them! Kaleb, I have not told anybody except 'my charts,' but one day, I swear they assembled the word "hi" with the sparkles! I thought I was hallucinating! I didn't show anyone. I waited. Three days later, the word disappeared! If I continue to feed them sparkles, they continue to communicate with me." Tesshu pauses and looks directly at his friend. "So, what do you think now, Kaleb?"

Even the sharpest ear cannot hear an **ant** singing.

—*Sudanese Proverb*

CHAPTER 14

A WALK ON THE DARK SIDE

While Sir Rush is folding his laundry, Savi sets the table for the evening's dinner. She places a vase of wild starflowers at the end of the table so that everyone will have comfortable eye contact with each other when the guests are seated. Savi makes sure Sir Rush's cushions are on his chair and keeps a few pillows handy in case the two young girls are short like him. She prefers to be prepared. One never knows exactly how the Echo Youths will appear. Savi is well aware both Girlfriend and Neighbour have mastered thought-form shifting, and perhaps, they will appear the same height as Sir Rush for him to feel more at ease. Everything is now in order, including his laundry. The two friends set out to find fiddleheads.

Savi carries a compass, garden snippers, and two containers to hold the fresh green fiddlehead gems.

Sir Rush totes binoculars and a "song meter," a very cool gadget he hangs around his neck. The song meter identifies birdsong in real-time. He belongs to an amateur wildlife acoustics club, and this spring's project is to try and capture the music of a female sparrow, which is a rare sound indeed. A few weeks ago, he placed recorders on trees within ten feet of a nest that a female was building. He hopes there is enough time to show Savi these recorders after collecting fiddleheads.

He also carries a snack of rye crackers and hard cheese. Sir Rush rarely leaves his home without a morsel of food stashed somewhere in his belongings. Since living in the Woods of Facuzi for the past ten years, he finally understands the rhythms of curiosity this unique forest constantly offers. He dislikes being hungry when he is curious; thus, he learned the value of preparing and packing nutritional munchies ahead of time.

A southern breeze carries wet earth fragrances to their nostrils. Once they are out of viewing range of his cabin—being somewhat obscured by numerous trees, maples, oaks, firs, and arbutus—they pass through a field of cheerful wild daisies. Luckily a path is beaten through this growth, for it is difficult for Savi to walk where new buds are beginning to show themselves. Although Savi visits Sir Rush every three days, she comes to his cabin via the east-west route, more commonly known as the Emery trail.

Before arriving at the wetlands, where oodles and oodles of wild emerald green fiddleheads sway in the late afternoon sunbeams, they pass through a darker area of the Woods where the Cuzies live, stuck in various fears. Many trees—fir, larch, and cedar—make up this part of the Woods. The late afternoon tree shadows trick the eye because the Cuzies often move to and fro through the tree shadows. Of course, the emotion of fear thrives in the dark, constantly testing these Cuzies. When the origins of their fear are known, these Cuzies find themselves slowly moving into the more lighted areas of the Woods. Usually, no more than ten of their type are at the annual Pit Festival. For those who do make it to the Festival, their life takes on a whole new meaning.

To feel the full effect of this section of the Woods, Sir Rush thinks it appropriate to talk about long-ago fears. And, since he is beyond this consuming emotion, Sir Rush rather enjoys telling a story from his past related to trepidation. Today, however, he feels like listening to a story.

"Savi, do you remember a time in your life when you were so full of fear—you froze?"

"Yes, when I hung out with a Vog gang for two years."

"Two years? How old were you?"

"I joined at age 17. I haven't opened this door of my past for a while now."

"Well, since you have opened the door, can I go for a little walk into your mindscape of that time?"

"Sure, Sir Rush."

"Let us lock arms before you begin."

They link up and continue walking in the Woods.

"I was living in Rumble X6 for three months. Since both my parents died, I had no other choice. Back then, relatives were like foreigners—they were very cautious of whom they let into their backyards. That is why I had to live in a Rumble. I had nowhere else to go.

"My main fear back then was being alone—especially before I went to sleep. I shared a room with two girls my age. They had boyfriends who lived in another Rumble nearby. They frequently slept with their boyfriends. I often came home after partying to an empty place.

"At a party one night, I met a guy ten years older than me. At first, you know, he seemed okay. I can't remember all the things we talked about, but I do remember he often interrupted me when I was talking, which annoyed me, so I told him I wanted to hang out with other people. He got upset and became teary-eyed. *Weird,* I thought. I asked him if I had said anything to offend him.

"He replied, 'You are not allowing the other personalities who come in and out of me to talk, and it isn't fair; they don't have a chance to get to know you too.' I recall his face and body language shifted when he spoke this sentiment. My heart was beating rapidly. I knew I needed a smooth exit line to get away from him. He felt dangerous to me. He continued to ask me more personal questions, and with each question, it seemed his voice changed; or his eyes looked intense, then lost, then frightened. He was flipping in and out of personalities right before my eyes! He kept introducing these inner voices even by name! He had me mesmerized! Eventually, I came to my senses and realized I had better leave this guy immediately, or I might regret it. So, I gave an excuse I *urgently* had to make a phone call. He followed me, then got distracted by mumbling in his head. Shortly after getting rid of him, I left the party. Halfway home, I remembered my roommates would not be home since it was a Friday night, and they would be with their boyfriends. I felt quite anxious, yet longed for my bed. Somehow, I associated being under the covers with being safe.

"Rumble X6, an old barn where the animals used to sleep— we slept. As soon as I arrived, I went straight to bed, wearing my clothes. I wasn't into experimenting with drugs, but I felt different and thought maybe someone had slipped a drug into my soft drink. I found it hard to nod off. What blind trust we had with the party organizers. Laying there looking at the ceiling, I couldn't get the image of the weird guy out of my head. Bits and pieces of conversation replayed in my mind. I tossed and turned. I finally fell asleep around 3:30 in the morning. Unfortunately, my sleep didn't last for long. An hour later, I woke up from scratchy sounds in the hayloft above my head. I thought I heard footsteps, or I imagined I did.

"O my, Sir Rush, I froze in my bed! Seriously, I could not move. My eyes tried to adjust to the dark, my heart raced, and I could feel my blood pounding in my ears. I convinced myself the guy at the party followed me to Rumble X6 because he was mad at me. I didn't want to get out from under the covers. I remember my fear thoughts became louder than the noises I had heard that had woken me up! I don't know how long my inner dialogue lasted, but eventually, I convinced myself I had to go and investigate.

"None of us in The Vog gangs had any weapons—a rule strictly enforced by The Vog. They were constantly doing Rumble sweeps and body searches and taking any knives, handguns, slingshots, whatever they could find that they knew could harm somebody's body. Remember, The Vog was then, and still is now into harming minds. The only thing I had, which to me seemed like a weapon, was my fingernail clipper and file. I have to laugh telling you this now because the one I had was the smallest design on the market, only two inches! I grabbed it, pulled out the file, held it in front of me, and went to see about the noise. I walked to the barn door entrance. When I opened the door, a gust of wind slapped my body forcefully. The wind then circulated around me and went upwards to the loft. The loft noise returned, and I found out the source of my fear—only the wind moving in and out of the cracks of the barn! I crumbled to the ground and wept; how I wanted to be comforted by someone in that moment. I woke up three hours later, curled on the ground."

When Savi finishes her story, they hear a strange scream behind them. They turn quickly. Savi's heartbeat quickens momentarily, yet Sir Rush remains calm.

"Ah, a Cuzi just spilled. You triggered one, Savi. It eaves-dropped on our conversation. I could see it following us while you were telling your story."

"Do you think we should try to find it and see if it is okay?"

"No. Fear-filled Cuzies prefer to be on their own. It's how they get stronger. I hope you don't think I sound cold-hearted."

"You cold-hearted? Never, Sir Rush. Hey, thanks for listening. I truly enjoyed recalling the memory here in the Woods. I'm so blessed to be over the fear of being alone before falling asleep."

"Yes, you are blessed, Savi. And I'm blessed to have you as my friend." Sir Rush takes Savi's hand and starts to run. "Come on, the fiddleheads are waiting for us."

Ants are bizarrely unlike people, and yet there's a hint of
human behaviour at work in ant colonies. They are just
strange enough, while also being similar enough, to prick
the imagination. This has led thinkers throughout history to
compare ants to people. Why aren't we more like them? Or
are we actually more akin to ants than we'd like to believe.

—*Nathanael Johnson, Unseen City*

CHAPTER 15

THE HILLOCK

Girlfriend, Neighbour, and Sir Rush wake at 5:00 a.m., one
hour before sunrise. Since they agreed to leave for their
journey to The Hillock after sunrise mediation and breakfast,
it seems natural to take an easy pace this morning. When
assembled in Sir Rush's breakfast den, they will discuss any
last-minute arrangements. Sir Rush has already prepared a
simple meal of homemade potato bread, freshly churned butter,
lavender honey, hard cheese, and mugs of hot apple cider.

The sunrise over Mount Juniper for this day is spectacular. Multi-coloured bans of sunlight kiss them as all three drink from this glorious sight. The more one practises meditating with the sunrise, the more aligned one's vibrations become with the sun's offering of quintessence. Girlfriend and Neighbour, who started this practice at their mothers' breasts, know the importance of harvesting the sun's particles every morning. Their hearts fill with joy as pure as a crystal. This practice makes their minds more and more luminous like the sun itself! And often, they feel their souls are as vast as the universe.

For Sir Rush, on this day, he experiences a rare clarity. Most of his thought forms are absent while they are on the meditation rock. He contributes this profound sense of simplicity to the Echo Youths, who radiate like no others he has met. He knows their emanations surround him and give him this feeling.

However, no sooner have they all left the meditation grounds than Sir Rush once again lives up to his Echoes of the Sun Community "name." He skips down the path towards his home while whistling his song—I'm rushing, I'm rushing—running faster and faster. He then stops abruptly, slaps his thighs, and begins to laugh profusely. By the time Girlfriend and Neighbour catch up to him, he is wiping tears from his eyes.

"Are you all right?" inquires Neighbour.

"Oh yes! Yes! Yes! I am more than all right. I am expanded!"

He has such a broad grin on his face. They haven't seen him so elated.

"What were you laughing at?" Girlfriend curiously asks.

"Oh, my fine, young friends. When I finished my meditation, I had a surge of electric energy like I hadn't felt so precisely in such a long, long time. As you may have noticed, I rush around every day, everywhere, and for the first time, while running down the hill, I popped into my astral body and saw myself objectively—for the first time, ever! I found myself hilarious, especially how my head led my body while running! My expression looked like a mixture of serious intent and joyful oblivion. When I stopped, my astral body reunited with my physical body, and the laughter felt so rich it brought tears to my eyes. Thank you both for bringing this gift to me. I will always remember it."

"Gift?" They ask instantaneously.

"Yes, your mutual gift of clarity. When I go to the sunrise by myself almost daily, I rarely experience this particular feeling. I know your positive influence and your radiations excelled me to a new vibrant space inside myself. I can't wait to tell Savi and Una."

"Una?" Again, they speak at the same time.

"Yes, Una. Sorry, this isn't the time to talk about him now. I feel like skipping some more. Do you care to join me?"

"Sure," Girlfriend exclaims.

"I'm with you, Sir Rush. I'll follow Girlfriend, and she can follow you."

"Okay, here we go."

What a delightful sight to see Sir Rush skipping down the path towards his little abode with Girlfriend and Neighbour trailing close behind. From the perspective above, one would quickly think they were all flying down the hill!

By the time they arrive at the end of the path, they are laughing and out of breath, falling into each other's arms, exchanging morning hugs.

"I think you two deserve a hearty breakfast. I do hope you are hungry. I sure am."

"I'm ready," says Neighbour.

"If breakfast is as good as last night's dinner, I can't wait," adds Girlfriend.

A feeling of pride comes over Sir Rush that sparks him into his usual rushing-around self. He tells the girls to meet him in the den in twenty minutes. He also advises them to wash their hands and tidy themselves before coming to the table. They are grateful for his fatherly affection, even though he is like an excited child, eager to be helpful. Girlfriend and Neighbour walk to the guestroom at a slightly quicker pace.

"Isn't he delightful, Neighbour?"

"He sure is. I love the way he is compact in his body matter. It makes everything he does precise. But you know, what moved me about him is when he told us the story last night, about the choice he made a long time ago to dedicate his life to serving the Solar Consciousness. Imagine being a successful person and giving up all your material possessions to accept the responsibility asked of him by the Invisible Mentors through Relaxella. And he didn't even approve of her back then. He had to cultivate a lot of faith to change dramatically, don't you think, Girlfriend?"

"Yes. It is also interesting Sir Rush is still very active in organizing community events. Remember he told us he would be in charge of this year's Pit Festival. I guess his experience as a businessman didn't all go away, and he does this in such a smaller body."

"What do you mean smaller body, Girlfriend?"

"Don't you remember him telling us how when Relaxella gave him one opportunity to shape-shift, he chose that of a midget?"

"I don't remember him saying this."

"Yes, he told us—no, wait a minute, he only told me when we were doing the dishes and you and Savi were outside looking at the evening stars. Being taller than shorter folk, he had compassion for them. He wanted to have a body with a reasonable height to relate better with the Cuzies when he accepted his assignment to live in these Woods."

"Wow, I like him even more now," says Neighbour. "Did you know Savi was a street kid and even belonged to a Vog gang for two years?"

"Really? I didn't know."

"I guess they were telling us different parts of themselves when we were alone with them. I am sure they knew we would share their info sooner or later. Meeting Relaxella was like seeing a bright light in a dark room for Savi. When she heard an unusual woman would be giving a talk to Vog gangs about 'shielding,' she went. Because of her ability to steal, Savi—whose nickname back then was Quick-fingers—initially went to the talk to take her ideas and turn them into techniques to aid her negative habits. Little did Savi realize how much of an effect Relaxella had on her when she finished her talk. Savi told me almost in tears last night how she felt overwhelming unconditional love from Relaxella and longed to embrace her. However, she didn't want other gang members to know, so she ran ahead and waited for her.

"When Relaxella stepped onto the last path, furthest from the rec hall, Savi jumped out from a bush and yelled at her to stop. Relaxella slowly turned around. They made eye contact. Relaxella did not say a word. Savi told me she felt like every mean bone in her body turned to mush, and she cried as she had never done before. Relaxella took her in her arms and held her while she released a lot of anxiety. Relaxella held her tear-stained face in her gentle hands and told her she needed someone to help her keep the gardens tidy at her home. From that moment on, Savi never looked back."

"She is special. Thanks for telling me about her past. O, dear, we only have five minutes to wash our hands and comb our hair. Let's make the beds after breakfast, or we will be late."

Sir Rush places everything harmoniously on the table. Then, anticipating Girlfriend and Neighbour coming into the room for breakfast, he looks in the mirror, fixes his hair, and hopes they will be pleased with his cooking skills, just like the night before.

Sir Rush fills his mug with his favourite hot morning beverage—hot apple cider—for the second time and stops his pacing when the girls appear. As the girls walk in quietly, the sun comes out from behind a small cumulus cloud and lights the breakfast table with an eloquent soft light, touching freshly picked purple coneflowers arranged as the centrepiece. Girlfriend and Neighbour sit at the table and close their eyes. They begin to calm and centre themselves before eating. Sir Rush feels nervous, hoping everything is fine since they didn't make any breath-taking sounds at his display when they entered. Aware of his self-consciousness, he noisily lands in his chair, then looks at them and sees the corners of their mouths go up ever so slightly. Closing his eyes, he begins to follow the breathing patterns of his guests. Being a rather noisy nasal breather, he hopes he doesn't disturb his friends. Sir Rush keeps opening his eyes to see if they are finished. He knows the importance of blessing food before consuming it, but living alone, he often forgets. The fifth time he opens his eyes, he sees their hands rise up from their laps. Their right-hand palms face up, and their left-hand palms face down. He copies their movement. He feels the heat from their hands. He enjoys the sensation so much that he misses the feeling when they return their hands to their laps. Girlfriend and Neighbour open their eyes. They can't control their giggles; his hands are still in the air! When he realizes what is happening, he quickly brings his hands to his side. He almost spills his mug of apple cider! All three let out a sigh of relief and then laugh full and robust.

"Your hospitality is wonderful, Sir Rush," Neighbour joyfully says. "Relaxella has asked us to keep a diary of our adventure, and I am honoured it is my turn to write notes about you."

"Dear one, if I would have known you wanted to write about me, I would have been sure to tell a story or two about my ancestors. Now there is no time. What a shame."

"O, I'm sorry, especially if this means a lot to you. Perhaps we can make time this morning if you want."

"No, no, my young friends. I don't want your hand to get sore from writing about me. And besides, it is already the 8th hour of this wonderful morning, and we must leave soon. Maybe, you could squeeze a story out of me while we make our way to The Hillock."

Neighbour loves his suggestion.

The three friends eat their breakfast in silence. By being fully present in the moment with the nourishment before them, they can assimilate the intricate minerals and enzymes inside the foods. Once again, he feels the two young friends' energy fields influencing him. He never ate so little at breakfast in a long time! By being present in the moment, he finds the air he swallows along with the food fills him up faster than usual.

After breakfast, he hands them each a small sack of food he prepared the night before and tells them to do their best to fit the goodies in their packsacks. He insists they will need some nutrition during the walk to The Hillock. Girlfriend and Neighbour are initially grateful for the food, yet by the time they walk to the guest room, they feel the extra bundle will be too heavy to carry with them. They gently drop the bundles on their beds and watch how the mattresses bend.

Girlfriend puts her hand to her forehead, pretending she faints, and then plops on the bed beside the food. Immediately they giggle.

"I mean, really, Neighbour, this is a bit much, isn't it? It's too heavy. If we edit the food bundle, he might be insulted. Do you agree?"

"Yes. I think Sir Rush has packed us a lunch like he will eat it himself. He is kind. I, though, prefer the lightness of our knapsacks yesterday. I don't want to feel burdened while we are on this part of our adventure. What should we do?"

Girlfriend suggests they accept the gift of food for now and then hand a portion of the food over to him at some point during their walk to The Hillock. They know how much he enjoys eating, so they surmise he will be hungry within the hour because he didn't eat very much for breakfast.

They finish tidying up the guestroom, removing bed sheets, pillowcases, and towels and putting them in the hamper. Then they put fresh linen on the beds, clean the sink and toilet bowls, sweep the wooden floor and leave the window slightly ajar to air out the room.

They fasten each other's knapsacks on their backs and walk out the front door. Sir Rush is nowhere in sight, but a horse stands nearby.

"O, aren't you a pleasant surprise," says Neighbour. Sir Rush comes running out of his house and goes directly to the horse.

"Well, look who shows up after the party is over. Girlfriend and Neighbour, I would like to introduce you to Una."

They walk closer to Una, extend their hands to shake hands, and quickly bring them back to themselves. They both wonder what came over them. Una moves his head around in a circle and shows his teeth. Sir Rush says he is laughing, and they are not to be alarmed.

"I guess my horse friend has arrived in time to accompany us to The Hillock, right, Una?"

This time, Una moves his head up and down, which means yes. They both like the feeling of the horse and are greatly relieved when Sir Rush suggests they put their packsacks in the side bags strapped to his body.

The walk to The Hillock will take them just under three hours at a steady pace. They need to reach their destination before high noon. Sir Rush assures them they will have enough time, providing they don't run into any needy Cuzies along the way. He does not explain the origins of Una.

Everyone in The Echoes of the Sun Community has a transformation story to tell, and sometimes it is more important not to tell someone else's story, as tempting as it might be. After one's transformation, they have access to "magic" but are trained to use magic wisely. Sir Rush knows his most immediate responsibility—to ensure Girlfriend and Neighbour have all the appropriate instructions to make the next part of their journey comfortable and safe. They can find out about Una another time.

At precisely the 9th hour of the morning, Sir Rush clears his throat and calls attention to himself. He steps onto a rock that makes him taller than the rest of his company, with a packsack on his back appearing almost half his size. He tucks his tanned baggy pants into well-worn boots. His blue and green long-sleeved tunic top secured at his waist with a yoke belt gives him a handsome look. The belt has an unusual buckle, which looks three-dimensional depending on how the sunlight falls onto it. When he adjusts his belt, he remembers Savi will give Girlfriend and Neighbour their belts. He looks around for her. He adjusts his Tilley sunhat, which casts a slight shadow over his right eye, and makes him look a little mysterious. As he is about to speak, Savi comes running onto the scene, a little winded. Parts of her long brown hair look like they are standing up!

"I'm sorry I am late, everyone. Luna, my dog, decided she wanted to chase chickens this morning. I had the hardest time catching her. It is not like me to be untimely. Please accept my apology."

"Savi, you are not late. I haven't said my goodbyes to my surroundings. Yes, I accept your apology, although it is unnecessary to give one. By the way, you look beautiful, as usual."

Una makes a horse sound, rolls his head, and shows his big teeth. Sir Rush clears his throat again. He tells the Echo Youths how grateful he is for their visit to his home and speaks about the honour he feels to lead them to The Hillock. After carrying on for a few more minutes with various details, Sir Rush asks everyone to join him in singing the Community song. He knows the vibrations of singing always harmonizes people, and words sung in gratitude give invisible protection. Here is the song they sang.

We are The Echoes of the Sun,
united in our minds.
We work with each other
and never speak unkind.

We are The Echoes of the Sun
united in our hearts.
We work with each other
to lighten the dark.

We trust, we care,
We live knowing deeply
Our lives are to share.
We trust, we care,
We live knowing deeply
Our hearts are fair.

We are The Echoes of the Sun
united in our motion.
We work with each other
with deep devotion.

We are The Echoes of the Sun
united in our views.
We enrich each other
to support our hues.

We trust, we care,
we live knowing deeply
our lives are to share.
We trust, we care,
we live knowing deeply
our hearts are prepared.

We are The Echoes of the Sun
united in our mirth.
We sing with each other
and trust in our worth.

We are The Echoes of the Sun
united in our love.
We work with each other
to bring the peace of the dove.

We trust, we care,
we live knowing deeply
our lives are to share.
We trust, we care,
we live knowing deeply
our hearts are prayer.[15]

---

15 See musical arrangement in Appendix 2 at the back of book.

When they finish singing, a deep silence brings a wave of peace to everyone. Deeply touched, Sir Rush is grateful to begin walking with this tranquil feeling, so he jumps from the rock, adjusts his knap-sack, and as he kisses Savi goodbye, she quickly gives him the two belts. He motions with his arm for the Echo Youths and Una to follow—choosing not to tell the Echo Youths that it has been one year since he has gone to The Hillock, not wanting to activate thoughts of doubt in his ability to lead. He knows he has to keep calm, no matter what happens.

Girlfriend and Neighbour walk beside him. They feel a huge difference in his energy field, and oddly, he isn't rushing or talking. Una doesn't need any coaching to follow.

Girlfriend leans into Neighbour and whispers, "I want you to know while Sir Rush was talking, I activated my gift of Space and saw fairy-like beings surrounding us. I think there is a lot about this man we don't know. Maybe the fairies report to him when the Cuzies need support. Maybe he talks to the fairies? This adventure is getting very cool, Neighbour. And it's hard to believe this is only our second day!"

A hillock is defined as a small hill, but "The Hillock" is not any small hill. Nature has specifically adapted The Hillock to receive only those who honour solar consciousness. Thus, The Hillock only understands the vibrations of The Echoes of the Sun Community members. Therefore, those who have cleared their Meridians by the Point-by-Point Invention are able to enter. There are one hundred and forty-two people inside the Realm of Thagara. Girlfriend and Neighbour will be the youngest members to participate in this mission work once they arrive. As Relaxella refines her Invention, the more unrestrained participants become, the more they can be of service to the Community. Personal issues no longer have any relevance. Girlfriend and Neighbour are the most refined individuals to go into the Realm. Their mutual gifts of clear sight and their independent gifts of Space and Glow will aid the Realm of Thagara in ways not conceivable even to the Invisible Mentors.

After the foursome stop at Lake Boji for a mid-morning snack of rye crackers topped with almond butter and apple slices, they are excited to continue, perhaps because they can see The Hillock clearly, and its presence makes them feel close.

"I find it amazing The Vog have no clue about the magic of The Hillock," Neighbour expresses.

"Shhh. Please, don't mention The Vog around me. The images they conjure in my mind disturb my equilibrium. Don't you realize if they ever discover The Hillock, The Echoes of the Sun Community could be in much danger, Neighbour?" Sir Rush seems uncharacteristically upset.

He stops on the road and stares at Neighbour, awaiting an answer.

Neighbour looks at Girlfriend for support. Neighbour then puts her arm around his shoulder and apologizes. "I'm sorry if I have upset you, Sir Rush. I didn't mean to, honestly. I was imagining if The Vog were open to even a few of our practices, they wouldn't be negative, aggressive, controlling, and constantly living in frustration. It disturbs me to see people who have not had an opportunity for a peaceful life as we have. Without a doubt in my mind, solar consciousness is for everyone, and it saddens me that it takes a long time for people to catch on. Once again, I am sorry if I have upset you."

"I appreciate your sentiments, Neighbour. Your heart is large and pure. Before I became a member of the Community, I saw many problems The Vog created. Even though ten years have passed, I experienced a lot of pain and saw a lot of pain done to the earth. I guess I can still get triggered, even by the name!"

"Do you want to drum it out of you? I have heard drumming releases anger. Although we don't have a drum, I suppose you could use the earth as your drum?" suggests Girlfriend innocently.

"I am grateful for your offer, but we have no time to lose. Is there a song you both know? I would love to hear you both sing. Singing always soothes me."

"I know—let's sing Centre of You," suggests Neighbour. "Do you know this song, Sir Rush?"

"Indeed, I do. Savi taught it to me. She learned it when she first came to The Echoes of the Sun Community."

"Let's hold hands and sing," suggests Girlfriend.

Deep inside the centre of you,
You hold a vision of what is true
Your thoughts, your feelings, your actions must shine!
To help this world at this critical time.
Deep inside the centre of you.[16]

"Neighbour, you certainly can reach those high notes better than I can."

"Thanks, Girlfriend. I find your alto voice very soothing."

"Hey, what about my singing voice?"

"I loved the way you sang with depth the words—Centre of You. I could feel the earth moving!"

Sir Rush is pleased with Girlfriend's comment. "Did you like our song, Una?"

Una moves his head up and down, showing his big not-so-white teeth.

---

16 See the musical arrangement in Appendix 3 at the back of the book.

The sky becomes more of a gorgeous blue after they sing together.

Sir Rush suggests they follow along in a single file since the path will narrow around the next bend. When he turns on the trail, Neighbour notices his furrowed brow and asks him what he is thinking. Both Girlfriend and Neighbour have a great way of bringing people back into the present moment. He stops.

"Funny, you should ask that question. I was thinking one of the best ways of continually moving forward is to compare yourself with those who are more advanced, for this gives you an incentive to make a further effort. Unfortunately, many people cease to evolve simply because they refuse to compare themselves with and model themselves on those who are more forward-thinking.

"You two fine young Echo Youths are delightful models for me. Your constant enthusiasm and attention to detail in the moment bring me a continuous bouquet of positivity! I want you to know I will think of you often as you begin the next phase of your journey. Now, I want to challenge you both. Since we have only a half-hour left to reach The Hillock, let's run for a few moments up the hill. Are you ready?"

"I sure am," says Girlfriend.

"I will run!" Neighbour exclaims.

Then Girlfriend adds, "Be careful not to pop out of your body. We don't want to be late for our destination."

Sir Rush and Neighbour laugh at her comment.

He replies, "Cute, Girlfriend, very cute. The race starts now!"

By the time everyone reaches the summit of The Hillock, they are hot! They rest momentarily on the ground under the shade of a large cedar. The green grass cools their cheeks.

Girlfriend turns, smiling, to their treasured guide. "O, Sir Rush, you are a great man. You have been a wonderful host and companion, and I am sure my dear friend Neighbour will agree. We, too, will think of you while we are away, and hopefully, you will feel our love and respect from the distance."

"Thanks, Girlfriend, your words are kind. Look at the sky. I feel I am drinking blue reflected light. I cannot tell you what the colour blue does for my soul. You know the Realm of Thagara has blue light too, do you not?"

"Wow, really," says Neighbour. "Amazing. Blue is my favourite colour."

"Yes, it has a blue sky, and it also has an internal sun. I think you are in for many a surprise. Please think of me sometimes when you look at the blue sky in the Realm. Let this be our channel colour to send each other thought waves from our hearts. Oh, and one more thing, here are the belts you are to wear when you are in the Realm of Thagara. Never take them off. These belts are for your protection and to help you adjust your frequency in the Realm of Thagara."

Clasping hands with child-like excitement, Girlfriend, Neighbour, and Sir Rush look deeply into each other's eyes.

"Are you ready?"

"Ready." The Echo Youths speak together.

"Repeat after me."

In the corner of our eyes,
We see the opening
We dance for the joy
The new world brings.

After repeating the little chant three times, Girlfriend and Neighbour remove their boots. The blades of grass, swaying with excitement at their feet, tickle them into a dance. They hold hands and slowly raise their arms up, enhancing harmony between them to include any invisible beings watching. Laughter at once grows from their mutual joy. Then, between gasps and giggles, Girlfriend asks Sir Rush, "What do we do now?"

"We dance!"

The sound of the growing wind is the music as they hold onto each other, spinning in a circle. Perhaps it isn't *really* a dance, though they love the freeing feeling of moving together in space. A vortex of energy begins to manifest all around them. The wind is picking up speed and volume.

"I don't remember being told a cone of wind energy would manifest for you two." Sir Rush speaks a little louder than usual.

"Maybe the ritual changes slightly each time it opens pending on whom it is opening for," suggests Girlfriend.

"An intelligent answer. You never stop surprising me," admits Neighbour.

They continue moving in a circle, although sometimes they let go of each other's hands and twirl.

Girlfriend comments, "Maybe our dancing is creating this vortex of wind."

"Yes. I feel we have harmonized our thoughts, feelings, and actions. It is time now to receive. Let's slow down." Sir Rush speaks almost breathlessly.

All three gradually stop and stand still, holding hands. They close their eyes and feel the sunrays penetrating their minds. Waves of calmness envelope them.

Una stands off to the side. He wishes he could transform into his other body at this moment, but his time for thought-transference[17] is almost over in his life, and he dares not take an unnecessary chance. Una sees the Wind Being coming in from the western horizon. He begins to speak—as horses do—to indicate to the others to open their eyes. Sir Rush knows Una's way of communicating. He opens his eyes to see an incredible energy form moving gracefully towards them. He firmly feels he has to get out of the circle to not get in the way of the Wind Being. Its magic would take over from here. He knows his duty is over. He gently lets go of their hands and tells them to hold onto each other and close their eyes.

The sun goes behind a cloud at this precise moment, and the wind picks up its intensity. The feeling of the wind circulates, even in between their toes. The sun comes back. The Wind Being surrounds Girlfriend and Neighbour. Sir Rush then instructs them to let go of each other's hands. He tells them to trust. They are to keep their eyes closed, and by the time he counts to three, they are to fall backwards. It is essential no fear exists. Girlfriend and Neighbour never feel the emotion of fear. Everything is exciting and adventurous to them!

With confidence, they leap up into the air at the count of three! The Wind Being reaches forwards with its palms. The girls land softly into a feeling they will later have trouble expressing in words. They can no longer hold their excitement with their eyes closed—they have to look!

"Wow! We are high above the ground, Neighbour!"

"This is soooooooooooo beautiful, Girlfriend. How lucky we are!"

Now out of the vortex, Sir Rush does not have a chance to say a vocal goodbye to his two new lovely friends. Instead, he stands and watches the Wind Being gently preparing the opening to the Realm of Thagara. Little do Girlfriend and

17 Thought-transference is the same as shape-shifting.

Neighbour know how fast they are spinning! Yet, they do not feel any dizziness. Only from outside can one view this degree of intense force the Wind Being is generating.

From the north and south, two other Wind Beings come forward. They are much smaller in stature than the one holding Girlfriend and Neighbour. Each of these smaller Wind Beings trail a ladder behind themselves. Each ladder has seventy-seven rungs. They quickly place the ladders gently on The Hillock. The earth gives way. It softens and melts to create space. The Wind Beings apply only gentle pressure to the ladders, which slowly carve their way into the pliable earth. Inside, clasps for the ladders appear. The two Wind Beings secure the ladders to the clasps and vanish quickly.

Then the graceful significant Wind Being places the two friends gently in the opening. Magically, two precise sunrays touch the centre of their hologram buckles when they are on their feet again. They both feel warmth enter their solar plexus. The Wind Being winks at them and disappears.

"Look, Neighbour, our buckles are shining!"

"Amazing. A sun ray activated the belts! Come on, Girlfriend! I can't wait to get down there."

"Neighbour, everything happened so fast. I am afraid I am a little disorientated. What about Sir Rush?"

"Before we go down the ladders, let's mutually send him a thought-beam of gratitude."

"Great idea, Neighbour. Imagine it is on a blue beam."

Unexpectedly, after the two Wind Beings placed the ladders into the earth, Sir Rush flew up into the air by the force of the wind and landed on Una! As he adjusted his weight, the thought-form of appreciation from Girlfriend and Neighbour flowed into him. He smiled deep and said to Una, "I am blessed again. What a lucky guy I am."

Together the two best friends move with bare feet down the ladders, giggling and feeling ever so carefree.

By the time they reach the last rung of the ladders, they have slowed their pace. They feel their Meridians move through their legs. They look up to see how far they have come down, and see the opening of The Hillock magically shut. Everything is happening so fast!

As the light vanishes from above, they adjust their eyes to the ambiance of the Realm of Thagara.

Little do Girlfriend and Neighbour know they will never return to The Woods of Facuzi the same way they have arrived in the Realm of Thagara.

End of Part 1

PART II

Sometimes it's important to work for that pot of **gold**. But other times it's essential to take time off and to make sure that your most important decision in the day simply consists of choosing which color to slide down on the rainbow.

—*Douglas Pagels*

CHAPTER 16

HEART QUARTERS

Relaxella is taking it easy this morning. The warmth of the early day inspires her to sit in the garden with a cup of tea. She finished her meditation with her assistants much earlier. She feels a calm wave of gratitude moving through her, and she knows whom to thank—the Invisible Mentors.

She loves to recite various prayers that touch her heart, mind, and soul. Sometimes, when watching sunlight passing through delicate flower petals connecting her with wonder, she spontaneously says a prayer aloud. Some days speaking a prayer isn't enough, so she dances, and dancing makes her feel she is actively in prayer.

After the warmth of today's prayers envelops her, she thinks about various details regarding what recently occurred at Heart Quarters. She also looks from time to time at notes from Jenerrie and Parli to help her understand the finer points.

The start-up process for Tesshu and Kaleb has been a little hectic, so since a month has passed, she has given them a five-day break. If the young men feel too different from their peers or family, it will be counter-productive. They need to integrate slowly with the processes they are undergoing here and in their respective homes.

According to the assistants' notes, the two contestants seem to be getting along amicably. Kaleb, from the start, is more doubtful and slightly aggressive. He certainly asks more questions! Tesshu, the quieter, more serious one, has an open and compassionate heart. His assistants observed he helped Kaleb get through a Meridian more than once.

Relaxella hopes they will become great friends; however, it is never certain personal and social harmony will be achieved with new friends when someone clears old information stored in cellular memory.

Pleased with her assistants' attention to detail thus far, Relaxella decides she will also give them some time off soon. She puts their transcripts down, finishes her cup of tea, and lovingly now thinks about the gifted teenage Echo Youths and their exceptional parents.

She knows Girlfriend and Neighbour are presently merging into the vibration of Thagara. She can imagine the awe they will experience in the Realm. Since she has known the girls all their lives, her deep connection to them sometimes feels grandmotherly. For years, Relaxella has witnessed their exuberance for The Echoes of the Sun Community vision. They are naturally born leaders who will in time advance the Community's aspirations. Neighbour wanted to take some paint supplies with her to capture her impressions; however, Relaxella wisely advised her only to carry essential items in her backpack. Relaxella assured her when she returned, a studio would be available for her to paint to her heart's content.

Recently, Una dropped in for a short, timely visit. Knowing Relaxella is under a lot of pressure to manage the two blessings she received from the Invisible Mentors, he cherishes she is always glad to see "him." They conversed about synchronicity events, how they are developing sharper mental skills, and how they interpret the current manipulations of power The Vog practice.

On this recent visit, Una shared the delight he felt when he saw Girlfriend and Neighbour embraced by the Wind Beings before entering the Realm of Thagara. He had never witnessed such exactness before. Una mentioned how the girls stayed calm and entirely trusted the process and how he felt humbled by the power of nature spirits.

Una spoke to Relaxella of his deep admiration of Sir Rush and how Savi helps him more often. He hinted he thought they were falling in love with each other. Relaxella is pleased to hear this news. Savi came from a troubled past, and having a meaningful relationship with Sir Rush would be fantastic for her.

Life never fails to astound Relaxella. She embraces every day as a gift. Over the years, there were many times while developing the Meridian Figures she was on the verge of abandoning the project, and then someone new would show up and provide her with the support needed for The Echoes of the Sun Community vision.

Relaxella lives in a mental state of "providence." She deeply trusts currency will arrive to support her and the Community. When the Community is abundant, with great enthusiasm, she propels the collective vision further or helps others who are not so fortunate. When the currency is lean, she manages the difference with a positive attitude. Abundance cycles are never too much and never too little. Always, they find balance in her life.

A few weeks have passed since she visited her private garden other than a Sunday. So, today she takes some time this morning to look into the eyes of her plants. Walking down the mosaic stone pathway, she recalls Davey's last visit with her, wherein she mentored him on how to care for seeds. He adores the seed nursery and asks many intelligent questions about seeds. His hands are so tiny compared to hers; thus, he managed to pick up one seed at a time and plant it in the prepared nursery pots. Not once did he show frustration, even when he spilled a container of basil seeds. It took them a while, but they managed to pick them all up. He told her, "One day, I will invent a magnet that will be able to pick up fallen seeds."

On that Sunday together, they planted twenty varieties of herbs alongside the perennials since Relaxella is determined to have a lush herb garden this year. Davey, in amazement, held one of the tiniest seeds on the planet—the mustard seed—carefully. Then, together, they tossed the wild mustard seeds into an area where the sunlight falls all day long. Relaxella informed him, "One mustard seed can eventually become a tree! The tiny mustard seed has the strength in its DNA to provide ample foliage, branches, and resting places for birds when matured." Davey wondered, "*How old will I be when I can see and hear the birds visiting?*"

As the day has a more open feel, Relaxella decides she will arrange a singing rehearsal with Sophia. Music is a sweet balm, and all her assistants love participating in this activity. Four young men recently joined the choir; two bass and two tenors. Her female assistants are pleased to hear male voices mingle with theirs. Earlier in the week, Sophia had suggested to Relaxella that she wanted to prepare everyone to sing their

Community song, *Once Upon A Solar Time,* harmoniously at this year's Pit Festival. Relaxella agreed immediately. Singing always unites the Community, and Relaxella has a strong premonition about this year's Pit Festival needing vocal harmony.

She leaves her garden space with a beautiful feeling of tranquility. Jenerrie waits patiently just outside the breakfast room for her. While sharing morning pleasantries, Jenerrie tells her she heard the Heart of Communication in the Realm of Thagara recently experienced tremors. Relaxella assures Jenerrie that the mini quakes are not to worry her. In fact, the tremors often push forward work activity in the Realm.

After breakfast, Relaxella desires to be in her own space and let the day unfold without any plans other than singing class later in the afternoon. Sometimes, she finds it is essential to flow in the moment and let her intuition guide her without questioning where it is leading her.

The sun produces etheric **gold,** and the Earth fixes it.
For billions of years, its rays have travelled
through space and penetrate to the depths of the
Earth, where beings turn it into matter.

*—Omraam Mikhaël Aïvanhov – Daily
Meditations August 13, 2017*

CHAPTER 17

WELCOME TO THE
REALM OF THAGARA

"Are you sure you are ready for this, Neighbour? Relaxella did tell us the last time she counselled us if we had any doubts, we didn't need to go into the Realm. To become an ant for a while is something I never imagined I would be doing at our age. I am curious what all of our other Echo Youth friends would think if they knew we had permission to do this."

"Yeah, I guess we'll have plenty of stories to tell upon our return. I hope our newly-required gifts can be with us while we are in ant bodies. I would love to experience the Glow at least one time while we are here— 'in' the Earth." Neighbour smiles at Girlfriend.

"So, why are we waiting? Let's play thought-form transference!"

Before entering Level 1 of the Realm of Thagara—there are seven Levels altogether—they prepare their consciousness with silence. Girlfriend and Neighbour know that to carry on any conversation with their soon-to-be "insect" friends, they will have to visualize the dimension carefully to not appear too tall, dense, or extra long-legged in comparison.

Mirroring each other, still in their human bodies, they delicately uplift one of their symbols, located on their foreheads. A tiny, almost invisible ring traces their hairline, wherein the symbols are embedded into their scalps. Whenever anyone from The Echoes of the Sun Community wants to change their consciousness—shape-shift—they consume one of their symbols. Everyone has a different symbol. However, after they remove one, it will not grow back. Everyone has a different number of times they can shape-shift, except for Girlfriend and Neighbour. Their ability to shape-shift is unlimited!

"This is going to be fun!" Neighbour announces as she slowly loses her physicality.

"Yes! Nothing like an adventure," adds Girlfriend. They wait briefly for the change to take place. Within seconds—they land in what they assume is Level 1 of the Realm of Thagara.

Edwige and Earl are patiently awaiting any new arrivals.

"How many are we expecting today, Edwige?" Earl, the head ant guard for this day, inquires of the administrative secretary.

"Let me see here. Hmmm, the list isn't grand, Earl, only two Echo Youths. They should be arriving shortly. I'd say our job has been pretty relaxed for the last while," she says, smiling. "Do you agree, Earl?"

"Yes, I'd say you're right on there, Edwige. Not too many at one time, not too little to get bored of our own kind. I rather like it when new members of our tribe arrive here. I enjoy watching them adjust to the vibration of this place. And even more curious is their reaction when they discover who the 'real' ants are in this underground 'Queen-dom.' What are the names of the Echo Youths, Edwige?"

"Hmmm, let me see. They are called Girlfriend and Neighbour. What strange names! Do you agree, Earl?"

"Yes, I'd say you're right on there, Edwige. I'm always pleased when we are on the same shift. I'd say that there is nothing like having a friend who thinks the same; it makes for fewer arguments. What time is it, Edwige?"

"Hmm, let me see—10 wands to the 12th pentacle. They will be arriving soon! I'd say it's time to call in the Welcome Committee. Do you agree, Earl?"

"Yes, I'd say you're right on there, Edwige. You sound the bell, and I'll open the gate."

The shift to an ant's body is swift and painless. The two friends stabilize themselves and test their voices. Neighbour breaks the silence.

"Wow, Girlfriend, you look great with all those legs. How do you like the size of my abdomen?"

At first, Neighbour's voice sounds like she is in an echo chamber. The reverberation is too much for all her legs to stand on. She falls. In turn, Girlfriend tumbles, and they laugh, and soon both of them are kicking their new six appendages wildly in the air.

"O, stop, Neighbour, stop, I'm frantic! Where is this laughter coming from?"

"Maybe our antenna."

The two laugh even more.

"O, Girlfriend, isn't this amazing, and we are probably bald, too!"

They marvel at how extraordinary—their human faces remain intact within this new identity!

They quickly turn themselves onto their legs and awkwardly find their balance when they hear a husky voice ask, "Are you prepared to come in?"

"Yes, yes, we certainly are. Ready as we ever we will be. If you only knew where we came from—ah, never mind; thanks for opening the gate. My name is Girlfriend, and this is—"

Earl interrupts, "—Neighbour. Strange names you both have. We have been expecting your arrival. Come on in and join the colony."

Girlfriend and Neighbour walk briskly through the open gate. They sneak a peek at each other, and with a language known only to "forever" friends, they understand they are excited, eager to talk privately again, and, most of all, grateful they are together in this new way.

Earl beckons to the Echo Youth ants. "Come over here. I want you to meet Edwige before the opening ceremonies begin."

"Why is there a ceremony?" Neighbour is curious.

"Well, because you have both arrived! We have been waiting for you for quite some time! Many rumours are circulating about how clear and bright you two are. I am honoured to be the first to greet you into the Realm of Thagara. Ah, here is Edwige, my assistant for today."

Earl winks at his partner for this morning. "Edwige, my pal, I want you to officially meet Girlfriend and Neighbour who normally reside on the Earth, not *in* the Earth if you gather my meaning. Girlfriend and Neighbour, this is Edwige."

"Pleased to meet you both. Are you not being formal, Earl?" Edwige twinkles her eyes at him.

"I'd say you're right on there, Edwige. Let's move to the opening ceremonies. Everyone agree?"

All ant heads nod simultaneously. They gaily walk over to a space carved into a vast "miniature" auditorium. Edwige finds their new guests' seats ideally situated to see every detail of the up-and-coming performance.

Today's Welcome Committee consists of fourteen Obedi-Ants. These ants have overcome behavioural problems. Before, they were called problem ants and they lived in another section. Onta, the Queen of the colony, made sure they didn't cross over into her managed area until she trained them. Most of their problems were because they didn't know how to co-operate. The Queen trained these Deliqu-ants to get along with each other. When they mastered their differences, they graduated and became Obedi-Ants, never to repeat their unruly ways.

The Welcome Committee has the responsibility to give out and explain the map of the colony to newcomers. They make maps from old ant skins. When an ant dies, the skin preserves its nervous system, which holds the intelligence of ants, the memory of territories travelled, the location of colonies destroyed en masse, and where various junctions of nerves meet. There are snacks at these junctions for travellers and worker ants, often consisting of bits of orange peel, crumbs of grains, and a few morsels of sugar. Obedi-Ants are allowed to finish leftover scraps of snacks other ants did not devour, a secret they do not share.

However, the best reason to be an Obedi-Ant is the honour of creatively welcoming guests to the Realm with a dance performance!

Today's Obedi-Ants form two lines, with the first ant on both the right and left sides dressed in a mauve-coloured costume. The second ant on the right side has an indigo costume, and likewise, the second ant on the left side has an indigo costume. The pattern continues with the other colours being sapphire blue, turquoise, apricot-orange, dandelion-yellow, and finally, ruby-red. Once seven ants are lined up, the colour pattern continues seven times. Even though there are only fourteen newly-trained Obedi-Ants for this particular spectacle, all Obedi-Ants who have performed this role participate in the ceremony. The hum of ants breathing permeates the performance space. When this vibration immerses all, the dance of colour begins.

The patterns weave in and out at various speeds. For an instant, a grid forms then erases and appears again somewhere else in the performance space. Sometimes, when the movement is fast, the grid seems to remain constant and herein a bright golden light pulses.

Girlfriend and Neighbour marvel at the sophisticated dance before their eyes. Just as they are getting accustomed to the patterns, other ants enter in groups of seven; their costumes are silver. Their movements are vertical to the horizontal patterns of the "kaleidoscopic" ants, and at every seventh ant, the dance routine changes.

The spectacle is beautiful! A vivid, moving grid! Then suddenly, without any warning, all forty-nine colourful ants and the silver-costumed ants stop. Onta, the Queen of the colony, appears as a blazing bright, tall, golden ant. She stands a whole ant-body above everyone else! Onta pivots in and out of the grid spaces quite rapidly, yet eloquently. Finally, entering the middle of the performers, she jumps rapidly up and down in the air so fast a slight cooling breeze can be felt. When she stops, everyone in the Welcome Committee collapses.

Their multi-coloured costumes spread open, forming star shape after star shape. What a sight! Once again, Onta then dances gracefully in the tiny spaces between the performing ants, and within no time, their ant bodies form the words:

WELCOME TO THAGARA
GIRLFRIEND AND NEIGHBOUR

Although slightly puzzled over such a display for them—since they didn't even know these ants—Girlfriend and Neighbour are overwhelmed and suddenly feel shy.

Neighbour leans over and whispers to Girlfriend, "You have always been more articulate with words. Can you say something appropriate?"

Girlfriend whispers back, "Neighbour, if we beam them with our mutual good feelings, it will speak louder than any words I can muster at this moment. I am speechless too."

So, together, Girlfriend and Neighbour look at those looking at them and smile delightfully. They nod, and they laugh, and then they nod again. And now every ant head nods, and every ant laughs with them. Oh, what a splendid feeling!

Onta moves her antennae, communicating she wants to speak to the guests.

"Girlfriend, Neighbour, we are pleased you have reached us safely. We have waited a long time for your arrival. As our ancient texts have described, the day the two Echo Youths— who have the gift of clear sight and shape-shifting consciousness perfected, arrive in Thagara—will be the day all can rejoice, as the Golden Bow will start to pulse. Now it is time for us to give you a welcoming feast."

Every ant scurries here and there, and shortly, Girlfriend and Neighbour are seated at a heart-shaped table with Onta and a few elder ants. Even though it is hard to imagine in human terms what they have on their plates (only a few crumbs) will fill them, the density of these minute particles of food is a surprise once they start to consume them. Moreover, they can taste each cell of a crumb!

Onta encourages a few elder ants to sing ancient songs about the Community when the meal finishes. Kira and Mira sing a song about the necessity of working together, harmonizing actions, and remembering to be joyful. Others, like Imagin-Ant, tell a story of how to see with our inner eye. However, the highlight of this gathering is when Cogniz-Ant speaks an Ode to the Golden Bow.

O Golden Bow!
You are already magnificent!
Diligently, with devotion, we create your base.
Every day we see you shine
is a day to remember your grace.
What golden light you will give.
What sumptuous joy we will feel.
Every day we make you gleam
is a day closer to our dream.

O Golden Bow!
You will link dimensions like never before.
Your brilliant light will be the bridge.
And through the Earth, you will go,
way, way, way into space.

The invisible world is your partner,
this dimension we all share.
We are the humble earth-movers
caring for your presence to emerge.
A new destiny for the visible world!

O Golden Bow!
You gather us together in a continuous dance.
A symphony of lustrous beauty!
You will rise victorious!
As our daily sun forever caresses our hearts,
you will appear like an arrow before us,
but not sharp or piercingly mad.
You will only be virtuous and loving
To every, every hue–min.

When Cogniz-Ant finishes speaking, Onta thanks him and asks everyone to pause for a moment of silence to honour the ancient Ode to The Golden Bow.

When the little silent ritual finishes, Onta tells Girlfriend and Neighbour they will be a while in Level 1, acclimatizing to the Realm's vibrations. Eventually, they will be ready to continue their journey through the other remaining Levels.

In all the Levels, they will collect pearls of wisdom. When Neighbour asks what they can expect to see or receive in each Level, Onta tells them it isn't their custom to share this information. Everyone has to experience the Levels in their own way.

Onta asks Edwige and Earl to bring them to a resting area away from the cleaning up noise. They marvel at how the inner sun of the Realm of Thagara shines so brightly. Of course, Neighbour loves the blue sky, too. The Echo Youths find out the colony will sleep at the same time, dreaming the same dream repeatedly—the vision of the Golden Bow rising.

Girlfriend and Neighbour will stay in Level 1 for thirty days to understand how the ants construct, communicate, and work together.

When you start being enthusiastic about whatever
it is you like, that is the **Gold**en Age for you.

—*Michael Winterbottom*

CHAPTER 18

SYNTHESIS PART 1

It is a beautiful day in May. Forty-four days have passed
since Tesshu and Kaleb began their journey of clearing their
Meridians and their corresponding blocks. The last time they
were at Heart Quarters, The She insisted they go through the
Triple Warmer Meridian[18] at the same time when they returned.
She also insisted they study notes on this Meridian beforehand,
as it is usually one of the harder ones to get through.

Tesshu and Kaleb no longer need their assistants to help them
put on the Meridian suits. They walk out to the platforms and
stand before their game consoles. They enter their passwords

---

18 Triple Warmer Meridian: Helps to regulate our stress and immune
    system responses. If there is excessive activation, our fight or flight
    response kicks in.

and watch the figures download their Meridians and corresponding remaining blocks. They look up and wave at their assistants, something they do every time they start the game if they didn't see them personally before. Often though, Jenerrie and Parli are there to greet them, especially in the morning. If they are busy, they can count on Omni and Coral to help.

"Hey, Kaleb, I am excited about clearing the TWM.[19] How about you?"

"Yes, I am. Last night, it was a bit of a stretch for me to make notes; still, I did. It brought back some issues I used to have doing school homework. It's strange though the name, Triple Warmer."

"I hear you. I gave a lot of thought to how I want to approach going through this Meridian. The info I read said the emotional imbalances that can impact this Meridian are fear, greed, and grief. So, I wrote down a list of other words often spoken together, and I came up with; body, mind, and spirit, which affect fear, greed, and grief. I thought we could talk back and forth using these three words as our stimulus."

"Sounds like deep thinking, Tesshu."

"Perhaps it's too complicated—but before you say no, have a listen to what I wrote last night."

"Sure."

"We often push ourselves too far to accomplish more than a twenty-four-hour day allows. Some of us would rather build paint chip sculptures to forget all the responsibilities demanding our attention. Some of us would rather dull our senses with substances that bring imbalance to our minds over time. I trust our Meridians—the connectivity in our cells—will create streams of healthy vibes in us when we believe diseased body parts are perfect. Thus, unwavering best choices of foods will

---

19 TWM is the short form for Triple Warmer Meridian.

fuel us, and vast amounts of self-control will enable us to feel we can accomplish anything—like pushing yourself to do one more chin up."

"Tesshu, I like what you wrote. So are you thinking about approaching this Meridian through a dialogue we originate in the moment?"

"Yes, Kaleb. Associative thinking multiplies the impact of our brain's ability to collect and connect dots in new ways, generating breakthrough ideas. Perhaps we will undo fear, greed, and grief stories without going through them again."

"It would be awesome not to have to recall such stories."

"And did you know, Kaleb, associative thinking is, at the core, all about curiosity? It's a potent tool to give a new spin to an existing idea."

"You're so smart. Okay, I will add to what you said momentarily. Remind me again the last words you wrote were—"

"One more chin-up."

"'Chin up, young man.' My father used to say those words a lot to me." Kaleb pauses, reflecting. "It bothered me until I understood he wanted me to feel prouder about myself."

"I have always been proud of my body even though I am more of a thinned-boned guy. Sure, it was awkward when I went through puberty, but I didn't have a lot of self-consciousness."

"In high school, I used to know this extremely self-conscious girl who always checked how she looked in the mirror or windows, even her face on her cell phone! All her peers thought she was beautiful. How odd to be obsessed with one's body image."

"Body image! Point noted!"

"Speaking of points, Tesshu, what point are you in?"

"I am dwelling in point 7. The electrical pulse has attacked the rim of the circumference. The flow is stalling. This Meridian has got me guessing."

"What is your first guess, Tesshu?"

"I guess I'll carry on. Ha. Gotcha! Now I'm through point 7. The snake has found its victim; the bird has hit a hollow spot in flight. There is stillness."

"You're sharp, Tesshu. It makes me wonder if there is any other information I need to speak about for *my* point 7 to clear so I can overtake you."

"Hmm, overtake me! You are competitive."

"I'm competitive sometimes, yet often I sit and pout and mis-understand what my life is all about. Frequently I wake in the morning and deny the harsh realities going on, even in the next apartment. And then I wonder, what am I trying to embrace? After all, a nuclear attack will not hold me in one place. So, I carry on with a forced reply at times. Those days even a dog's lick could not heal my inner sore. I'll 'suck around' in my emotional puddles, and then when I've pouted for too long, I'll drive myself with a desire to break the hold of my misbehavior. The process itself, the waiting, the holding power, truly makes me feel I am not educating my time appropriately, and the world could pass by my window without saying goodbye. The association with the word 'body' is action. Realizing there is a force lifting us forward to touch each other's hearts, not with 'arms,' but with wide-open compassionate eyes."

"Impressive vocal inspiration, Kaleb. And you thought you weren't a deep thinker. When you spoke, it sounded like you let go of some grief. Where are you now on your TWM?"

"Point 15! I passed you. What's our next challenge?"

"Eh, correction. We are both in point 15. Would you care to take on the mind now?"

"Certainly, Tesshu. We only have eight more points to go through on this Meridian. What did you want to say about your mind?"

"My mind knows me better than I know my mind."

"I'll agree and add my mind sees me better than I see my mind."

"I think I like my mind better than my mind likes me."

"Yes, I feel my mind more than it feels me."

"When I think of my mind, my mind thinks of me."

"I'll agree. When I know my mind, I know my mind knows me."

"Mind you, Kaleb, I just peeked at your Figure, and I can see we both have only one more point to clear."

"One more point. Let's listen sincerely."

"Okay, spirit, point us to you."

"We are ready to clear—"

"Clear what, Tesshu?"

"To clear any concepts that are no longer wise."

"To clear any beliefs that hold us from paradise."

"My spirit is wise even though I am not old."

"My spirit is free even when I am not bold."

"My spirit is sometimes as vast as the stars!"

"My spirit is my avatar!"

"Kaleb, I have cleared this Meridian. Yes!"

"Me, too! I enjoyed dialoguing with you!"

Jenerrie and Parli enter the mini-theatre.

"Quite an impressive conversation you two created. We have it recorded in case you might want to listen another time."

"Thanks for the compliment, Jenerrie." Tesshu smiles at her warmly.

"Well done, young men." The She emerges from the back of the mini-theatre. She has been quietly observing them.

Tesshu and Kaleb turn quickly.

"From what I just heard, you both did your homework on this Meridian. Your ability to tune in to each other is outstanding. I feel you are both ready to learn a more recent technique I have developed called Synthesis."

Kaleb speaks in a frustrated tone. "Excuse me? I feel now that I have cleared my TWM, I am on top of the game and could accomplish a lot more if I stay."

"Kaleb, I ask you to have an open mind."

"Okay, sorry. Sometimes I'm stubborn."

"Don't be hard on yourself, Kaleb. You just made it through one of the most challenging Meridians to clear. I am pleased you are excited to continue to undo blocks. Once you are out of your suits, Jenerrie and Parli will take you to the Outflow Room. See you soon."

After removing his Meridian suit, Tesshu notes how light he feels. He loves the process of associative thinking through a Meridian. For Kaleb, speaking out loud made him feel intelligent. He enjoys getting to know Tesshu, and as he doesn't have any friends on the outside he can converse with so profoundly, he feels good about their growing friendship.

Once in the outflow room, The She opens a window to keep a fresh supply of air circulating. She adjusts the light frequency minimally. The assistants place a thick burgundy cotton mat in the centre of the room. Jenerrie arranges a feather pillow to support her head when she lies down. The young men are waiting by the door for instructions. Before lying down, The She encourages them to come near her and then she speaks to them gently.

"You are here now in this room to experience hands-on work with—my Heart Meridian. This part of your process is an exceptional learning procedure. I will put myself through a recall of a life event that happened to me years ago. As you know, I have cleared all my Meridians. This event does not have any negative emotional effect on me. It is a memory I choose to retrieve to demonstrate the Synthesis technique."

The She lies on the mat and aligns her spine carefully. She instructs the boys to sit comfortably on either side of her.

Tesshu and Kaleb observe her entering into a calm state. They sit on pillows to help keep their spines straight. The energy flow of the Heart Meridian moves from the shoulder down the arm to the baby finger on the palm side. Jenerrie places an image of the pattern of the Heart Meridian beside the young men so they can quickly locate the points on her arms. Jenerrie leaves the room with Parli.

"The memory I will speak aloud is called *A Change of Heart*. When I reach various details of clarity, you will feel a pulse on the point you are touching. You then proceed to the next. There are nine points to clear."

"I am not confident I will find the points on your arm precisely." Tesshu is concerned.

"I agree with Tesshu. Could anything go wrong if we are not touching exactly in the right place?" asks Kaleb.

"Thank you both for your concern. Nothing will go wrong. Please trust your intuition as we go through this process. Let's begin."

Tesshu and Kaleb are ready to watch her mouth form vowels and consonants into words. They are prepared to see her face frown, smile, twitch, and even cry. The She closes her eyes.

"I activate now with conscious precision the memory—*A Change of Heart*."

The She places her hands over her heart momentarily. When her hands return to her sides, she tells the young men she is ready to begin. Tesshu and Kaleb find point 1 on her Heart Meridian and gently apply pressure.

"What does it mean to make a vow? Preparing for my marriage ceremony with my husband to be, we discussed vows at length before we both wrote our own. We researched various cultures and traditions. I studied a variety of vows that are part of many people's unions for generations. I was amazed how the *final* vow, which spoke about death, affected me. I wondered about the origin of the common words *until death do us part*. I again researched cultures to see if there were other phrases I could say instead. Finally, though, I chose those five words, as did my husband.

"Even though I memorized all the promises we decided to declare publicly, I still made a mistake when speaking the final one at our ceremony. I said—*if death—we will part for sure*. It sounded so matter of fact. Why I added *for sure*, and how I expressed the words made many of our guests giggle, and others shuffle in their seats. I took a quick inhale. He smiled to help me relax my worried face. I exhaled slowly and spoke the words correctly—*until death do us part*. He was pleased.

"My blunder became a topic of conversation at our wedding reception, as my husband and I were both psychologists, and most of our guests were our colleagues. When a chance to dissect hidden meanings in conversations showed up, my associates loved to explore such diversity. It was food for our kinds of minds. Oddly, those five words created an unexpected theme during our reception party.

"We raised glasses of wine on more than one occasion with my blunder shouted like a slogan. My husband and I found humorous ways to make light of *death*, which is such a 'perceived' serious subject.

"Later, cuddling and reminiscing about our delightful celebration, we wondered if the married guests, later at their homes, said those precious words to each other—until death do us part, or the words that made up the last vow of their marriage celebration—without fumbling."

Point 1 pulses. Tesshu and Kaleb look at each other and move together to press Point 2.

The She continues telling her story, eyes closed. "My husband and I started to have a reputation as a couple that enjoyed talking about death and its mysteries. We hosted many dinner parties wherein we freely spoke about this subject, as our guests were always curious about our perceptions and our research.

"Over the years as a practicing psychologist, I gave advice to many people with different backgrounds, from investment bankers to schoolteachers to criminals released from prison terms. All of my clients had one aspect of their strained mental health in common; they all had a fear of dying—every one of them. This profound subject—death—was now magnetizing itself to me through my clients.

"My associates inevitably referred people to me. My practice multiplied. Who knew there are so many people afraid of dying?"

Point 2 pulses.

"Seven years into our marriage, my husband had a *change of heart*. He decided he no longer wanted to continue his psychology practice. He was in his mid-forties, and life pushed him to speak out about injustices he perceived through his patients, which affected his greater need to become a voice of conscience for people. He attended rallies, shouted at politicians trying to deceive people, and began to socialize with others who were stronger than him in their convictions for justice.

"He brought people over to our home from all walks of life. Our dinnertime conversations continued to be entertaining. He became more animated in his way of being. Our marriage was still healthy and stimulating, even though we sensed we were turning a corner."

Now points 3 and 4 pulse.

"Then it happened. My husband had left the house for the day. I was doing some warm-up exercises outside to prepare myself for my morning jog. I reached down quickly to tie my shoe, and instead, I had a massive heart attack. Luckily, a woman walking her dog saw me on the ground and called for an ambulance. The emergency doctors frantically defibrillated my 40-year-old heart, trying to get it ticking again. An arsenal of devices designed to measure many aspects of my body were near me. It boggled my mind to witness myself lying on the hospital bed with all the medical equipment surrounding me. How could I see myself? Where was I?

"Death and dying are not something most physicians deal with very well, to begin with, so, when I regained consciousness, I remember the two heart specialists looking at each other as if to say—'you tell her she died and came back to life.'

"Strangely though, I already knew this phenomenon happened to me! I had seen myself leave my body. I heard back and forth conversations with my doctors to bring my heart back online. I had died for a full three minutes!

"I told the doctors I went to the most beautiful place I'd ever seen—an idyllic world where an overwhelming peace slowly entered me, and I could see such golden light everywhere I looked. I never dreamt I would experience such magnificence. Light of pure, unconditional love pulsed in my body—it was the most incredible sensation.

"Weeks later, my husband informed me, the two specialists found out about my work—coaching people through their fear of dying. They wondered if I had fabricated my 'idyllic' experience to get more business. Insulted by their accusations,

I demanded a written apology. Prior to the letter arriving, one doctor had already written a paper on his experience having me as his patient. My reputation started to receive more negativity than I deserved.

"A few years after my near-death experience,[20] I often felt I understood spirituality differently from my husband. My accounts of my experience in 'another world' were sometimes too much for him to hear.

"It is not to say I prayed more, although I thought and felt I needed more stimulation in this area of my life than he did. I needed to revisit fragments of what I saw. I didn't want my heavenly experience to go away. He didn't understand my need to take a lot of time to meditate or walk in a forest by myself. He thought I was escaping reality.

"Even before my NDE,[21] I imagined I had angels watching over me, and I wanted to have a clearer awareness of their presence in my life. Then, one day, when walking alone, I had a deep knowing I had to let my husband go. I was being called in my life to serve differently."

Tesshu whispers, "Kaleb, can you see points 5 and 6 pulsing without us touching them?"

"Wow, Tesshu, I do. Amazing!"

"One day, while meditating, I received a profound vision of the Meridian Figure. I knew without a doubt I had to follow this vision and make it real. I hired a computer scientist, programmers, and assistants to help me capture the vision.

"At this same time, my husband was called to be a leader for an environmental group. Our paths were changing, and we both had to follow our callings. When I told him I could no longer be a wife to him, he was deeply disappointed. However,

---

20 A near-death experience is when a person physically dies and is then brought back to life.

21 NDE is the short form for near-death experience.

he accepted graciously. We did not divorce. We left each other amicably and have remained friends ever since.

"Again, I attracted people into my life who had serious issues with the fear of dying. Once they cleared their fears through the Meridian Figure, they became more useful in their lives and decided they wanted to help the vision of The Echoes of the Sun Community."

Points 7 and 8 pulse.

"It is without a doubt *A Change of Heart* is a memory of a time in my life wherein I received a second chance to see life from a different dimension, a different lens. When you understand there is no turning back, you leave those you have loved if they cannot embrace your changed self—which is never easy to do."

Tesshu and Kaleb release point 9. They are genuinely thankful they now know more of who The She is—and was. The She brings her arms to her heart, momentarily. Then, when a full smile fills her face, she opens her eyes and lovingly makes eye contact with Tesshu and then with Kaleb.

"How are you feeling?" Tesshu breaks the silence.

"Wonderful. Thank you both for being so present. You followed the nine points on my Heart Meridian precisely. I am very pleased with your progress. Kaleb, I sense you have something to say."

"I am amazed and confused at the same time. Is there a reason you chose *A Change of Heart* for a memory? I can relate to what you were saying, as my parents have passed away, and I have some fear of dying. In fact, while you were talking, I had flashes of how I experienced my parents' death. Ah, never mind, there I go again, rambling in circles with my thoughts."

"Take it easy, Kaleb. Nothing is wrong with how you think. I chose *A Change of Heart* because I have seen my husband's presence for the past couple of days. Then, before I went to check on you both in the mini-theatre, I recalled a conversation

I had with him years ago about death and dying. I felt his presence this morning strongly. The Heart Meridian is mighty. Our inner emotional heart is always available to us as guidance.

"I also know the earlier in life one studies and accepts dying without fear, the easier it is to have a life filled with meaningful purpose. Every time you are here working with the Meridian Figures, a part of you is dying. Memories are opened, understood, and released. They no longer have any impact on you.

"When you both experience being the receiver of the Synthesis technique, you will quicken the process to clear your remaining blocks in the Meridians. The artificial intelligence in the Figures helps you to move many memories, but AI cannot assist you with releasing fears around death and dying. Synthesis is the way forward. When the technique is complete, meaning all nine points on the Heart Meridian have spoken, you begin to live in the manner of a truth-seeker. This technique also increases leadership qualities, compassion, and discernment in your lives. You will sharpen your natural intuitive abilities. Life and its synchronicities will begin to make more and more sense. You will receive everyday qualities of mindfulness you never dreamed possible. Kaleb, we would like you to experience the Synthesis technique first."

"Why me?"

"We know you have not fully processed the anxiety, sadness, and loneliness you feel since your parents' death."

Tesshu comments, "Kaleb, this is a gift to you. I look forward to you telling me about your experience when it is over. I am keen to experience the technique too."

Jenerrie and Parli arrive.

"Tesshu, you are free to go back to your Meridian Figure or do whatever you choose," suggests The She.

Jenerrie asks, "Tesshu, do you want to walk in the gardens and have lunch together?"

"Sure, Jenerrie, sounds good. See you later, Kaleb."

The **Gold**en Age is the most implausible of all dreams.
But for it men have given up their life and
strength; for the sake of prophets have died and been slain;
without it the people will not live and cannot die.

—*Fyodor Dostoevsky*

LEVEL 2

After the first month of initiation into the Realm and receiving many reports, Onta comes down from Level 4 to announce the Echo Youths are now ready to start their journey upwards. She arranges for a few elders to join her, and together they walk Girlfriend and Neighbour to the entrance of Level 2.

"Your ability to adapt to the collective consciousness here in Level 1 is impressive. The Elders have guided you well, and they feel you are prepared to go forward. You have learned to pass on information when collective work is being done, a most important skill. This map will guide you both as you make your way through the seven Levels. There is much to discover. Along the way, you will help us in ways even we do not understand."

An Assist-Ant to Onta gives them each a snack bag. Onta reassures them food will always show up for them when they are hungry.

"I currently operate out of Level 4. I will see you when you get there."

Girlfriend and Neighbour bow to Onta, even though it isn't necessary. Onta departs with the Elders. They are alone now, and the silence evokes wonder.

On three entrance walls, 5D instructions appear—a section written in their spoken language, another in picture language, and a third area written in musical language. They choose to study the picture language format since their ant brains resonate with images more efficiently. There are several apricot-orange puzzle pictures. They move the puzzle pieces around with their six legs to form one picture. When they finish, an image of a library with shelves full of books appears. Neighbour accidentally touches the centre of this image, and the entrance to Level 2 opens.

"Amazing; like being in a library," expresses Girlfriend.

"The books, though, are not tangible."

"You're right, Neighbour. They are just floating in the air of this space."

"I've got an idea. Perhaps if we stop moving, one of the floating books will stop, too, in front of us."

"Kind of like when we twirled in the Woods of Facuzi, and while we were motionless, everything around us stabilized?"

"Yes, Girlfriend. Let's try."

Just as Neighbour thought, a book pauses in front of each of them when they stop moving. At first it is awkward using their front two legs as hands, but they catch on quickly and are able to turn pages. It feels like their brains are drinking the knowledge from the books! Finally, after absorbing three books full of information, stories, and historical facts, they are tired and hungry but still curious.

Girlfriend remembers the map they received when they first arrived. "Let's rest, and view the map while we have our snack, Neighbour. Perhaps it will help us sense the size of this environment and where we should go after here."

"I wonder how long we are supposed to be in each Level."

"Me, too. You have the map, right, Neighbour?"

"Yes, Elder Confid-Ant gave it to me. But Girlfriend, I am really hungry. Let's eat first."

"Sure. My head is too full of information anyhow."

The two "Gal-Ants" eat their snack with gusto. While eating, they reminisce about their journey and reflect on how they miss their respective families. When they finish the snack, they take a moment of silence and send their parents a telepathic communication expressing they are happy and safe.

Surprisingly, after eating the snack, they fall asleep, lying on their ant-abdomens, all six legs folded in upon themselves. While the two friends are napping, the map Neighbour carried wiggles its force out of the bag and places itself on her thorax, just above the hologram belt. Neighbour awakes from a sensation. The map is pulsing! She untangles her long legs and, reaching for it—cannot believe what her eyes are seeing—is it the map or is it the Glow? Her Glow? Neighbour gently touches this pulsation, and before she can wake Girlfriend to show her the Glow, she disappears.

If speaking is silver, then listening is **gold**.

—*Turkish Proverb*

CHAPTER 20

SYNTHESIS PART 2

"Kaleb, I will now guide you through the nine points on your Heart Meridian. Parli and Coral will apply gentle pressure to each point. You may not even feel their touch. All we ask is for you to tell us anything you see or understand. This process will take as long as it has to. Our attention and unconditional love are only for you now. Our clarity will be an asset to your process.

"I will coach you with questions if I sense you need support. Try not to overthink or edit your thoughts. Allow whatever has to come up. Sometimes the mind has to go through the swamp before finding the garden. Do you understand?"

"Yes, I understand. Thank you. I am ready."

"I didn't get to say goodbye in any meaningful way. I went to work at Pete's Garage early, my usual routine. I promised to phone my dad during my lunch break, but I forgot. Shortly after I arrived back home from my day at work, a police officer came to my door and told me my parents had been in a car accident. They died instantly.

"The officer asked me if I had any siblings or relatives I could be with nearby. As I am an only child with no grandparents and my aunts and uncles live far away, I told the officer I had no one close. He asked if I wanted a priest to check on me now and again. My parents and I didn't practice any religion, so I wasn't comfortable with his idea. In hindsight, it would have been much easier on me if I had received some counselling. However, some part of me—probably the stubborn part—thought I could work out my feelings independently.

"I had one friend whose parents helped me arrange the funeral. Afterward, it took me a lot of time to be comfortable in my own skin. My friends didn't know how to talk with me either."

Kaleb pauses. The She senses he needs prompting.

"Please summarize your relationship with your parents."

"I had a good relationship with my parents despite choosing my own path in life. I didn't follow my dad's career of being a lawyer. My mother was a schoolteacher, and I didn't have it in me to teach. They gave me a lot of freedom, which was cool. Sometimes they criticized my choice of friends, but probably most parents of teenagers do the same. I also didn't go to college or university. My parents were not so keen on this decision, as they were both highly educated, but they allowed me to follow my heart. They died two years ago. I miss them every day."

Point 1 pulsed. Kaleb's breathing patterns are normal. The She, Parli, and Coral can see his eyes moving back and forth behind his closed lids. Many times, Coral feels the urge to ask him a question. As an empath, she can feel a lot of what he senses. However, she holds her tongue.

The She prompts him again. "Kaleb, did they have an open or closed casket funeral or were they cremated?"

"Open. Although they died instantly, their heads had no damage. I wanted to see their faces again." Kaleb's body starts to twitch. He is trying to hold back tears.

"We are here for you, Kaleb. Feel free to release your grief with us."

Kaleb curls up onto his side and cries deep, deep sobs. Parli rubs his back. Coral gives him tissues and strokes his hair. The She has her eyes closed and sees what he is seeing. A tear comes to her; she wipes it away undetected by her assistants. She speaks compassionately at the right moment.

"Kaleb, my next question may be hard to answer. Do you in any way feel responsible for their death?"

Kaleb rolls over onto his back, opens his eyes, and asks through tears, somewhat aggressively. "Why are you asking this question? What do you know?"

"I can see pictures in the minds of others, Kaleb. You must know this about me by now. I saw an image of you working on the family car the day before they passed. You were under the car, making adjustments. Again, I ask gently, do you feel responsible for their deaths?"

"Yes, I do!" he shouts.

Parli and Coral are surprised at his tone of voice; however, they maintain the connection with his Heart Meridian.

"Every day, I have the thought, it is all my fault! Some days it isn't easy to get out of bed and come here to work on my inner life. I show up, but I am not always confident I will succeed every time I am here. A shadow of guilt is always hanging onto me. It crowds my mind and makes me doubt my ability to do the right thing or make the right choices."

Points 2 and 3 clear.

"We are here for you, Kaleb. Feelings of guilt can make us feel undervalued, of little worth, or judged. Rest assured, we are not judging you. You have cleared three points. You are progressing wonderfully. Please, focus on your breathing and see what surfaces for point 4."

Perhaps five minutes go by. Kaleb is viewing his inner movie. He suddenly thrashes his arms in the air. This time, Parli and Coral move away from him until Kaleb stops moving. His eyes are closed, and it is like he is fighting an invisible force. They gently put their fingers back on point 4.

"Kaleb, what are you seeing?" The She asks calmly.

"I see my messy apartment. I see how I walk around in a daze sometimes, trying to figure out what I can do with myself. I see the faces of my past friends who no longer know how to relate to me. I see the only framed dusty family picture hanging crooked on the kitchen wall. I see how lonely I look. It is like I am watching a movie about my pathetic life! This technique is too much! I've got to get out of here!"

Kaleb stands up abruptly, almost knocking over Parli and Coral. He is looking for the door. The She signals to Coral to go to his side. Coral quickly steps in front of him and places her hand gently on his upper chest. His heart is beating rapidly. Coral speaks almost in a whisper to him. He has to lean into her to understand what she is saying.

"I can sense you deeply, Kaleb. You feel like you have no control of your sensations or actions right now. But you do. I had a strong response, too, when I went through the Synthesis technique. All the fears of watching my grandfather die came to me precisely. Kaleb, if you lay down again, we will assist you in clearing this deep sorrow you are carrying."

"Yeah, then what?" He looks at The She and continues. "You go on and on about how wonderful Tesshu's life and my life will be once we go through the Figures. It seems to me I will have to take on more of your ways in my lifestyle. I will have to be more responsible, more this, more that! I don't know now if I want all this change in my life! I'm not so sure this Synthesis technique is for me. Why do I need to look at the death of my parents—again? I prefer to stop this process now and go home."

The She is now beside him and Coral. Parli is standing near the door.

"Kaleb—guilt, doubt, and self-judgement are self-destructive. We see you as too special to allow such heavy feelings to overtake you at such a tender age. I am not here to brainwash you or suggest that you become someone who doesn't suit your inner world. Completing the Synthesis technique through the Heart Meridian has never been easy for anyone. Once fears of death and dying are cleared, limitless joy awaits you."

"Sorry. I just can't accept this gift right now. I feel like I am being rewired too quickly. Please allow me to leave. I will try and come back in a few days when I feel more certain of myself. I feel like visiting the graves of my parents now. Maybe I will cry a little more on my own. I mean no disrespect. I just know right now, I am not equipped to deal with what else may show up."

Parli opens the door for him.

For Kaleb, his deep-seated feelings of guilt, which he has not completely cleared, make him have his own—change of heart.

The **Gold**en Age is before us, not behind us.

—Shakespeare

CHAPTER 21

SEPARATION

Neighbour is somewhat stunned to find herself in a new section of the Realm of Thagara—alone. She feels a little insecure without her dear friend, Girlfriend. The delicate ant skin map stretches out beneath her. She lowers herself to see if she can figure out where she landed. While there are plenty of lines and scribbles, she is standing on a heart symbol. "Ah, I must be in Level 4—The Heart of Communication."

She wonders if what she saw only moments ago is the Glow or if something on the map triggered the same visual effect. However, the action around her instantly draws her into the present moment, so she doesn't have time to contemplate. The fast-paced movements of four ants, in particular, mesmerize her as she watches them move a peculiar green shape and place it down gently in a central area near her.[22]

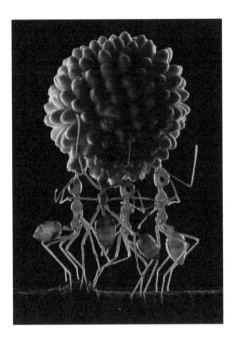

Listening closely, she hears sounds, like earth language words. Then she hears human laughter.

"Pretty impressive, isn't it?"

She turns quickly to see where the voice comes from and almost falls over in shock. A little hue-min shape, a petite man, way smaller than Sir Rush, is standing beside her!

"My, what are you?" exclaims Neighbour curiously.

"Oh, I apologize if I have surprised you. My name is Dig."

"Are you a—or am I a—are you a short person in an ant's body—no, I mean, am I a short ant in a hue-min body? No, no, no, I am all mixed up. What's happening? Am I hallucinating? Girlfriend, where are you?"

---

22 Image of ants holding up a green object was found on Facebook on a site called My Life Is (Bangladesh). Permission granted by site owner.

As Dig laughs, his little hands hold his straw hat and his belly. "Slowly, young one, slowly. You can say I am a short hue-min, although I am six feet in height when in my regular body shape. Exactly five inches taller than you are when you are in your normal body."

"Are you Sir Rush's twin?"

Dig laughs again, "No, I'm not."

"I can't believe I am seeing a little hue-min, and I am in an ant's body, and we are communicating." Neighbour is baffled.

"I sincerely thought Relaxella would have told you about me. Let me start again. My nickname is Dig, and my real name on the earth is Duncan Denomey. I am twice your age. I am the first man to go through The She's Point-by-Point Meridian Figure Invention. Back then, I definitely wanted to serve and be effective in the Realm, so I volunteered to come down here. I have heard her invention has dramatically changed since I went through it. I have lived in the Realm for fourteen years. It is strange to know Relaxella never mentioned me. I fear her memory skills are weakening. This issue is nothing I can influence from where I am standing.

"I lead many teams of hue-mins here in the underground. We knew you would be arriving soon. Not too much surprises us, although Level 4, where we are now, had another tremor. I guess the force reverberated into Level 2, and that's why you landed in this place ahead of schedule. Anyhow, Queen Onta shared with us how you did exceptionally well the last thirty days and are very quick to notice the social habits and mannerisms of the real ants. I will tell you why this is extremely important shortly.

"Now, though, we need to help you come out of being in an ant body, even though you have not lived in this thought-form for very long. We will assist you in returning to a hue-min form, although tiny like me. It is important not to be larger than the ants."

Dig stops talking when he notices Neighbour is again mesmerized by the movement coming from multiple directions.

"Dig, I am overwhelmed! I am seeing more little hue-mins walking this way!"

"We call ourselves hue-ants, Neighbour—our collective nickname in the Realm. They are arriving to support the change you will go through."

Dig, knowing what she is experiencing, gives her more information. "The Echoes of the Sun Community members appear as ants to the real ants that share an existence in the Realm of Thagara with us, or rather, we with them. Because we appear to them as part of their collectivity—behaving like one organism—we utilize their diligent working habits and get a lot done! The hologram belt we are all wearing is a way to differentiate us from them. Did Sir Rush tell you what it is for?"

"He said the belts are for our protection, and it helps us adjust our frequency in the Realm and to 'wear the belt at all times.' Is there anything else I should know?"

"If you look here on the underside, you can see a very tiny electronic chip. This chip creates a holographic image of an ant on our bodies, visible to the real ants. Thus, the real ants—whose group mind consciousness we have tapped into for aiding our work—are in the illusion that we are ants like them. Remember that when you transform into a hue-min shape, you must continue to wear your belt; otherwise, the real ants may not be kind to you. Are you ready for the change?"

"Why can't I do it myself? I can shape-shift, you know."

"I knew you would ask that question. It's different down here. The frequencies are so demanding that we have found with the support of hue-min collectivity, the shift is easier. Also, if we do not help you, the hologram belt disappears!"

"Fine, I will accept your help to put me back into a hue-min form. Wait! Hmmm, this is embarrassing. Can you make sure I have jeans and a blouse on, please?"

Those nearby, who are present to help her, all laugh politely.

"Do not worry, Neighbour. You will have clothes on when you transform; however, you must visualize what we are all wearing—this simple gold-coloured uniform with a hologram belt."

"Do I need to wear a hat like yours?"

"Good observation. No, you don't. As you can see, many chose not to wear a straw hat. Okay, it's time, dear one, to prepare your consciousness for the change. You know where to locate your symbol on your normal body, so when I say 'now,' imagine fully you have removed your symbol. The Echoes of the Sun hue-ant group mind will bring you back into your real hue-min body; however, it will be more compact. Your body will feel strange for a little while."

Dig motions for the others who have gathered to form a circle around Neighbour. They all link hands and raise their heads.

"Now!" shouts Dig.

An intense light beam from the sun in the Realm of Thagara reacts with the thought forms of the group hue-min mind, and Neighbour re-forms! Everyone cheers. Neighbour looks down at herself. Even though it is tiny, she has her body back, and she is grateful she isn't naked! Suddenly, tears trickle down her little cheeks.

"Neighbour, do you feel any pain?" Dig speaks compassionately.

Neighbour leans on his body and tries to gather her emotions. She finally finds the words and speaks into his chest. "Where, oh, where is my best friend, Girlfriend?"

I'm right here now and I want now to be the **Gold**en Age…if only each generation would realize that the time for greatness is right now when they're alive…the time to flower is now.

—Patti Smith

CHAPTER 22

KALEB'S DECISION

Kaleb knows he is more sensitive ever since he started clearing his blocks through his Meridians. Sometimes he feels energy coursing through his body in multiple directions at once. Even before experiencing Synthesis, Kaleb often felt overwhelmed after a session with the Invention. From time to time, Coral encourages him to speak with her one-on-one, but he doesn't want to go over details he discovers about himself again at the end of the day. His social life is nil. He can't find a decent job. Pete told him he would always hire him back; Kaleb, though, isn't into working on cars anymore. And with Coral, even their mutual attraction doesn't give him enough nerve to ask her for a date.

Kaleb faces many aspects of himself simultaneously and needs more time to assimilate all his changes, especially after receiving a partial Synthesis session. In addition, the daily decisions he needs to make for himself often increase pressure in his chest. Also, he can't stop judging himself for not being courageous enough to finish Synthesis. Being a loner has its strengths and weaknesses and vulnerable moments. He needs a distraction from his heavy thoughts. He has so much restlessness churning inside—after experiencing the Synthesis technique, he goes to a Vog rec hall without knowing what to expect. That decision happened two days ago.

Today, Kaleb has another pounding headache as he waits outside a Vog rec hall, where he promised to meet Ben. He doesn't trust what Ben will do to him if he doesn't turn up. He knows the first day he met the gang, a few of the members followed him home. Ben, an emotionally-unbalanced man, has a lot of testosterone-filled followers who do whatever he tells them to do. Kaleb feels caged in a vortex of voices. He can't decide whether to tell Tesshu about Ben. In the first month of working on the Figures, Kaleb and Tesshu often hung out after the sessions, getting to know each other. Then Tesshu had difficulty with his parents, so he could not see Kaleb as much as he liked.

Kaleb looks up in time to deflect a slap to his head. He catches the hand and turns the action into a simple handshake. "Ben, how's it going?"

"We are glad you showed up, Kaleb. Let me get right to the point of today's meeting, as we don't have much time to spare. Did you decide if you will lead us to The She's quarters or not?"

Kaleb hesitates to give him his answer. He looks down at his feet, shuffling back and forth.

Ben grabs the back of his neck and squeezes hard. He then shoves Kaleb forward and says sarcastically. "Do you need more time to write in your journal to find your answer?"

Today, five followers are with Ben, and they all laugh at Kaleb, as they know talking about his journal writing touches a sensitive spot in him.

When Kaleb ventured into a Vog rec hall for the first time a few days ago, he accidentally dropped his knapsack, and his journal slipped out. Ben, who always notices new arrivals and inconsistencies in characters, jumped on the chance to bring Kaleb into his power. When he saw Kaleb looking around nervously, reaching for his journal, Ben stepped on his hand before he could tuck the journal into his knapsack and called out, "What is this? Hey, guys, come here, quickly." He held up the journal while Kaleb looked on helplessly.

At that first encounter, all the others in the gang immediately surrounded Kaleb. Ben slowly opened the journal and read aloud a random passage from Kaleb's writing, expressing his feelings about The She and her Invention. There were plenty of sarcastic "ahhhs" and "ohhhs." Kaleb could sense Ben's curiosity and jealousy mounting simultaneously. The more Ben read aloud, the more angered Kaleb got, until finally, Kaleb bravely lurched forward and pulled the book from him.

"Are you embarrassed we are reading all about your f e e l i n g s?" Ben seemed to stretch this word out, encouraging the others to laugh longer with him. Kaleb was humiliated that day, which is how Ben often weakens new "potential" members into his group. Some of the guys begged Ben to read more; however, he knew when to stop.

"No, I will not read any more of his journal notes—this time. I will insist, though, you start visiting us regularly so we can get to know you and this person you call The She and her Invention. Are you writing a fantasy story or a real story?" Ben and the gang stared at Kaleb.

"Listen, guys; I can't get into it right now. It's the first time I have come into a rec hall. I just want to play a few virtual reality games to unwind from my day. Perhaps, I'll tell you about my writings another time. Let me go."

They did let Kaleb go, as he asked. However, Ben began to scheme with a few of his steadies how they could get Kaleb to talk. Ben had a feeling what he had read in his journal was real and not some fantasy story Kaleb made up. The more he thought about if there was a highly sophisticated technological invention Kaleb knew about, the more he wanted to meet the mind behind it.

Despite Kaleb's pounding headache, he fumbles with his words and tells Ben. "I almost didn't meet you today, but I didn't want to upset you. How about you and a few of your guys come to my house on Saturday. We can talk about the Invention. I have a massive headache right now, and your neck grip just made it worse."

Surprisingly, Ben agrees. He lets him leave.

As Kaleb walks home, he wonders if he will get a bruise within the next couple of hours from the pressure of Ben's grip on his neck and, if anyone asks, what he will tell them.

Kaleb again contemplates whom he can confide with now regarding his decision. Finally, when he reaches his street, oblivious of anything and anyone around him, he realizes he has no one to help him make up his mind—he has to decide on his own.

Again, he briefly entertains telling Coral. He understands whatever way he chooses to go, whether to continue with the Meridian Figure or go deeper into the world of Ben and his Vog gang, he has to be fully committed to his decision. He also knows commitment scares him, which is the root of his indecisiveness, guilty feelings—and today's massive headache. Surprisingly, when he turns the corner to his house, Tesshu is walking toward him.

"Kaleb, how are you? I haven't seen you at the Estate for a few days. You okay?"

"Hey, Tesshu, nice to see you. I'm taking a break. After Synthesis, I think a 'switch' flipped in me."

"I heard you didn't get through the whole process. Jenerrie told me it happens many times with others. You can continue, you know."

Kaleb shuffles his feet. "Yeah. I know. Not now, though. I need some space."

"I miss you. It's not the same without you going through the game simultaneously. Is there anything else happening with you?"

Kaleb rubs his neck. "Tesshu, I…I…have been hanging a little at The Vog rec hall, playing virtual reality games. Please don't tell The She. I need a distraction for a while. I promised Parli I would be back there next week."

"Whoa, the rec halls? I have heard—

"Never mind what you heard, Tesshu! I can handle myself."

Tesshu is surprised at Kaleb's sharp tone of voice. "Kaleb, you sure you don't want to talk with me about whatever you are going through?"

"Sorry, no, I don't. I have to go home now. I have a huge headache. I appreciate you coming around to see how I am doing."

"Sure, Kaleb. Take it easy. See you next week."

Praise, like **gold** and diamonds, owes
its value only to its scarcity.

—Samuel Johnson

CHAPTER 23

THE SEARCH

Onta, the Queen Ant, spends most of her time in Level 4. Daily she processes information to direct actions. She is pleased Dig found Neighbour, and her conversion to a hue-ant turned out to be easy. Onta spends time with Neighbour privately to encourage her not to worry about Girlfriend. However, the two Echo Youths have been friends since they were four years old and are practically inseparable. Neighbour could not shake the idea—she had to try and find her.

After analyzing reports sent to Onta from her Assist-Ants, she asks Dig and Neighbour for a meeting.

"There has been movement detected in Level 3—the Solar Ray. Perhaps Girlfriend is caught in the vortex of the Ray.

Many before her have often gotten lost there, including you, Dig. Remember?"

"Yes, Onta, I sure do. I was in there for days, it seemed. That is how I got my nickname, Dig. I carved the pathway to Level 4," he says more for Neighbour to hear than Onta.

"Exactly. For years, Level 3 has been the most troublesome to get through for many who have come here to help. Yet, that Level works on our 'will.' You, Dig, know this more than any other hue-ant."

"Are you thinking I should go and look for Girlfriend?"

"Yes. Neighbour is confident with her help, the two of you will find her."

"Onta, there is plenty of work to do here. How will you manage without me? There is a risk we won't find her, and we could get caught in the vortex, which manifests without warning and can last for days."

"This is a risk I feel I have to ask you to take. Girlfriend is an important part of our vision; however, Neighbour, you must understand that the journey you are on is bigger than one friend. I know that sounds harsh, but you must trust whatever happens to Girlfriend is her fate. However much we might try to save someone, each soul who comes into the Realm of Thagara has its destiny. So, keep positive, Neighbour, and talk to her through telepathy, as you know how."

"How many days Onta?"

"Only three. You both must return if you do not find Girlfriend by then."

Neighbour protests. "If we don't find my best friend in three days, I will continue to look for her on my own!"

"I firmly forbid this idea, Neighbour. You must return together. I will see you here within three days, hopefully with Girlfriend by your side."

Just as **gold** is burnt, cut and rubbed examine my words carefully and do not accept them simply out of respect.

—*Gautama Buddha*

CHAPTER 24

THE SHE IS QUESTIONED

Two officers from The Vog arrive at Heart Quarters without warning. Jenerrie does her best to convince them The She won't meet with anyone unless they have an appointment. They rudely shuffle past her and let themselves into her office. The She stands up immediately, comes away from her desk, and walks toward the intruders with a force that makes them stop. Crossing her arms with feet planted firmly, The She demands why they have disrespected her protocol—of making an appointment to see her.

"We have our orders to ask you a few questions. And besides, we don't have the habit of making appointments," says Officer Grey.

"And as you know, we work from our timeline, not yours," contributes a nervous Officer named Stanner.

"And we do not answer to you. You answer to us!" Officer Grey powerfully verbalizes as he leans forward into her energy field. He is in charge.

"I have been through various interviews with your side over the years. What is it you need to know now? I have nothing to hide. I have said this over and over. I welcome any of 'your kind' to come and see our work. However, you rather report from the outside based on hearsay rather than personal experience. Then you create false news stories about us. After fourteen years of dodging your antagonism, how do you expect me to feel now, especially after you barged in without an appointment or even introducing yourself!"

Officer Grey knows he is up against a strong woman. Although his training is in verbal antagonism, he senses immediately he has his work cut out for him.

He speaks. "I am Officer Grey. This is Officer Stanner—satisfied? Don't answer. We've heard about The Hillock, and we insist you to take us there. We know this is a way 'your kind' go into the secret chambers in the underground, and it is about time The Vog sees what you do there."

"Officer Grey, it will do you no good for me to show you The Hillock. You do not understand! The world of which we are all part is based on the laws of Nature. The Hillock obeys these laws in ways that even confound us. I've said this to your reporters in the past and I'll repeat it now. The Hillock opens *only* when someone has cleared their harmful emanations, course feelings, and any thought forms not in correspondence with vibrations that radiate utter respect for all living beings. Also, a huge factor is that you, Officer Grey, will never enter The Hillock unless you first go through a Meridian Figure. Point-by-Point is a vehicle to get clear and to get there! This is what I have tried to tell your side for years! Your 'ears' are never in the moment with me." The She's patience is waning.

"Then tell me how long it will take for me to go through one of your, what did you call it, Figures?"

The She takes his request seriously and saunters around him, scrutinizing his body. Officer Grey is a very overweight, pompous man who doesn't have the faintest idea who he is up against, and The She knows it and uses this to her advantage. He is now visibly uncomfortable and slams his fist on her desk.

"Stop whatever you are doing, now!"

"My, my, my, you sure are fussy. First, you want me to tell you how long it will take for you to go through a Meridian Figure, and then when I start to try and make the calculation— you cut my concentration. I'll have you know I am an astute observer. Since you have one point open on your fourteen main Meridians, that shows me you have three-hundred-and-sixty more to unblock. From what I can gather about your body mass, it could take you at least two years, if not longer, to go through a Meridian Figure and get clear, according to my truth. I'll have you know those who come to me for assistance, who do not honour The Echoes of the Sun Community are not prospects I entertain. Also, a long list of people from our Community requested to go through the Figures before you. I like to respect first-asked, first-served if you know what I mean. It is now your decision. How can I help you?"

The She has him cornered and loves it. However, she also intuits this Officer will withdraw and leave in a huff. His partner, Stanner, watches quietly. When they first arrived, The She had observed Stanner's blocked Kidney Meridian in over-drive with fear. She knows she won this round, yet she also perceives they will return to riddle her with questions.

Pointing his finger at her, Officer Grey exclaims, "I'm telling you, this is not over yet!"

"Well, I insist the next time you do want to meet with me, you make an appointment! I am a very busy woman. If you don't, you may wait longer than your patience can tolerate. My assistant will see you to the gate and out of my estate!" The She calls out in a firm voice, "Jenerrie get these men out of here now!"

Where **gold** speaks, every tongue is silent.

—*Italian Proverb*

CHAPTER 25

ALONE

When Girlfriend wakes up from her ant nap, she can't believe Neighbour isn't right next to her. She calls out her best friend's name. Only her voice echoes back. The floating books are still active, and now they are annoying to look at. She doesn't have time to absorb any more information. She needs to find Neighbour. She sees a tunnel and hopes Neighbour is exploring inside. Fearlessly, she enters the tunnel, and a current of air instantly sweeps her up. Landing on all six legs, she thinks, *I must be in Level 3, because the predominant colour here is dandelion-yellow, not apricot-orange. But I sense I am alone.*

There are no floating books here, only symbols spinning around her. Each time she tries to catch a symbol, it goes right through her hands, which are actually ant feet! Then, she notices the symbol of an arrow is appearing more consistently than any other symbol—and it keeps pointing up.

"This is incredible! They are the ancient rune symbols! I remember studying the runes with Relaxella in my first year of training with her. Now memory, help me; what does the arrow stand for? Come on, talk to this brain, however small it is. Courage! Victory! The rune is telling me if I have the courage, I will have victory!" Girlfriend speaks louder. "Neighbour! Where are you?"

The currents are circular, and they continue to pull her upwards. The symbols re-appear like waves in front of her.

"Wow! I just somersaulted in an ant's body! I'll have to remember and tell Neighbour later. Neighbour—ah, my sweet, sweet friend, how I miss your company, your comforting shining eyes, your way of being with me, no matter what mood I am in."

Girlfriend listens deeply for any recognizable sound. She has no idea the speed or the distance she is moving. She finds it very difficult to stop her ant body. However, fatigue comes over her, and she needs to rest.

"The feeling of calmness, serenity, is what I want right now. A gentle feeling of peace inside is what I need. The current is relentless, though! It keeps pulling me upwards and too fast! I am so tired from all this tugging on my ant body. Whoa, what is that sound? I don't understand! Why am I moving more rapidly? Hopefully, after this wave stops, calmness will arrive. What is happening to me? I am not scared, but I will yell in case Neighbour is nearby. Help!!!!!!!!!! Help!!!!!!!!!! Neighbour, can you hear me? Neighbour! Neighbour! Can you hear me? Help!!!!!!!!!! Help!!!!!!!!!!"

Why are you so enchanted by the world
when a mine of **gold** lies within you?

—*Rumi*

CHAPTER 26

TESSHU'S CONFLICT

Tesshu is pacing the floor in the living room. His father has his back to him. He is looking out the front window into the mid-afternoon light. His mother is sitting on the couch, fidgeting, crossing and uncrossing her legs, taking short sips from her hot coffee.

"Dad, look at me. I can't agree with your decision. I loathe the policies of The Vog, and I think you are compromising your truth for the sake of this new job. I know you can do better than this contract. Don't you know Warea Ridge is the sacred land of The Echoes of the Sun Community? The Vog has no right to start a project there.

"You and Mom insist I am involved in something like a cult every time I go to Heart Quarters. You don't see the limitations you have thinking this way. To me, you being employed by The Vog is working for a sect! They have never displayed any willingness to see into other dimensions of reality. They hold onto their beliefs and make sure everyone else does too. They always want to control our actions. In my opinion, they do not work for the common good of people. They do not act inclusively, like The Echoes of the Sun Community. They make their plans exclusively."

"Enough, Tesshu! I don't want you speaking to your father this way. He has lived a lot longer than you, and he knows what he is talking about."

"Well, then tell me how you want me to talk? Like a son, who doesn't know the truth when I see it? Do you want me to perpetuate the lie so many of your generation are stuck in? I'm not going to do it, Mom. You raised me to be honest, and I am. Yet, you both cannot open yourself wide enough to take all of me in."

Tesshu is visibly upset and continues to pace the floor. His hands travel through his longer-than-usual locks. He likes the feeling of air swishing around his forehead when he jerks his head back to take his hair off his face. Since being involved with The She's Invention, he has let go of specific rules he had on himself, one of them being tailored haircuts every month. He wishes his parents could embrace this newness he embodies rather than feel threatened. However, at this moment, Tesshu's parents are avoiding each other's and Tesshu's eyes.

"Kenji, Amber, you have never even asked me to arrange a meeting for you to meet The She. Not once have you shown the least bit of interest in why I go there almost every day. I thought we went through all this scrutinizing with the ant colony project I have developed for three years now. Haven't I proven myself to you both? I spoke to you many times at dinner about her, and I know I have told you she is very open to meeting you, but still, you have not shown any interest. How do you think this makes me feel, as your son?"

"Tesshu, I said, enough! I will not tolerate any more of this kind of talk from you." Amber is distraught. Whenever she does not have an answer, she always resorts to "enough."

For Tesshu, in this delicate moment, it is enough. He takes in a deep breath.

"Okay, since you have had enough, I can say we are on even terms. I have had enough of the two of you living in your lack of courage. I can guarantee you I will be out of the house on Monday. Dad, you have made it very clear regarding your decision. The tension in this house is so thick that I am afraid you will facilitate short-circuiting me and all the inner work I have done to date with the Point-by-Point Invention. I will sleep away for the next two nights, so your vibrations won't provoke me. I sincerely feel you have left me no other alternative.

"Dad, I have wanted to say this to you for a long time—I know the currency you will be making on this contract is more than you have ever earned in twenty years of your career. I also know this would relieve some of the financial burdens this house and family require and set you up for your retirement years. Your decision makes me more adamant not to live under this roof, knowing we would be 're-financed' with currency from The Vog."

With these parting words, Tesshu runs upstairs to his room. He puts together an overnight bag. He has a digital wallet with enough in his balance if he has to sleep in a hotel room. His thoughts override his emotions, but he will not allow himself to feel what his parents are feeling. He knows he has made a firm decision thus he must follow his truth. He feeds the colony, waters the plants, and then locks both the ant colony door and the door to his room. He runs down the stairs. His noise is the only sound in the house. When he reaches the front door, his father stops him by placing a hand on his shoulder.

"Son, please don't be extreme. We love you, and we don't want to see you go like this. Please let's talk it out a little more in a little while. Go for a walk, and when you return, we'll start all over again. I apologize for your mother. I know she is sorry. We are both uncertain in our lives with all of the changes to my business. I beg you to stay and work it out with us. I know it has not been easy for you in the last while, but please, Tesshu, don't walk out on me now. I need you, Son."

Tesshu looks deeply into his father's eyes and says, "I have to, Dad, because I need to honour my truth. I love you, too. But sometimes love is tough; you have said this to me more than once—remember?"

Tesshu turns and walks out the front door. Kenji has one foot inside the house and one outside on the porch, but he stops himself from chasing after Tesshu to plead with him again. Amber joins her husband. They watch the back of Tesshu as he swings his knap-sack from shoulder to shoulder as if clearing the energy in his aura. Amber begins to cry, and Kenji consoles her in his arms.

They deem me mad, because I will not sell my days for **gold;** and I deem them mad because I think my days have a price.

—*Khalil Gibran*

CHAPTER 27

PEER PRESSURE

When Tesshu reaches the end of his street, he decides what to do. He first thought about going to Heart Quarters, but since he isn't scheduled to attend on a Saturday, he hopes Kaleb is home and will welcome him. Recently, Kaleb confided to Tesshu that he spent time in the Virtual Reality Halls on the north side of Rumble X46. Sensitive Tesshu prays he will not have to go looking for him there.

By the time he arrives at Kaleb's house, he has cleared his mind and emotions. Kaleb is surprised to see Tesshu when he opens the door.

"Hey, Kaleb, how's it going, man?"

"Tesshu, my pal, what a surprise to see you here on a Saturday afternoon. I thought you were busy this weekend.

Every time I invite you over, you always have some excuse, and now you are here. Good to see you. Come on in."

Ben and a few of his steady buddies are sitting in the living room. Kaleb introduces Tesshu to Ben and his followers. Tesshu's heart rate instantly escalates when he looks into Ben's eyes. He is sitting in Kaleb's only lounge chair, legs spread wide, with a sheepish grin on his face after every exhalation of the cigarette he smokes. Tesshu is uncomfortable yet doesn't want to show it.

Tesshu moves slowly around the smoke-filled living room. He is not sure if he will sit down. George and Jim, Ben's allies, shift grudgingly to make a space for him on the couch.

"It's okay. I don't need to sit. I won't be staying long. So, have you guys been hanging for a while or what, Kaleb?" Tesshu is trying to sound cool. He doesn't know the slang of The Vog gangs, and whatever he does hear through gossip, he is never sure if he is up to date.

"Who is this weasel, K?" Ben loves to intimidate anyone on his first encounter.

Tesshu looks at Kaleb, indicating strongly with his thoughts not to give too many details. However, Tesshu does not realize Ben knows who he is since he has squeezed information out of Kaleb earlier regarding The She and her work.

"Ah, yeah, Ben, this is Tesshu. He is a friend I met when I worked at Pete's garage. Tesshu, this is—"

Kaleb doesn't have time to finish his lie. Ben is immediately angry with Kaleb for making up a story, knowing Ben is aware of their relationship. He jumps out of his seat, grabs Kaleb from the couch, and throws him against the wall. George and Jim instantly take a stance on either side of Tesshu. Kaleb tries to appear fearless. The cigarette dangling in Ben's mouth almost burns Kaleb's nose. Through gritted teeth, Ben tells Kaleb he does not like it when someone lies to him. Kaleb apologizes quickly. Ben relaxes his grip and turns to Tesshu. Although Tesshu's heart beats rapidly, he feels a surge of courage coming through him as the pictures of his most recent argument with his parents slip into the present moment. Tesshu stands tall and reaches out to Ben, who surprisingly takes Tesshu's hand and grips it forcefully.

"So, you're Tesshu. Kaleb, the wimp here has been talking about you. Take a seat."

Tesshu, not wanting to make this guy angrier, says, "Sure, good idea."

"Kaleb, get us a few cool ones, will you? Make it quick."

Unlike Kaleb, Tesshu finds the strength not to be affected by his hard edge. "Hey man, take it easy on Kaleb. He is a good guy." Tesshu surprises himself at how confident he sounds.

Jim, who now stands where Tesshu was, steps forward, looking like he could hit Tesshu for his boss; however, Ben gestures for him to sit.

"So, Tesshu, Kaleb tells me you are also involved with this Invention some weird woman created."

"Yes, I am. But I don't think she is weird."

"So, give me some details, man. What do you think, this is a party or something?"

"I'm sorry to upset you, Ben. I can probably answer any questions you may have, based on my experience so far. There are a lot of details, and some of them may bore you. What do you want to know specifically?"

"I hear already you are tougher with words than Kaleb."

Kaleb returns to the room with five beers and distributes them to everyone. Tesshu is not into drinking alcohol, but he thinks it would be wise not to be too different around these ego-pressured individuals. Tesshu decides to take one swig and then eventually tip the bottle over.

"Kaleb, why don't you take a seat by your pal, Tesshu. This way, I can watch your reactions to his answers. George, move to the floor."

"Sure, boss, not a problem."

"Tesshu, what I want to know is how many untouched assistants are working with you?"

Ben, George, and Jim burst out laughing. They all tug at their crotches.

"Gees, Ben, I don't know. I haven't asked them such a personal question."

"But what about Jener—? Ah, what did you tell me her name is, Kaleb?"

Kaleb almost chokes on his sip of beer. He isn't expecting to be dragged into this so quickly. "Ah, Jenerrie, Ben, her name is Jenerrie."

"Kaleb, what did you say to this guy about her?"

"I'll answer for you, Kaleb," says Ben. "K here tells me Jenerrie tends to spend more time with you than him." Ben is leaning forward into Tesshu's space.

"She is assigned to me to help me with my progress. What are you hinting at, Ben?"

"Like I asked with my first question, I want to know how many virgins are flowing around there."

"Gosh, Kaleb, what the hell are you doing with this dude? Man, I don't like the thought forms I am picking up with you guys. You better let me know what is happening, or I'll, I'll—"

Ben is furious. He grabs Tesshu by the front of his shirt and brings him close to his face, as he did to Kaleb only moments earlier.

"You little brainy ant worshipper, I know who Jenerrie Ernel is!"

This news makes Kaleb's face go pale.

"I knew her long before either of you ever met her. We used to be sweethearts when we were sixteen."

George interrupts, "Ah, come on, Ben, you were only with her for three weeks, and the farthest you got with her was holding her hand."

"So, maybe I feel like making up for lost time now." Ben releases Tesshu and flings him back onto the couch.

"Lost time?" Tesshu says sarcastically, shaking off Ben's energy. "It's been at least eight years. Not once in any of our discussions has she mentioned you."

"That doesn't mean she doesn't remember me."

"Seriously, Ben, I can sense you are wondering if we are dating. We aren't, but we are getting to know each other slowly. I respect and admire her. She is, though, a very in-demand person. I am lucky if I get to share five minutes with her. So, I am not into asking her anything on your behalf."

Kaleb is astounded at the verbal courage Tesshu displays in front of Ben and his steadies. He has no idea Tesshu can articulate with aggressive dudes. He feels a smile forming on his lips but suppresses it as soon as he realizes what this expression will indicate to Ben if he sees his smirk. Kaleb has enough issues with Ben. He doesn't need to create another problem by showing he is pleased—Tesshu more or less just told him off.

Ben has not anticipated such verbal competition with Tesshu. He can't find words quick enough to come back at him. He guzzles the remainder of his beer, burps, tugs at his crotch, and then throws himself onto his feet. With this elevated position over Tesshu, he looks him straight in the eye. "Well, then, you will arrange a meeting for her and me to see one another again."

"Not possible, Ben. You don't know who you would have to deal with first before ever seeing Jenerrie off-hours. Her boss would need to know a lot about you, and if you were not willing to give her information or meet with her first, I am confident she would not let her number one assistant visit with you—especially alone."

"How come you sound like an authority on this subject, man? You don't get it, do you?"

"Get what, Ben?" Tesshu surprises himself again with the boldness of his response.

"When I want something, I do not stop until I get it!"

"Well, I can't help you, man. Why don't you write a letter if you truly want to see Jenerrie? Kaleb or I could deliver it to her for you. Then, if she is inclined to give you some attention, she'll respond."

"Write a letter! Listen, ant brain, I don't have time to write a letter. You may regret you have not been cooperative, unlike my new pal, Kaleb. And for the record, Kaleb is not going back for another session. He is into hanging with us, aren't you, Kaleb?"

Tesshu looks at Kaleb with disbelief. Kaleb is showing facial signs of stress. His eyes are shifting, and he is biting his lower lip. Tesshu touches his shoulder.

"Kaleb, what has got into you? You can't quit with the work you've been doing on yourself."

Kaleb shoves Tesshu's hands off of his shoulder and replies angrily.

"Don't tell me what I can do or not do! I am so tired of everyone wanting me to be how they think I should be. I am hanging with Ben and his gang—Peer Pressure. I am into what is happening with them. I suggest you leave, my friend, before you see a darker side of me; I have been hiding from you ever since we met. I will not hurt you, Tesshu. Ben, can he go now, please?" Kaleb sounds desperate.

Ben senses Kaleb's fragility, and surprisingly, he agrees it is a good idea for Tesshu to leave. Kaleb breathes a sigh of relief.

Tesshu is stunned by what transpired in the last half hour, including what he previously went through with his parents.

He doesn't even want to think about where he will sleep this night. He pushes himself slowly off the couch and knocks over his beer. He leaves without apologizing for this action.

Tesshu walks around a few blocks to let go of the heaviness in his mind. At four o'clock in the afternoon, he finally lands at the Chatterbox Cafe on the West Side of town. He wants a cup of coffee. He hopes the ambience at the café will be a good distraction to help him get his emotions unstuck.

Many characters are at the café. Tesshu knows he needs to be in "this movie" for a distraction. Once settled, he scans the crowd. There are a couple of older loner types, a few chatty teenagers, a middle-aged couple, and when he sees the intense-looking man with his two children, he decides they will be the main characters in his impromptu script. The man is reading *Connections*, a weekly paper that lists an abundance of choices of things to do other than stay home. He has a coffee in front of him. The two children sitting with him, whom Tesshu assumes are his children, have ice cream floats.

The girl looks nine years old, and the boy who sits beside his father is probably four years old. The man does not have a ring on his finger. He keeps looking at his watch and then the door. The young girl seems to anticipate her father's head coming up from the newspaper to look at the entranceway, and she, too, turns to look in the same direction. The children blow bubbles in their floats, and then all three simultaneously look up at the door. They laugh. As they laugh, a woman enters the cafe, notices them immediately, and sits beside the girl. Tesshu can't figure out if the woman is nervous or shy. The children smile at her and shuffle in their seats. They watch their dad's eyes shine when he talks to her. She keeps moving her hand through her hair as if smoothing out her aura. He wonders if those children see auras or remember seeing them. He wonders if anybody at this moment even thinks about the invisible energy around people's bodies. He wonders if people see their Meridians in a dream or on their lover but don't know or trust what they see. He feels good about what he knows now about his mind, body, spirit, and Meridians. A part of him wants to stand and make an announcement. However, what could he say without sounding ridiculous? Who would hear him? Tesshu watches various people coming and going, "the extras on the scene."

Tesshu's deep need for a distraction keeps his imagination going. He decides the man has recently met this woman and is, at this moment, introducing her to his children. The woman smiles a lot. Her eyes are large like his children's. Tesshu feels they have recently started to fall in love, and he knows out of anybody in this cafe, this group of four will be the ones he can ask for help if he decides to step into his script. He knows this is so because they are the people who have the most light coming out of their eyes. However, he refrains. He drains his coffee and refuses a refill. He stretches his arms upon standing. The foursome all look at Tesshu at the same time. They are the only clients in the cafe who notice him. Maybe he is invisible to the others except for this group of four and the waitress. He smiles at them, and they return a smile. As the director of "his movie," he freezes their energy into a snapshot. He absorbs the warmth of love they are emanating to move him out into the cooling evening air.

Once outside, he breathes deeply. The caffeine has smoothly lined his veins. His heartbeat feels intense again, yet not the same as when he was at Kaleb's or with his parents. He decides to go to The She's and see what will happen. What does he have to lose? Besides, sooner than later, he has to tell her and Jenerrie about Ben and the scene that transpired at Kaleb's house and what just happened at his home. He senses another chapter in his life is opening and instinctively knows he will be going deeper into another reality he never imagined he could enter. This thought excites him to such a degree he finds himself running with a grin on his face—not even the wind can wipe it away.

Where children are, there is the **gold**en Age.

—*Novalis*

CHAPTER 28

TEMPORARY HOME

When Tesshu reaches the gates of The She's estate, Venus, one of the first planets young Echo Youths learn to find in the early night sky, is already out. Heart Quarters is misty, the way the warmer day air mixes with the slightly cool evening wind. Tesshu has never been here past the 17th hour. He pushes on the gate to see if it will give, and to his surprise, it moves. "This is unusual," he says out loud.

"Unusual? I knew you were coming here."

Tesshu is startled at the sound of a familiar voice. "Jenerrie! Whoa—hey! What do you mean, you knew I was coming here?"

"Tesshu, I am linked to you even when you are not with us. As you are now spending more time here, I can tune in to your thoughts and feelings with greater accuracy. After dinner, I went into my room and did an exercise we call 'remote-viewing.'[23] I felt such disharmony coming from your thought forms I knew something wasn't right. So, I came to the garden to walk and talk to you peacefully to ease your mental suffering. I received a few pictures—an argument with your parents, an encounter with Kaleb and some other men I have never seen before—" She pauses. "Although one man gave me an eerie feeling I haven't had in years. Then I could sense a quickening of your energy as if you were running, and I knew you were heading this way. I apologize if I frightened you."

"Frightened me? Not you. You could never frighten me. You don't know how glad I am to see you."

Tesshu reaches out to embrace Jenerrie, something he never did before. To his surprise, Jenerrie melts into his arms. They stay together longer than he imagined would ever happen. This moment feels so comfortable to Tesshu—the first real warm connection he has had all day. Tesshu merges into her embrace; he rubs her back and gently squeezes her closer. She gives no resistance. Her hands massage his neck and lovingly caress his long black hair. Her touch seems to ease the pressure on his brain from the long day of disagreements. He sighs deeply, thinking, *she is a perfect height for me.* Tesshu then gently releases himself from their hug and looks her in the eyes, filled with tears of joy and thankfulness.

"Come inside, Tesshu. I will ask Parli to tell Relaxella you arrived—unexpectedly." Jenerrie locks the gate behind them. When she returns to Tesshu's side, a ripple of energy flows through Tesshu's body. He trembles slightly, and Jenerrie notices. "Guess we charged each other a bit there, hey, Tesshu."

"You can say that again."

---

23 Remote Viewing: The practice of seeking impressions about a distant or unseen target by sensing with the mind.

They giggle softly and stroll together on the garden path. Tesshu can feel the heat from her hand without touching it.

Although it is hard for Tesshu to tell Relaxella and Jenerrie that Kaleb is now hanging out with a Vog gang, he has to let them know. Naturally, this news saddens Relaxella; however, she consoles Tesshu by telling him, "There is a natural order to life, despite one's fears and doubts. I trust he will be back with us again soon."

Relaxella sympathizes with Tesshu's home situation and suggests he can temporarily live with Sir Rush in the Woods of Facuzi. His exploration of the Point-by-Point Figures will continue, though perhaps not daily. Sir Rush has an old truck he will fix for Tesshu to get to Heart Quarters unless he prefers the longer walking route through the Woods. Tesshu looks at Jenerrie and winks. She picks up his picture of driving the truck with her beside him. Relaxella knows they are attracted to each other.

Tesshu's plans work out the next couple of days as he, Relaxella, and Jenerrie have discussed. He knows his parent's patterns like clockwork. He prefers to pack his things when they are not around, so he arrives back home on Monday morning after they are both gone for the day.

He enjoys boxing items for which he no longer has any use. He labels, tapes, and stores them in the basement of their house. He manages to edit many things as he decides he will only take essentials. The main problem to solve—is how to move the ant colony unnoticed.

For Tesshu to get the ant colony to the Woods without it falling to pieces and, more importantly, to move it at a time of day when his neighbours won't see him, he devises a plan that works, as he imagines. However, he doesn't discuss it with Relaxella, as he thinks she would disapprove.

Although he feels bad about starting the fire in the shed of Mr. Baxter—a retired accountant—four houses down his street, Tesshu knows it will draw attention away from his home so he can leave unnoticed. Years ago, his dad told him that Mr. Baxter stores old Vog tax receipts in the shed. Tesshu trusts Mr. Baxter will not suspect him after word gets around that he has left his parents' home. Tesshu's problem of going unnoticed becomes more important than the guilt he knows he could perpetuate. Therefore, early in his plan, he concentrates on his essential purpose—to move the colony safely.

Together, with Sir Rush, they carefully mount the ant colony onto a cart and come down the steps from his bedroom. They exit through the back door and gently place it on the truck. Tesshu knows he will be entering into another facet of The Echoes of the Sun Community, even though he isn't a member. It doesn't matter. When they arrive at Sir Rush's home, they slowly take the ant colony off the truck and place it in a shaded area in his backyard.

Before going to sleep the first night in the Woods, he feels a powerful urge to talk to his parents, to let them know he is all right. Unfortunately, Sir Rush doesn't have a cell phone, nor does Savi, and there isn't any reception when he tries his own. Fortunately, he had taken a moment to leave a tender note on the kitchen table, which said, "Please trust me, I will be in touch soon. I am safe. I love you."

Mr. and Mrs. Tanaka will probably let only a few days go by before asking the authorities to help locate their son, especially if they do not hear from him. Then things will get challenging around Heart Quarters. Tesshu is sure his parents will direct The Vog there.

Despite all the abrupt changes in his life, as he lays in his new bed, he feels a sensation of peace he has never felt before. Whatever he has been through with the Point-by-Point Invention thus far is now positively affecting him. Little did Tesshu know or even imagine he would be living in the Woods with a highly-respected member of The Echoes of the Sun Community only four months after getting involved with The She's Invention.

Dare to love yourself as if you were a
rainbow with **gold** at both ends.

—*Aberjhani*

CHAPTER 29

RETURN

Dig and Neighbour search for Girlfriend in Level 3 for three
days. They hear her voice from time to time, but there is
such a force of swirling energy they can never hear the sound
long enough to follow it. They feel stuck and defeated. Dig
has so many responsibilities in the other parts of the Realm of
Thagara that he knows they need to return and report to Onta.

"Neighbour, I know this is not what you want to hear, but—
we have to stop looking for her. We have to trust Girlfriend is
being watched over, and no harm will come to her. It's time we
go back to The Heart of Communication, where we first met."

Neighbour asks for a moment to be alone. She needs to
compose herself. She feels deeply saddened they cannot find
Girlfriend. Plus, her adventure won't be as fun without her. Dig

gives her some space. He takes out his portable seismograph to record the motion of the ground where they are standing. He will look at the data later and report his findings to Onta.

"I am ready now, Dig. Thanks for trying to find Girlfriend with me."

"No luck, Onta. I'm sorry. We did our best. We have to trust that Girlfriend is safe. We never know what is happening all the time in the Levels." Dig is disappointed. He feels he has failed Onta's expectations and, more so, Neighbour's.

Onta consoles them. "I have no doubt you both looked thoroughly around for her. I am confident we will know what happened to her soon. Maybe she will arrive here in Level 4 today. Let's stay positive and hopeful. Sorry to change the subject, but, Dig, you are needed desperately because the colour mauve is the last to assemble, and the other workers have been waiting patiently for your direction. Neighbour, I would like you to stay with me for a while. I have some things you can help me with if you agree."

"I would be glad to stay with you, Queen Onta. I am exhausted emotionally and physically from our adventure. We were constantly fighting strong currents. I can't even imagine what my best friend Girlfriend is going through. I am amazed and grateful Dig, and I arrived all in one piece! Thanks again, Dig, for helping me. Your courage and ability to focus are admirable. I have learned a lot from you." Neighbour gives him a hug.

"Onta, Neighbour, it has been my pleasure serving you both."

And with those kind words, Dig bows to them and goes on his way.

All that is **gold** does not glitter,
Not all those who wander are lost;
The old that is strong does not wither,
Deep roots are not reached by the frost.

From the ashes a fire shall be woken,
A light from the shadows shall spring;
Renewed shall be blade that was broken,
The crownless again shall be king.

—*J.R.R. Tolkien*

CHAPTER 30

WOW!

The first night at Sir Rush's home, Tesshu's sleep was very restless, despite feeling peaceful before he nodded off. He dreamed his ant colony had broken wide open and thousands of ants scattered, and swarmed in all directions. There were more ants in his dream than in the colony, and some were crawling on him. He woke up in a cold sweat at the crack of dawn.

Sir Rush, being a light sleeper, heard Tesshu's thrashing movements. He got up and prepared a hot cup of cocoa for him. "A nasty dream, Tesshu?"

"Yes and no. I mean, I love my ants, but I don't love how they crawled all over me in my dream. They are probably adapting slowly to their new environment and perhaps communicating their frustration to me through the dream. I don't know. I feel a kind of anxiety from them I haven't felt in a while. I will go now and check on the holding tank."

"Tesshu, relax, relax. Drink this nice cup of hot cocoa before you go outside. The light is breaking the surface. Please, let's have a small meditation together to welcome the sun."

"Yes, all right. I will take your advice. It's almost like the ants sometimes take over me. Ever since I started to communicate with them, they appear in my dreams when some significant change will happen to me. For example, they were present every sleep for a week before I left my parents' house. In last night's dream, though, they were aggressive."

Tesshu shakes his head as if shaking ants out of his hair.

Being very new at this "business of ants," Sir Rush proceeds to make Tesshu laugh about his circumstance. When the sun rises in its full glory, Tesshu forgets about the urgency to visit the colony he felt when he first woke up. Now, happily making fry bread for breakfast with Sir Rush and listening to his entertaining stories, his mind is freer. Sir Rush hasn't had good two-way communication with another man in a long time, so not surprisingly, he is in no rush to do his errands and chores this morning. By the time they each finish three cups of cocoa, three poached eggs topped with fresh chives and cilantro, and fry bread coated with fresh strawberry jam to add sweetness to their morning, they are ready for a full day's work.

"Sir Rush, I'll clean the dishes after checking on the colony; I feel them calling me again."

"Never you mind about the dishes, my new friend. I'll do them gladly. You're settling in. By the time your stay is up here, I'm sure you will have helped me—and us—in better ways than doing the dishes." With a motion of Sir Rush's hand, Tesshu leaves the little bungalow, smiling gratefully.

When he reaches the colony, the ants' activeness is very evident. Tesshu grabs his magnifying glass, the one that makes his ants ten times larger, and proceeds to look closely at them. It seems like every ant has a piece of sparkle in its mandibles. They are bringing the sparkles to a specific area—outside the container! Tesshu wonders out loud, "What? How is this possible? The lid is on. Did the corner crack when we put the container down?" He hollers, "Sir Rush, come out here and see what is happening!"

Tesshu sees a communication is starting and knows Sir Rush will appreciate this phenomenon. Within seconds after Sir Rush arrives, one word has formed. Sir Rush looks at Tesshu. His mouth drops open.

"Well, I'll be. I've seen it with my own eyes."

"Ah, I know you're fascinated, but...eh...we have to work fast to get the ants that escaped back in the tank. Perhaps when we put the colony down, we created a small crack."

"You're not suggesting I pick up the ants one by one?"

"No. If you go and get a tablespoon of your delicious strawberry jam, I will put the jam inside the tank, and you can watch how fast the ants will go inside to eat. There is no time to waste!"

"Right! There is no time to waste! I will be back before you can count how many escaped!"

While waiting, Tesshu observes the ants have stopped their activity with the sparkles. Instead, they are now moving in a circle around the word they created.

Sir Rush seems to be taking longer than necessary. When he appears again, Tesshu understands why—carefully holding the spoon of jam, he is also carting a box full of equipment and almost topples to the ground more than once, so Tesshu runs to his side. He grabs the spoon.

"Looks like you have another idea? What is all this equipment?"

"I will tell you after you put that red sweetness inside the holding tank. Go on. Do it quickly! I don't want those ants anywhere else except in there."

It doesn't take long for the ants to smell the jam and move back into their home. When Tesshu turns around, he is surprised to see Sir Rush has already assembled the equipment.

"What is all this for?"

"This is my recording equipment. I have an array of microphones, acoustic sensors, and geophones that assist me in listening inside the earth."

"Geophone? What is it?"

"A geophone is a device that converts ground movement into voltage, by recording and analyzing the data."

"So, you want to listen to my ants?"

"Yeah, why not? I am a wildlife acoustician; well, not a professional. I am a hobbyist. I love studying the sounds of nature and recording them with this equipment. These acoustic sensors may help me hear your ants 'speak.'"

"Cool! You are always surprising me. Your discoveries will support my project for sure! How does it work?"

"With any luck, I will pick up vibrations, and I might be able to decode a language, even if it is only the heartbeat of your ants. I think this would be a fine discovery."

Tesshu now takes this microphone and places it directly on the formed word. He watches Sir Rush fine-tune the dials, frown, equalize the sound, and frown again. Even though he finds Sir Rush comical when he looks serious, Tesshu knows it would show disrespect if he laughs out loud. The guy is super-focused!

"Move it slightly to your right, no, my right. Slowly, more, a bit more, slowly, yes, there! Stop!" Then, with a gasp, Sir Rush exclaims, "WOW! I can't believe it. It's Girlfriend!"

"What did you say?"

"I said, 'It's Girlfriend!' She is crying out for help. Come and listen. You can hear her shouting."

"But, if I go over there, I will have to let go of the microphone."

"Of course. Wait, I will come to you, and then you come here and put the headphones on."

Tesshu hears the same phrasing as Sir Rush heard.

"What is happening to me? Help!!!!!!!!!! Help!!!!!!!!!!!!!! Neighbour, can you hear me? Neighbour! Neighbour! It's Girlfriend. Can you hear me?"

As Tesshu concentrates on the sound, his eyes look at the ground near the word the ants formed. He assumes all the ants have gone back into the container to feed on the jam, but then he sees a different form of sparkling movement. He quickly takes off the headphones and runs back to the word on the ground.

"What are you looking for, Tesshu?"

"I thought I saw an ant moving, refracting light."

"Oh, this is wonderful. It must be Girlfriend! She is above ground! Her hologram belt is sending signals to us!" Sir Rush paces back and forth until Tesshu shouts—

"—Stop! You might step on her! You might step on Girlfriend!" Tesshu is frantic.

"Of course! What am I doing? I must think straight. We have to find her, Tesshu!"

"Listen, Sir Rush, you are overly anxious, and I'm sure this ant energy field we are in is affecting your own. Go back to what is familiar to you. I will take the magnifying glass and search for her."

"The hologram belt will be around the petiole, the section after the thorax."

"I know where the petiole is, Sir Rush."

"Of course, of course, you know. I gave the belt to Girlfriend when she was still in a hue-min body."

"I sure hope you can explain a few things to me after this emergency is over."

"For sure, I will. Now get to work!"

"Yes, Sir!"

When Girlfriend spirals out of Level 3, she finds herself in the palm of a hand. Looking up, she sees a magnifying glass very close to her legs. She kicks her six legs wildly in the air. Then she rights her body and starts to crawl on the palm. The palm accommodates her movements. Soon she crawls on a slightly hairy thumb. Finally, she stops and adjusts her hologram belt slightly with two of her legs. When she looks into the magnifying glass, she sees white teeth; someone is smiling at her!

Tesshu is balancing Girlfriend on his thumb.

By his side, Sir Rush is breathing heavily. "Here, here, put her in here."

Tesshu carefully puts her into the metal box and says, "What's next?"

"Well, I owe you an explanation. Are you ready to know more about The Echoes of the Sun Community?"

"Yes, for sure. First, I have to find the gap where the ants came out and fix it."

Sir Rush picks up the magnifying glass and quickly finds the gap. "It's right here. I actually saw it earlier. If you need my help, let me know. You are better at this kind of thing than I am. I will pack a little picnic and saddle Una. Then, we will go to Savi's house and tell her about our discovery. She will be thrilled! After, we can all walk through the Woods of Facuzi to Heart Quarters, and Relaxella can see Girlfriend, who will be back into her hue-min form by then."

An inner smile comes to Tesshu. He will be glad to see Jenerrie again. Even though only two days have passed, it seems like weeks since he gazed into her lovely blue eyes.

An inch of time is an inch of **gold**.
But you can't buy that inch of time with an inch of **gold**.

—*Chinese Proverb*

CHAPTER 31

PREDICAMENT

Kenji Tanaka slouches in his swivel chair behind his new oak desk, looking at the paperwork awaiting his decisions. He is anxiously biting his fingernails when Julie, his secretary, walks in without knocking first.

"Kenji, are you okay? You look pale."

Kenji quickly removes his fingers from his mouth and feels a hot flush of colour come over his skin. Shuffling in his chair and with eyes fidgeting, he moves the papers on his desk to appear busy. He then briefly makes eye contact with her. "I'm okay. I haven't gotten a lot of sleep lately."

Julie moves closer, her beige lace bra showing slightly through her tight tanned blouse.

"Any news about your son, Tesshu?"

Kenji looks up quickly; his eyes meet her huge breasts first. Damn, he hates it when she is so close to him. From the first day he met her, he never enjoyed her frequency. He, however, cannot avoid her since she has been appointed his secretary and has had a senior position within The Vog for years.

"What do you mean, Julie?"

"Has he come back home?"

Kenji leans forward on his desk, making her move back, but she doesn't move very far. Then, looking around nervously, he lowers his voice and says, "Julie, who told you he left home?"

"My research."

"Be specific."

"If you insist. The President, Mr. Clarence Billet himself, asked me to do a current review on you and your family. Any time The Vog hires someone into the organization, we keep an eye on you until we can fully trust you. You should know by now how The Vog works, Mr. Tanaka."

Kenji thinks to himself *I can't stand her sarcasm.* Then out loud, "Julie, details. You're on my time."

"If you insist. I found out through a nosey neighbour; Tesshu hasn't been seen around your home for the last three days and—"

"Enough!" Kenji stands up and pushes his hand through his hair—an action he has often see his son do. "Get to the real point for coming in here."

"Well, I am here to give you my condolences."

"Condolences! You make it sound like Tesshu is dead!"

"Well, many stories are circulating about the 'inventor lady,' and who is currently participating with her."

"Whoa, hold on. You have read too many false news articles. I don't believe the woman is holding my son against his will. On the contrary, he is doing some—soul searching, that's what he calls it—you know how young people are, and this woman seems to be helping him. Wait a minute, what am I telling you all this for? I think you should leave."

"Not so fast, Mr. Tanaka. I still haven't told you the other reason I came in."

"Please get to the point. You can see I have a lot of paperwork to complete."

Julie moves around the desk and into his "personal bubble" again. She enjoys thoroughly intimidating him with her overbearing energy. "You have an appointment today with the President at the 17th hour. Would you like me to call your wife and tell her you might not be home for dinner?"

"No, thank you. I can handle my personal affairs. Now, if you don't mind, I have to get back to work."

"Very well, Mr. Tanaka. I'll call the President's office to confirm you have agreed to the appointment." She turns on her high heels and loudly exits.

Through Love all that is bitter will turn sweet.
Through Love all that is copper will be **gold**.
Through Love all dregs will become wine,
Through Love all pain will turn to medicine.

—*Rumi*

CHAPTER 32

THE CONTRACT

Officer Grey returns a week later to Heart Quarters with the President of The Vog. He took The She's words seriously and made an appointment, as he did not want to embarrass himself, let alone the President. The She had to shuffle many appointments to accommodate them. She has no choice but to meet them. Jenerrie opens The She's office door to let them in.

Followed by Officer Grey, the President saunters into The She's office, examines her uncluttered desk, and then looks at her up and down. "You still appear young as ever. You must be doing something right, Relaxella. Seems you have changed your name since you were my student. I hear you prefer to be called The She. Is this another code name like so many in The Echo Community?"

"We are The Echoes of the Sun Community. If you do not mind getting to the point of your visit, Mr. President—or should I call you by your first name, Clarence?"

The She does not like this man who is twelve years older than her. He was her Political Science professor when she was attending University. She loathed going to his class as his arrogance irritated her. She constantly disagreed with his concepts of justice, liberty, and democracy. And, more than once, he kicked her out of his class, considering her too outspoken. He became a politician the year she graduated. Years ago, when she started creating her Point-by-Point Invention, Relaxella lived in a city under his political jurisdiction. He often sent inspectors to her business to ensure everything she was building was up to code. After putting up with his intimidating tactics for five years, she finally moved to the countryside, wherein his political arm could not reach her. Luckily, Relaxella outsmarted him back then, and now she intends to do the same one more time. *Some people are relentless,* she thinks, and almost tells him so.

"Relaxella, sorry, I will not call you, The She. I was impressed walking up the pathway to your office. I can see you have created quite a nest for yourself and your assistants. I have been following the press closely regarding your work. You are a very busy woman. There is not much I do not know of what you have been doing."

"I am surprised an intelligent man as you, believes in the press, Clarence. I have done much more extraordinary things than the papers have ever managed to document. Please don't say you know me. You will never know me because I do not make time for people like you to *get* to know me. Again, remind me why you are here."

"Two-fold. First, Mr. Tanaka asked a favour of me to visit you and see if you could tell us where you have kept his son."

"The way you phrased your words sounds like you think I have him locked up! He is living in the Woods with one of our elderly community members. He needs time out from his parents, as many twenty-one-year-olds do. He is finding his way and his parents are aware he is trying to figure out his purpose in life. Please rest assured the next time Tesshu is here, I will insist he calls them. I do not like to pressure young adults, Clarence, unlike some people I know. I trust this answer is satisfactory. What is the second reason you are here?"

"The contract. We are pleased you have verbally agreed to let us in on the latest phase of your Invention."

"I thought I was quite clear with Officer Grey. He can start once his name comes to the top of the waiting list."

"We are not on the same timeline as you, Relaxella; you should know this by now. When we want something, people move for us. I am sure you realize if you do not co-operate, many of your delightful assistants who have been with you for the last five years will soon find themselves in Rumbles."

"You are still such a controlling man, Clarence! I can't believe you are using a threat to get me to agree to your demands. Seems you *do* know something about me—that I will always protect those who have worked with this vision, for without them, it would never have the success it does. I cannot meet with you until the Pit Festival is over. We have been planning our annual Festival for months; it is a Community priority. Under no circumstances will I take time out to show you my Invention until after we finish our event."

"Okay, I will agree. However, I insist you let me come to this—what did you call it?"

"The Pit Festival, Mr. President."

"The Pit Festival? I must admit you have strange names for people, places, and things in and around you."

"I am not interested in your criticism. Now give me the papers to sign."

"Patience, my dear—patience."

Relaxella adjusts her frequency to sound charming. "Thank you, Mr. President, for honouring my request to meet again after our Festival. As you mentioned earlier, I am a very busy woman. I would be happy to sign the papers now."

Clarence indicates to Officer Grey to give her the contract. The She double-checks all information before signing. When she is satisfied, she writes one of her signatures—Relaxella. Little does Clarence know all her business dealings with the Point-by-Point business are signed—The She. This intelligent divergence will buy her some time in the future, as legal corrections will have to be made. Her defence will be—he did not want to acknowledge her "other name," The She. The more she can delay any of The Vog people coming into her space, the better it will be for The Echoes of the Sun Community. Relaxella hopes more urgently now that The Vog's "expiry date" is near. Any actions that propel negative frequencies of darkness and discord eventually find a way to balance back to the light.

"Jenerrie will let your office know the details for our Festival. However, I trust you will not bring along any of your press friends—it is one of our sacred Festivals. According to an agreement The Vog signed a long time ago with us, all spiritual practices are to be honoured without the insistent pulse of interviewers and camera flashes."

"Relax, Relaxella. Please don't remind me of what I already know. Officer Grey, make sure you follow up with her assistant."

"Yes, Mr. President."

After Clarence Billet and Officer Grey leave her office, The She opens all her windows and clears their lingering dark thought patterns with the power of her bright mind.

A friend is a treasure, more precious than **Gold**.
For love shared is priceless and never grows old.

—Anonymous

CHAPTER 33

RELAXELLA AND UNA

Relaxella is overwhelmed with responsibility. The pressures in her life are reaching a turning point, and she knows she needs the comfort of a familiar man's presence and arms embracing her, allowing her to be a little vulnerable. She always seems to have some form of mental breakthrough when comforted, and she knows whom to call on, but it is dangerous—for him. He has his duties in the form in which he chose to serve, and they both know he only has a few more times to change into a hue-min again before his symbols run out. Also, because of his nature as a radical, outspoken individual against The Vog twenty years prior, he assumes the role of Una for his protection, as well as Relaxella's and everyone else involved with the Community goals.

No one person controls The Echoes of the Sun Community vision. The Community isn't an organization collecting membership fees, a university, or a religion; it is a familiarity one can sense with another, a distinct look in the eyes, and a deep knowing each member is aligned with truth and integrity. The idea of honouring solar consciousness unites everyone. This consciousness thrives and grows from everyone's contribution. Everyone resonates with the frequencies of joy, gratitude, and respect for each other.

Not too many things upset Relaxella; however, after the visit with Clarence Billet, she wants to be in the presence of a man with a compassionate heart, a man who has a balance of feminine and masculine energy.

Relaxella arranges for Una to meet her in her quarters early Sunday evening when duties around the estate are less pressing. She asks Jenerrie to make sure a bottle of Château Lynch-Bages Pauillac Grand Cru Classé is available for them. Also, Vera and Vital need to be on call to cater food for their rendezvous. Relaxella rarely allows alcohol into her body. She knows the after-effects it has on her. Lucky, she is wise enough to prepare her Liver Meridian before she drinks, so she will not experience a subsequent lag of energy the next day. She also acknowledges that drinking a little red wine now and again releases her mind and allows her to laugh more deeply, which she hasn't been doing lately.

When Una arrives, he is a little wobbly on his feet upon seeing her. Coming back into a hue-min body is not as easy as it used to be. This time though, he managed to shape-shift without too much strain. They immediately embrace each other and sigh contently. He feels honoured to be with her privately. He enjoys the sensations of his male body, yet he admits he feels younger when he embodies Una, "the horse." Relaxella gives him a summary of her meeting with Clarence. They reminisce about their past—when the Science of Transformation influenced the consciousness of their generation. Little did they know back then it would lead to such proportions.

"Are you ready for the great awakening?" Una asks her with a smile.

She grins softly back at him. She knows they will dive into a deep conversation with this question, which they both love to do.

"I feel a mass shift in consciousness is hugely welcomed by many. Much will change, and it will seem like it happened overnight, although it has taken years for the transformation to emerge, the great awakening to awaken! What are your thoughts, Una? Twenty years ago, you were one of the most forward thinkers I knew. What does your horse brain think now?"

They laugh. Relaxella loves to listen to him. He is poetic, philosophical, charming, eloquent, and fluid when elaborating on a subject. At the same time, he encourages her questions and comments, which spark his ideas and imagination even more. Leaning back on the couch cushions, she puts her feet up. The lights are dim, their wine glasses half-full. He massages her feet with lavender oil mixed with a superb carrier oil of almond. She looks at him lovingly with warm and watery eyes as he shares his ideas.

"Many people have talked about 'living in the moment.' Yet how many truly experience this state of consciousness habitually? I feel the inevitable great awakening will enable this state of being to permeate the awareness of the common person. Their alignment with higher frequencies will support them to be more joyful, grateful, and less fearful. Many will benefit from the surprise and bliss of living in the moment, and welcome their soul's evolution.

"Surely those you have trained to overcome the fear of death and dying will assist this consciousness to permeate on a mass scale. I like to think the great awakening is like a cosmic shock, an event to make us aware of something out of alignment that existed before and is now corrected. This cosmic shock will help us return to stillness in ourselves.

"It is not as if we will all become 'one'—this concept is too far-fetched. Ironically, though, we will live with the feeling of oneness even with our differences. We will look at each other with a sense of awe that we even made it thus far. Many will experience The Science of Transformation with the one symbol everyone will receive—even members of The Vog—so they can choose to become a new person if they want.

"Even a single opportunity to shape-shift will be one of the greatest gifts the new life will provide. Many will give this possibility a great study because it would change the course of their atoms! They will have to deeply know that in choosing to shape-shift, they will not come back to the body they were born into but a new form of living 'death.' Everyone will choose independent of others' points of view, a sole—soul—decision. Perhaps some will experience the gift of shape-shifting only shortly before they transit out of their body and unite with the God of their Understanding. When they sense death approaching, they might choose to experience their transition as an aged bird dying in the hands of a child, or an iris vanishing naturally after sharing its beauty."

"You inspire me, Una. I love how your words take me to another shore. Do you think you could be a hue-min again—permanently?"

"Perhaps. If 'permanence' helps me better serve others in the new paradigm, I would. Being a horse, of course, is liberating."

"I know I have asked you before to describe what it is like to be in the consciousness of a horse. Please refresh my memory; it has lapsed lately, more than I like."

"First, I think we need to discuss what is happening with your memory. I wonder what is contributing to your forgetfulness."

"Una, I feel it is more than any single aspect in my life. I used to think it was because I am too organized—so many details take a lot of energy to remember! Jenerrie, though, arranges much of the business now. For example, did you know we have ordered the creation of ten more Figures? We will install them in the new studios being built."

"Impressive. I had no idea you were expanding."

"I have no choice. More people will be lining up to clear themselves with all the coming changes. We already have a long waiting list." Relaxella suddenly looks away. Tears come to her eyes.

Una hasn't seen her cry for years. He takes her hand and tilts her face so she can see his compassionate eyes. "Tell me what you really feel is happening to you."

"Perhaps the spiritual element of my heart is weakening."

"Do you still have memories of your near-death experience?"

"Yes. When I have time for myself, which isn't much lately, I used to love reuniting with this experience. It always brought me feelings of deep tranquility. Now, I can only recall one day in the past two months wherein I had a few hours in the morning in my garden alone."

"Perhaps, you need to slow things down, not expand."

"Una, how can I give the gift of time to myself? With the up-and-coming Pit Festival, Tesshu living in the Woods, and Girlfriend anxious for Neighbour to return, my assistants, Thagara beings, you—I hold everyone in my heart."

"You do hold everyone lovingly, Relaxella. I remember when you held me in your heart a little bit closer than the rest. Do you think you have taken on too much?"

"I do not feel I have taken on more than I can handle. It is just I know I can't do it alone anymore."

"What are you saying?"

"I want you back here beside me—beside us. You have always been part of my spiritual heart, and it is weaker now because I do not feel your everyday presence with me. I believe my heart weakness is causing my memory to slip. I would love to have you as my husband again."

"Is this why you asked me if I would consider staying permanently in a hue-min form?"

"Yes."

Holding her hands in his, Una looks deeply into her eyes.

"I have waited twenty years for you to want me back beside you. You have always been the only woman I truly loved. I would be honoured to go forward with you again—to help you with the expansion, pull weeds together in the garden, walk in the Woods of Facuzi, be entertained by Cuzies, and sing the ancient songs with others on a full moon night."

"Una, can you forgive me?"

"Forgive you? You did nothing wrong to me. I chose to honour your soul calling when you received your vision after your near-death experience. How could I not? Sure, I suffered for a while; nevertheless, I was lucky to have been able to become a horse."

They laugh, and he holds her close.

Relaxella can feel the strength of his heart beating close to hers. "Can you remind me now what it is like to be in a horse's consciousness?"

"Only if we ride together again—*until death do us part.*"

"I have my saddle. You are the reins I will hold gently so we can experience once again galloping to the rhythm of our hearts."

"I might insist, though, we begin with a trot. It's been a while if you know what I mean." Una gives her a wink.

The desire for **gold** is not for **gold**. It is for
the means of freedom and benefit.

—*Ralph Waldo Emerson*

CHAPTER 34

THE PIT FESTIVAL

The sky is clear. According to a report Sir Rush gave Relaxella, sunny skies will ensue all day long to support an ideal festival on the Autumn Equinox. Fantastic! Everyone loves the warmth of the sun. The prediction for the evening sky is also to be cloud-free, so all will behold the full moon's light. The sun will pass directly over the Earth's equator, causing day and night to be equal. Any aspect of the day out of balance with solar consciousness will shift to harmony.

Later, the celebration will carry on when the full moon emerges. Those who choose to continue the festivities will sit around a large bonfire, drinking hot apple cider infused with cinnamon and nutmeg spices. Sweetened treats topped with toasted almonds and pecans will be served, and festival-goers will sing songs of gratitude. Those who attend may choose to write a letter to the Invisible Mentors. In their letters, they might ask for the granting of a wish or help to release an aspect of themselves they no longer want to carry. Some may write that they want to let go of laziness; others might write to release the need for everything to be perfect. And still, others may compose a letter wishing for an abundance of friends to come into their lives. Then they will burn the notes in the evening fire—their wishes and prayers released.

Relaxella leaves Heart Quarters with all of her assistants and Tesshu, Girlfriend, Sophia, and Una—who is no longer a horse. Everyone is wearing colourful festive clothing. Relaxella is in a long flowing forest-green dress with tiny symbols of the sun and moon crocheted into the fabric. Her companions walk proudly beside her. Relaxella sees the parade of waddling Cuzies a short distance away coming out of the Woods led by Sir Rush and Savi. They, too, are dressed colourfully. The Cuzies carry their sculptures in various creative ways, super excited and delighted, eager for the arrival of this great awakening moment. There are one hundred and two Cuzies listed to participate in the ceremony—the most Cuzi involvement in recorded Community history.

Other Community members who live within walking distance also converge onto Warea Ridge, the sacred site for this year's Festival. Those who cannot physically attend the Festival can tune in by remote viewing. Everyone contributes in some form or another to make the event a lasting memory.

Sir Rush, the Festival coordinator, asked Eos, Estel, and Phoenix to organize the participation of the children. They are honoured to support the young souls with their high frequencies of abundant joy, purity, openness, and collective intuition in performing a simple dance for the opening ceremony of the

Pit Festival. Davey enthusiastically volunteered to be the leader of the dance.

The children are waving vibrantly coloured ribbons while everyone moves graciously towards the precise landmark on Warea Ridge. It is written in their history book, *Once Upon A Solar Time,* that one day, this sacred site is where the Golden Bow will emerge.

The children occupy the inner circle that is now forming. They have begun the opening dance, their movement free and inviting, ribbons caressing the sky. An invisible force seems to be guiding them.

The second circle forming is that of the Cuzies. They stand patiently waiting for their turn to participate in this extraordinary event.

Sir Rush and Savi join Relaxella, her allies, and other adult Community members to form a third larger circle; they hold hands and watch the children perform the opening dance. When Relaxella senses harmony, she nods to Sophia, who moves to the children's circle and encourages them to now hold each others' hands.

Sophia then provides the first note of the first verse of their Community Song—Echoes of the Sun.

We are The Echoes of the Sun.
United in our minds.
We work with each other
and never speak unkind.

We are The Echoes of the Sun.
United in our hearts.
We work with each other
to lighten the dark.

We trust, we care,
we live knowing deeply
our lives are to share.
We trust, we care,
we live knowing deeply
our hearts are fair.

When they finish the first verse—representing the physical plane—everyone closes their eyes and enters deep silence.

Then something happened Relaxella did not anticipate. An enormous bulldozer crests a hill, approaching loudly. Uniformed officials from The Vog walk beside in pace with the bulldozer, a mixture of men and women of varying ages—no children.

Relaxella keeps her cool, although she is upset about the President of The Vog arriving in such a fashion and so early to their sacred event! The invitation to his office asked that he come at high noon to enjoy their Community lunch.

The "golden" children huddle close to Sophia.

As The Vog approach, Tesshu thinks he sees his father amongst them. He dismisses the thought, but he still can't keep himself from looking in their direction every few steps to see if he is deceiving himself. The third time he looks, he knows it's his father, despite his uniform. He is nervous about making eye contact with him. Sir Rush puts his arm around Tesshu, sensing his anxiety. Tesshu relaxes; he feels Sir Rush is like a second father to him. Tesshu is unsure what his life will be like after this Pit Festival. He is grateful, of course, that he played a role in saving Girlfriend. And his ants, what will become of them? Is he now finished with this science project? Is it time to let them go into a natural home *in* the earth? Or could his trained ant colony somehow assist the Realm of Thagara in another way? He feels burdened by his thoughts taking him out of the present time.

Meanwhile, when Kenji notices his son, he starts running towards him, breaking from the close-knit group of The Vog. However, Clarence Billet sees Kenji running. He instructs an officer to stop him. The President walks up to Kenji, puts his hand on his shoulder, and says firmly, "You chose to be on our side."

The Vog group is now approaching closer and closer to the gathered Echoers. When Tesshu and his father finally make eye contact, tears are in their eyes. He loves his father, as Kenji loves him. However, their life path choices on who to serve are different. At least Tesshu feels good about his choice, and he can definitely see his father wrestling with his decision.

Meanwhile, in the Realm of Thagara, the hue-ants create a diversion so the "real" ants won't be able to participate in the Festival. Dig found a way to lead them outside of the base of the Golden Bow. He returns in time to be part of the Festival.

The majority of the hue-ants prepare to leave the Realm and say goodbye to the ant race. Some have lived and worked on the vision, like Dig, for fourteen years! They want to get "big" again; getting back in their hue-min bodies will be fantastic!

Onta trained Neighbour to organize the order of how everyone will emerge from the underground. Their timing to leave has to be exact. Neighbour is so excited! Soon she will be able to hug her parents, Davey and her best friend, Girlfriend! She was so happy to receive the message a while ago that they found her at Sir Rush's.

Onta, who *is* Relaxella's twin sister, will surprise Community members. Relaxella is proud of herself, Onta, Dig, and Una for keeping this secret—secret.

Relaxella has to trust The Vog will not move any closer to them. However, the noise of the bulldozer is still irritating everyone gathered. Relaxella whispers to Una, and together they walk towards The Vog to speak to Clarence. After only taking a few steps forward, the bulldozer stops. The noise of the motor ceases too.

Kaleb, who fought briefly with the driver, managed to pull out the key from the bulldozer ignition. He quickly runs and throws the key into a nearby lake. Loud grumbling is heard amongst The Vog while people point at Kaleb. He decides— in one brief illuminating flash of insight—where to place his loyalty, and with this impetus of courage, he breaks free from The Vog and sprints to the Echoers, relieved to reunite with them. He finds Tesshu; they hug firmly, like brothers. However, all the peculiar types in the second circle—the Cuzies—raise Kaleb's brow.

The children jump up and down joyfully, comforted by the quiet returning. Then, they join hands with the adults making a larger circle to sing the second verse that will help clear the emotional plane of all present.

Singing is a powerful tool for The Echoes of the Sun Community. They know that when the high voices of females and the deep voices of males fuse, they exchange extremely subtle elements. They imagine their voices are attached to a little kite on the end of a long string. The feminine voices meet masculine voices, and their harmonized sounds blend before returning, amplified and enriched. All receive unity in this fusion.

Sophia gives the starting note again, and their voices unite in singing the second verse with even greater force.

We are The Echoes of the Sun.
United in our emotion.
We work with each other
and never cause commotion.

We are The Echoes of the Sun.
United in our views.
We enrich each other
to support our hues.

We trust, we care,
we live knowing deeply
our lives are to share.
We trust, we care,
we live knowing deeply
Our hearts are prepared.

Even those of The Vog who hold dark and negative thoughts can hear the sincerity in the words as they listen to them singing. Even if they wanted to deny the good sensations created through the harmony of the Community voices, the beautiful ambiance keeps them quiet.

After they complete singing verse two of their Community song, the Pit grows to the size of the base of a 200-year-old Douglas fir tree! Everyone steps back! Before the Community sings the final verse, Relaxella instructs the Cuzies to throw their spill carvings into the Pit opening. Each Cuzi tosses their "creation" into a slopping channel—made specifically for the sculptures—and all feel a slight trembling in the Earth that gently widens the Pit's opening circumference. All the Cuzies create alchemy by throwing in their "mis-emotions" replications, making it is possible to transmute these objects into something else. The sculptures burn underground, creating a new energy source for the Realm of Thagara.

When the last carved sculpture lands below, a small explosion transpires. It is done! The Cuzies are so proud of themselves! They dance with joyful abandonment! Their enthusiasm influences the many others gathered, and they too celebrate the Cuzies' achievement.

The Echoers then prepare themselves to sing the third verse that will open a connection to the spiritual plane. This bond inspires the Invisible Mentors to work the absolute magic of assisting the Golden Bow to emerge through the Earth. Before this manifestation can happen, though, it is time for the hue-ants to exit from the Realm of Thagara.

For The Vog, standing there stunned, this next phenomenon shatters all their preconceived ideas of The Echoes of the Sun Community.

Out of the mist from the underground, led by Onta, the hue-ants appear one at a time and transform themselves back into their hue-min bodies. Cheers rise from the Community. Families recognize family members even though they have not seen them for years.

When Neighbour appears at the end of the line with Dig, the last two to walk proudly out from the Realm of Thagara, everyone bursts into loud applause of appreciation. Dig transforms into his six-foot body, picks up Neighbour under her arms, and swings her around. The crowd cheers even more. Girlfriend runs to her, and they immediately hug, then bounce up and down like four-year-olds. Next, Davey jumps into his sister's arms. When she puts him down, he gives her his colourful ribbon. Phoenix follows, and he embraces his daughter with deep love and care.

What is impressive is that even though all ants transform into hue-mins, they are all still wearing their hologram belts—now "larger." When Relaxella ascertains everyone who came out of the underground united with their families aboveground, makes an announcement.

"Families, I want to thank my dear sister Onta who is now by my side, for being an outstanding leader in the Realm of Thagara for the past fourteen years. Her quiet yet determined manner has helped our evolution tremendously. The writers in our Community will create her chapter to be included in our archives. Because of all of you volunteers who left your families years ago, we have been able to accomplish what we have as a Community. Thank you! As well, I want to share my appreciation for Dig, who devoted the last fourteen years of his life to making sure all seven Levels in the Realm of Thagara were operating in harmony with the divine plan of our Community. And finally, we are here today because of Girlfriend's and Neighbour's fearless contributions. Let us all go into the silence of gratitude for the final stage of the manifestation of the Golden Bow."

For Clarence Billet, the continuous visual of transformed beings walking out from inside the Earth is too much. He shouts, "Stop! This is enough magic for today! I order all of you to leave this area immediately! We declare this land as ours, and we are here to open ground for our project! We have had enough visual entertainment! All this dancing and singing, and then people walking *out* of the Earth—I don't even want to imagine what's next! You are all too strange! Now, move out of here before we do something drastic!"

As much as The She wants *to not* listen to President Billet, she knows it is wise to do so in this delicate moment. Everyone looks at her for guidance.

"Clarence, your face is very pale. Perhaps you need to sit down. We signed a contract wherein you were to honour our sacred Festival. And you know this is *our* sacred land, given to us when zoning in this area changed years ago. Now is not the time to claim this land as yours. I'm also upset you arrived so much earlier than invited. We are almost finished with the most important part of our Festivities. Please, I ask you sincerely, allow us to complete singing our Community song. What is about to manifest is magnificent! You won't believe it is possible. Come closer to the Pit and see the immense golden light that originates from inside our Earth. It is breathtaking!"

The President confers with "his people." Community members hear bickering amongst The Vog while he contemplates his decision.

Meanwhile, Relaxella quickly selects six golden children of various ages and gives them instructions.

Within a few moments, President Billet begrudgingly makes an announcement. "Okay. I will come forward and see what you all are so excited about."

The selected children walk toward President Billet. The Vog followers who surround their President move aside. Two of the older children gently offer their hands to the President and lead him closer to the Pit. He accepts their hands and holds them tightly. The other four children dance joyfully around him and coach him to walk where the Golden Bow originates. His steps are stiff as fear races in his blood. The children find it hard to get him to move! The closer he gets to the Pit, Clarence thinks he will have a heart attack! He has no control over his emotions. Relaxella then instructs Sophia to direct the singing of the third verse. She hopes the harmonious singing will ease the President of The Vog's anxiety.

> We are The Echoes of the Sun.
> United in our mirth.
> We sing with each other
> and trust in our worth.

We are The Echoes of the Sun.
United in our love.
We work with each other
to bring the peace of the dove.

We trust, we care,
we live knowing deeply
our lives are to share.
We trust, we care,
we live knowing deeply
Our hearts are prayer.

After they finish singing the third verse—unexpectedly, the bees arrive! The last alchemic reaction inside the Realm is happening! Hundreds upon hundreds of golden-coloured bees are flying out of the Pit! *(It wasn't the children's fault.)*

The children laugh because they are happy to be so close to seeing the Golden Bow come out of the ground and grow. What an intelligent sight! It is magnificent! It is so beautiful! *(It wasn't the children's fault.)*

O, the children are ecstatic! They love bees! Some children allow the bees to land on their bodies and tickle them with their tiny legs.

Clarence Billet is now closer to the opening of the Pit. The bees startle him the most. He is sweating profusely and feeling powerless. *(It wasn't the children's fault.)*

The children are running jubilantly in circles around him. He lets go of the older children's hands and waves his arms frantically. The bees see him as a threat, as his actions are not harmonious or fearless. So many bees swarm around him!

It isn't the children's fault when Clarence Billet falls to the ground, so full of fear, as he is allergic to bee stings! He protects his head with his arms, legs tucked into his chest. He cries out for help. Some of his Vog followers start to rush to him, but Dig, who quickly moved to his side first, stands tall with his arms spread out, insisting The Vog do not get any closer. Dig then gently talks to the bees, asking them to leave. In an instant, the buzzing air is clear.

"How are you feeling, Mr. President?" Dig is now on one knee, speaking softly to him.

"Honestly, grateful that I never got stung. But how can I be sure that the bees will not attack me again if I get up?"

"If you put on my hologram belt, they will not even know you are there. Give me your hand; let me help you stand."

Relaxella, Una, and Sir Rush gather beside Clarence too. Relaxella is content with Dig's quick intervention. And, of course, she knows the hologram belt will help him in more ways than one.

Clarence stands up slowly. As Dig is putting his hologram belt on the President, voices of The Vog from a distance are calling out—Are you okay? Can we get anything for you? Do you have any epinephrine?[24]

The President turns to his people and assures them he is feeling safe. The two older golden children again each take one of his hands. They slowly turn him around to face the Pit. A golden ray from the Golden Bow reaches the hologram belt when he stands still. The dark shadow that has long lived in the President lifts, and Clarence Billet wipes tears from his eyes for the first time in a very, very long while. The Golden Bow is activating a sacred fire in him—dormant for years. A feeling of peace envelops him, and more tears fall out of gratitude.

---

24 Epinephrine is a chemical that narrows blood vessels and opens airways in the lungs. These effects can reverse severe low blood pressure, wheezing, severe skin itching, hives, and other symptoms of an allergic reaction.

Relaxella speaks to The Vog followers. "You must understand, there is no way I, we, knew this would happen to your leader. We had no idea bees lived inside the earth! We invite all of you to join our circle. Please, we are sincere. The Golden Bow is for everyone." She turns to Echoers. "Those who have just arrived from Thagara, please give your hologram belts to our 'guests.' The Golden Bow's light will comfort their hearts rendered cold by hard times. We will assist your President in understanding leadership does not need to use fear as its weapon."

They give out the hologram belts, and many exchange hugs. The Vog followers are crying for the first time in years as well. Mr. Tanaka runs the rest of the way to embrace his son. Others from The Vog unite with family members who joined The Echoes of the Sun Community vision years ago. Now there is a renewed hope—division replaced by unity.

The rays of the sun have become **gold**en threads in me
connecting me to my higher self—ceaselessly.
I am grateful.

—denise bertrand

CHAPTER 35

THE GOLDEN BOW

Finally, the Golden Bow arrives in full sight! Anyone in union with what it symbolizes can see it any time of day, no matter where they are! It is the link with everything, beautiful, light, and pure!

The Golden Bow ushers in the Era of Fearlessness, Respect, Honesty, Joy, and Gratitude—the vision nurtured in the hearts of The Echoes of the Sun Community for generations!

What took eons to create—a Golden Bow, a Golden Age— now influences living beings slowly yet surely. There is no turning back! The great awakening has arrived!

Indeed, one can say—it is now truly, Once Upon A Solar Time.

It is never too late to find the **Gold**en Bow inside yourself.

—*feather*

10 YEARS LATER

A lot has changed with The Echoes of the Sun Community, while much remains the same, as no one can ever eliminate paradigms that perpetuate beauty, truth, and love.

Of course, it took a few years for old, negative, unsustainable behaviour models to weaken. There were some troubles in the transitions, especially with The Vog, but amazingly, Clarence Billet proved he could lead without force or fear. Within weeks of his "radiant" experience with the Golden Bow, he began planning the clean-up of the Rumbles. After two years of rewarding yet challenging work, Clarence decided to step down as President and fulfill a long-held dream—to become a carpenter. He built his own house and now lives a peaceful life in the countryside.

There is no free ride to inner freedom. Everyone understands all must work diligently with intelligence, honesty, and love with themselves and others to realize transformational desires. It is rare to achieve outstanding spiritual achievements in a few months or years; the effort sometimes involves more than one life!

Even if someone chooses to shape-shift, there is no quick ride to the top. Divine timing permeates all aspects of life. Now everyone knows with certainty that collective harmony is the elixir to shift humans to hue-mins—beings of peace.

Since many desire to make new life changes and educate themselves on living a collective lifestyle, they eagerly volunteer to create The Rays—branches of The Echoes of the Sun Community developing rapidly in many places, supporting the Expanded Vision.

Echoers let go of the tyranny of urgency The Vog imposed years ago. Instead, they move at a slower pace and benefit from simplicity.

Today, Relaxella and Una are having a *slow* lunch with Sir Rush and Savi.

"—and then my lovely wife said to me, 'Rushy, we're pregnant!'"

"Congratulations!" Una and Relaxella express simultaneously. Everyone hugs.

Savi, who is in a constant state of wonder, addresses URL—the nickname often heard when anyone wants Una and Relaxella's attention at the same time— "URL, we would like to register to stay at a Prenatal Birth Centre for the last trimester of our pregnancy. We haven't taken a break from our busy lives in a long time. Rushy has already discussed our plans with

Tesshu, and he is fine managing the Soundscape Ecology Club while we are gone."

"Definitely, you can be our guests! How many months are you pregnant?"

"Four."

"Good on you both for planning ahead. I will inform Vera and Vital, and they will make your stay memorable. By the way, we haven't seen Tesshu and Jenerrie for quite some time. How are they fairing with their two boys?"

"As any young family does—with patience. Jenerrie and I have become quite close, with our husbands working together daily. Jenerrie suggested we consider the Birthing Centre. As you know, she and Tesshu were the first couple to endorse the excellence of your work, URL. She told me that prenatal education provides great practical applications. I love knowing there is artistic and philosophical knowledge that I can teach our child during the prenatal period—in my womb—especially with my powerful creative imagination."

"I, too, am pleased with your decision," Una says, nodding. "Parents-to-be have the possibility to be real 'genetic engineers.' Relaxella and I agree that we must educate parents about the rewiring of the genetic code in utero, which has profound evolutionary consequences on future generations. When anyone is at our Prenatal Birthing Centres, you can participate in a plethora of activities daily—including singing to your unborn child. Sophia is still our teacher. We know singing works on the mother's matter and her child's growing body. Singing helps to harmonize our cells, pending the songs you chose, of course. If your voices blend pleasingly, your baby might come out humming!"

Everyone laughs, and Relaxella comments. "Oh, Una, darling, tell them what you and your team have been doing to enhance the beauty of our Birth in Peace Centres."

"By the time you arrive, we will have finished landscaping two acres nearby with multi-coloured flowers, shrubs, trees, benches, sculptures, and walking pathways. Even the labyrinth will be complete. We imagine mothers taking daily strolls in the gardens to nurture themselves and their babies by 'drinking' solar light, the only food of complete purity."

"We are so excited to participate in this aspect of the Expanded Vision. Thank you both for all you do for so many!" exclaims Savi.

"You're welcome, Savi," says Una. "Sir Rush, you are quieter than usual. How are you doing?"

Sir Rush, who now has a little "baby" belly himself from being well-fed with his own cooking, has watery eyes when he speaks. "I feel so blessed! Every day, I am immersed in gratitude. Every day, I feel the magic of life! Every day, my lovely wife surprises me with her inner and outer beauty. Even though I'm not rushing around like I used to, I still get a lot done in a day."

"How is your research coming along?"

"Fantastically! We conduct most of our experiments in the continually thriving Woods of Facuzi. Every day we are there, we hold a stethoscope up to nature. We listen to the heartbeat of the environment, making assessments and creating lines of communication with many earth species. As a result, a whole new science of soundscape ecology is developing at an incredible pace.

"After Savi and I welcome the birth of our child, Tesshu and I will write a course on listening to the language of bees. It is astounding how many queen bees have arrived in the past two years. They know we support their work; thus, they are not aggressive when we attach our equipment to their hives. His ants 'were' great teachers. Tesshu has innovated ways to communicate with the bees. For example, in our latest experiment, we built a glass structure with entrance and exit holes three feet wide around a hive. Daily he infuses the area with color and records their communications. The sound waves are the same every time the bees are encased in green light. An amazing discovery! Tesshu hopes to decipher their language or perhaps their song someday."

"I love it! Please tell Tesshu, Jenerrie, and their boys we would like them to visit us next week to discuss his observations."

"Rushy and Tesshu have wonderful chemistry together. They are remarkable researchers. And soon I am sure my husband will be a marvellous father! By the way, Relaxella, we heard you closed down Point-by-Point. Was it getting too much to handle?"

"Yes, in a way, it was. I dedicated twenty-one years of my life to this work. When I was at the forefront of my research, utilizing early AI applications with the Figures, I learned, applied, and developed the system profoundly. Those were exciting years!

"However, my team and I kept reviewing the data over the past seven years. We realized that going through the Meridian Figure game is no longer the vehicle necessary to become clear of thoughts and fears of dying. Humans are evolving faster and faster. Soon they will be like us—hue-mins.

"What surprised us the most was how the Synthesis Technique took over my business. After the great awakening with the Golden Bow, there were not enough Figures assembled or suits to accommodate the long waiting list, so we changed our approach and started our clients with Synthesis. We found out that when people vanquish fears of death and dying first, Meridian blocks disappear. Combining hue-min touch and compassionate listening is indeed the preferred healing modality. Synthesis offers this healing unconditionally. I give certified training to anyone who wants to become a Synthesis Practitioner two times a year."

"Also, if I may add, my love," Una winks at his wife, "after we renewed our vows, Relaxella and I rekindled a dream to open Transformation Centres in two phases. Phase I has taken more of her time; thus, she decided to close Point-by-Point."

Una stands up and reaches for site diagrams rolled up nearby. He lays a drawing on the table and gestures for everyone to have a closer look. They gather around.

"Here are the locations of two Birth in Peace Centres we already opened. This one, nearest to Heart Quarters, is where you will stay. It only took three years with a collective effort to build Phase I of the Transformation Centres. It is impressive how many birth specialists have come forward to support the Expanded Vision of The Echoes of the Sun Community.

"Land has been donated, too. There are plans for five more Birth in Peace Centres to operate within five years. We know prenatal education for mothers and their partners will continue to help raise solar-conscious illuminated children."

"Una, what is Phase II all about?" asks Sir Rush.

"In Phase II, we will build Die in Peace Centres. You can see here on the architectural drawings that we are modelling the building construction to be like hexagonal prismatic cells, otherwise known as honeycombs. Surely you can appreciate this synchronicity, Sir Rush."

Sir Rush nods, encouraging him to continue.

"One of our sayings is, 'dying can be sweet as honey.' Relaxella is tirelessly visualizing this concept. She wants to help those whose time is near to die without fear with a smile on their face, showing all loved ones present that their soul is at peace.

"Over the years, thousands of people have gone through Synthesis, and after doing so, many choose to become facilitators. Estel and Eos Ernel direct the Do Not Fear Death symposiums, and Parli and Omni manage them. Relaxella also lectures at these events two times a year, as many genuinely value her personal near-death experience." Una pauses, smiling at Sir Rush. "Rushy—I love your nickname, by the way—we are wondering if you can synchronize some of your nature recordings with photographs of wildlife, thus creating soothing virtual visuals for those ready to cross over."

"URL, I love this idea. And surely Tesshu will, too. Although it took us a while to record, we archived the sound of an 'antique' rosebud opening. Truly, the rose is the most beautiful song you will ever hear. We also found the 'voices' of butterfly wings, the gentle unfurling noise of fiddleheads, and even the laughter of morning doves. Do you know someone with a library of wildlife images for our collaboration?"

"Not yet. We are hoping you know someone."

"Then I will suggest Myrette. She often assists Tesshu and me. She shape-shifted into a hue-min photographer a while back, and her eye for detail is exquisite. She is also a whole lot less chatty. I am positive she will love to participate."

A knock on the patio door interrupts their conversation. Onta and Phoenix are standing, hand in hand, with an aura of joyous love, newly-united hue-mins radiate with each other.

"Are we interrupting?" asks Onta.

"Sister, Phoenix, how nice to see you both. Please come in. We are just looking over the architectural drawings of the Transformation Centres. We showed you them a few weeks back. Would you like to join us for tea and dessert?"

"We love dessert!" Onta and Phoenix say together, delighted. Everyone laughs.

Onta is the happiest in years since she is now engaged to Phoenix. She had quite a responsibility in Thagara and chose to live "on" the earth since that fateful day ten years ago. She met Phoenix when she volunteered to help Kenji and Amber Tanaka at the Golden Bow Resort. The day they met, Phoenix had a meeting with Amber as he was promoting Davey to be included in the evening entertainment for their guests.

Davey, now sixteen years old, is a well-known bike artist. His one-man show entertains children of all ages. He can even juggle with fire sticks while keeping his balance standing up on the bicycle seat! However, more importantly, he cultivates mustard seeds that can be grown in any soil. A six-foot forest of mustard trees is growing beautifully in the same spot he threw seeds down when he was only six years old! Anyone who visits Heart Quarters is welcome to sit on benches and marvel at how many species of birds gather to feast. Davey, however, still hasn't invented a magnet to pick up fallen seeds.

After Amber and Phoenix made arrangements for Davey in the entertainment schedule that day, Amber suggested Phoenix experience Onta's meditation class. So, he went. Phoenix often shares that he saw a golden aura for the first time in his life afterwards, and it was around Onta. His heart found solace with the quieter twin from that moment.

"Tell us your news, sister."

Onta brings out an envelope. "I received a letter from Dig. He asks me to share it with you."

"Go on," encourages Relaxella.

Dear Onta,

The Realm of Thagara is an underground paradise that never ceases to astound me. You would love the ambiance that is manifesting! As you know, we no longer tap into the ant consciousness. They have permanently moved from where we reside. We maintain our regular body dimensions.

The temperature is a steady "early summer day." The mists from the underground rivers rise before the sun and water all of nature perfectly. We are not shy of abundance here!

The seven Levels have expanded and house multiple hue-mins who choose to live and develop Thagara. Where possible, artisans build everything to last for numerous generations.

I am thinking about the tours again, Onta. I apologize for not giving you an answer sooner. I feel I am not the one to organize the tours anymore. There, I said it. It has been a hard decision for me to make. Many newcomers are constantly seeking my advice and wanting my guidance on how to set up a home "down here." And I want to continue to follow my passion for "digging," you know, finding more paths in this massive underground world. Don't worry. I have a solid idea.

Recently, Kaleb and Coral visited me. I asked them if they would like to take on the responsibility of organizing the Journey in Thagara tours and sharing The Echoes of the Sun Community story. They both are super excited to do so! I feel they will not disappoint. Coral is helping Kaleb be less intro-verted. He can articulate his needs more easily now with her by his side. Her empathic skills are fantastic. She knows how to give the right measure of information to whoever is seeking.

Kaleb needs to pass on his responsibilities with the Rumble clean-ups he has directed for the last eight years. And he con-fidently told me that he feels Ben, is now ready to take on this job with care and consciousness. Luckily there are not many more to convert to environmentally-friendly, fully-solar dwell-ings. Kaleb mentioned they would love to start the tours next Spring. Sound good?

On another note, I miss you. I am so happy you and Phoenix are engaged! You deserve someone to cherish you. I will be coming up for a visit soon. I trust we can meet again and share a few stories.

With deep love and friendship,
Your best digger, Dig.
P.S. Please share my letter with URL.

When Onta finishes reading the letter, everyone is silent, and together, they send a focused beam of love and appreciation to Dig in the Realm of Thagara.

Their silence is interrupted when Holly, one of Relaxella's newer personal assistants, enters the room. "I am sorry to disturb you and your guests, URL, but you did tell me to inform you if Azure and Lilac called. They are on the screen now. Shall I open the channel for all of you to see them?"

"Wonderful! We have been hoping to hear from them since they left for the Ray in the north."

And there they are. Two beautiful friends whose smiles always light up a room. Once their giggling subsides amid pleasantries, Relaxella asks them two potent questions.

"Are the 'old' suits working up there in the great white north?"

"Amazingly," Lilac and Azure say together, and, of course, they laugh in unison.

"Details, details, don't be shy."

"The shipment of Meridian suits that Point-by-Point game players used to wear arrived soon after we did," says Lilac. "It is amazing that the suits are upgraded to be independent of the consoles. All three-hundred-and-sixty-one light diodes that represent the points are embedded into the suits and light up awesomely! It is incredible how graphene, the most stretchable crystal, is woven into the suits, thus increasing the efficiency and speed of the sensors that activate the diodes. Graphene is an excellent conductor of electricity, and it also creates heat. And by the way, the twelve dancers are up to speed with the choreography Onta inspired them to create. And because of the heated crystals in the suits, they are never cold!"

Azure contributes more updates to the group. "And the virtual reality videographers tested all their equipment, and even though we will be performing outside, their cameras work! I am so glad we transported those solar cell cases you told us we would probably need, Una."

"You only have two days before Winter Solstice," comments Relaxella. "Is everything in order?"

"Yes, Relaxella. You can relax."

Everyone giggles at Azure's comment.

"Darling daughter," Phoenix says, smiling at her image on the screen. "Is it possible for you to create a live painting in such weather conditions?"

"For sure, Dad," replies Azure. "We are filming my part today inside, so Lilac and I can do our part together outside when the dance of light spectacle begins. Later the editing team will synchronize my painting with us, the dancers, the stars, and—the show-stopper—the crowning glory of the northern skies, Aurora Borealis! Civilizations have marvelled at this celestial phenomenon, ascribing all sorts of myths to the dancing lights—well, we are adding our 'generation' twist to the myth. The scientists up here who have been measuring solar winds for years assure us the mighty gales will arrive right on time."

Lilac and Azure are ready.

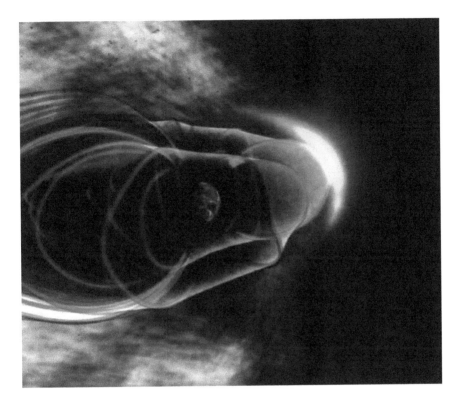

Solar Winds[25]

---

25 The artist's depiction of solar winds and concept of the Earth's global magnetic field shows the bow shock represented by the blue crescent on the right. The purple lines represent the magnetic field; Earth is in the middle of the image. Many energetic particles in the solar wind, represented in gold, are deflected by Earth's magnetic "shield." (Image credit: Walt Feimer (HTSI) NASA/Goddard Space Flight Center Conceptual Image Lab). www.space.com. Permission granted to use image by Mr. Walt Feimer.

APPENDICES

APPENDIX 1

I'm Rushing

feather aka denise bertrand   feather aka denise bertrand

I'm ru-shing, I'm ru-shing, I'm ru-shing when I get out of bed. I'm

ru - shing, I'm ru - shing, I'm ru-shing the thoughts in my head. I'm

ru shing, I'm ru shing, I'm ru-shing all day long. I'm ru-shing, I'm ru-shing, I'm

ru-shing when I sing my song. La la la la la la la la la la la la La

la la la la la la la la la la la.

I'm Rushing

APPENDIX 2

We Are The Echoes Of The Sun
by feather aka denise bertrand

We Are The Echoes Of The Sun

APPENDIX 3

Deep Inside

feather aka denise bertrand   feather aka denise bertrand

Deep in-side the   cen-ter of you, you   hold a   vi-sion of   what is   true. Your

thoughts, your   fee-lings your   ac-tions must shine!   To   help   this world   at this

cri-ti-cal time.   Deep   in - side   the   cen-ter of   you.

Deep Inside The Centre Of You

252

ACKNOWLEDGMENTS

I am so thankful to those who have inspired me to reach this dream of publishing my first novel. So many adults, including thousands of children I have taught, combined with my innumerable experiences throughout life, have blessed me and shaped the outcome of *Once Upon A Solar Time*. I am grateful to all of you—especially those who are still my friends since the age of fourteen—you know who you are. Thank you for encouraging me throughout the years to keep on developing my creative self through writing.

I respectfully acknowledge Omraam Mikhaël Aïvanhov and Dr. Natacha Kolesar, Mentors in spirit whose teachings continue to support my inner growth—and to the I.D.E.A.L. Society community—together, we learn how a "high ideal," while challenging, is worth every effort.

In particular, though, I want to thank the following people for the extra support offered while I was in the final year of writing my first novel.

My dear remaining sister, Marissa, whose loving phone calls gave me the courage to get back on track when I thought it was all too much. I appreciate how she treasures my creativity. Thanks for reading the first fifty pages a while ago and telling me you want to read to the end.

My brother, Simon, thank you for being there for me, no matter where my creative projects take me. My brother, Joe, for reading the first fifty pages and, from time to time, over the years, saying, "Hey sister, what about your book? You working on it?"

And, of course, my darling six nieces and two nephews and their partners, who, at different times during my process, told me, "I can't wait to read your book, Auntie!"

Appreciation for my friends: Slavka Kolesar for support on the cover design, Fernande Roy for insights on the colours blue and purple, and Sophia Hoffman (my "real" singing teacher for years!), who arranged the music of the three songs, "I'm Rushing," "We Are The Echoes Of The Sun," and "Deep Inside The Centre Of You."

Thanks to Emilee French and Desiree French, my drama students since 2014, for enthusiastically posing for the book cover and their wonderful mother, Rylee, for supporting my theatre work with children for the past nine years.

My dear friend and confidant Andrea McKenzie for her great ear, good practical advise and for sharing many laughs with me. Thank you, Andrea, for also giving feedback on the first fifty pages.

Thank you to my FriesenPress publishing specialist for your patience, as I often asked the same questions. As well as the FriesenPress Publishing creative cover and layout design teams. I enjoyed collaborating with all of you.

With deep appreciation, I sincerely thank my editor Lynn Thompson (Living on Purpose Communications), whose keen eye for details always surprises me. As well, she gently offered timely suggestions, spiced with good humour. She was never pushy about how I could improve specific chapters, and she always encouraged me to keep on going!

Lynn and I met each other while hitchhiking across Canada when we were twenty-one years old. We kept in touch for a few years through letter-writing but lost track. Then, forty-three years later, one fated day in March 2021, I received an email from her wondering if I was "the" denise bertrand she met a long time ago. What a wonderful life surprise. "Epic!" as Lynn often fondly says!

And finally, with my whole heart, I extend my deep loving gratitude to my mother, Theresa Bertrand, who passed peacefully in February 2021. I love to believe she "shaped" my imagination while I was in her womb! I also love to believe she is with my father, Simon Bertrand, and my other two caring sibling-sisters, Renee and Michele, watching over me and "somehow" reading my book in the invisible world.

Life is short. If you have a book inside you, I encourage you to write it. What a marvellous experience!

ABOUT THE AUTHOR

feather aka denise bertrand has been educating children, teenagers, and adults since the early 1980s. Her love for the performing arts started at the age of seven. She has performed in China, Vietnam, France, New York, Ecuador, and Canada.

At 18, she opened the first-ever Poets at Large Circle in her hometown of Amherstburg, Ontario. She organized Canada

Council-sponsored poets to visit her Circle and inspire locals to appreciate poetry.

At 23, she opened her first theater company, A.S.T.A.R. (After School Theater Arts and Recreation), in Toronto, Canada, in 1982. For seven years, denise wrote, directed, and produced one theatrical production per year with children 4-10 years old. During these formative years, she also developed her unique artistic expression as a performing artist, actress, dancer, and poet.

In 1986, denise received a Canada Council art grant to perform "The Meridian Figure—A Dance of Light" in China and Hong Kong with a computerized bodysuit that she designed outlining meridians and their acupuncture points. The bodysuit lit up in darkness. For three years, she performed this dance in many venues across Canada.

In 1993, she established herself on Salt Spring Island, British Columbia, Canada. Within six months, she opened the A.S.T.A.R. Gallery for the Performing Arts, where she conducted drama classes and held performing arts events for the wider public.

Then, one day in 1999, her life turned another corner when she saw an ad in the local newspaper requesting a Drama Teacher needed in Singapore! The company hired denise on the spot, and she was on the plane to Asia two weeks later. However, within one year, that company folded. So, denise braved the growing interest in drama education and opened her own company, Articulating Drama, in Singapore in 2000. Again, she was a sought-after educator, often traveling to four schools daily to teach her unique drama enrichment classes. She taught in eight of the eleven top private, government, and international schools, teaching upwards of 200 students a week!

Additionally, denise has conducted many public speaking workshops for adults, traveling to China, Vietnam, and Malaysia to give her one-of-a-kind workshops.

In 2007, denise moved to Phuket, Thailand, and re-opened her company, Articulating Drama, establishing the first after-school Drama Club in 2008 at The Phuket International Academy Day School. In seven years, she opened five drama clubs all over the island.

Three months after returning to Canada in June 2014, denise opened the first-ever Drama Club for children in a tiny village in the mountains of BC.

She travelled to Ecuador with 23 "transformational leaders" in 2015 to help local natives establish a clean drinking water program. Herein, she gave a drama workshop to Amazon native children, helping them express a local story through creative movement and drama. At this juncture in her life, she decided to ask her friends to start calling her feather.

In 2018, feather received a British Columbia Artist in the School Grant to direct the Creation Story of the Ktunaxa Nation.

feather has written upwards of 100 original plays. In 2009, she became a certified intuitive guide, and continues to support adults with their personal growth.

She also volunteers her time and expertise with an intentional community. Herein she is their self-taught bookkeeper, manager of their Community Shared Agriculture (CSA) program, and once a week, she cooks for up to 20 people. In her "spare time," feather enjoys going for walks in the forest, singing, golfing, tinkering, and writing.

Perhaps it is more evident now why it took 45 years for feather aka denise bertrand to write her first novel.

Please visit www.denisebertrand.com

Please visit www.air-feather.com

CPSIA information can be obtained
at www.ICGtesting.com
Printed in the USA
BVHW090747091222
653620BV00007B/9